Like echoes rippling through time, flowing in ever-tighter circles and drawing closer to a time when they can no longer remain hidden beneath deception and lies, dark family secrets are finally revealed, as they were always going to be, it was only ever a matter of when not if.

One reckless act, an unforgivable lie – unimaginable consequences.

To Oli
All the best
Olivia

A Family

By

Design

Olivia Rytwinski

PublishNation
www.publishnation.co.uk

For Aleks & Lily

Acknowledgements

Thank you to my friends, family and editor A J Humpage for their wonderful advice, feedback and support during the writing of this novel. I couldn't have done it without them. Thank you!

CHAPTER ONE

Lost

Until yesterday my life was perfect.

OK, maybe it wasn't perfect, but not a million miles off. I didn't know it at the time. Who stops to count their blessings as they rush to get the kids ready for school, travel to work, run the treadmill and step off at the end of a long and exhausting day? I had no idea of the nightmare to come. No idea what awaited me. Had I known, I would have kept Lyssa tight within my embrace.

CHAPTER TWO

One Day Previously
Wolfstone House
Benn Cady - Scottish Highlands

Cuckoo, Cuckoo.

I flinched and glanced as the bird hopped in and out of its doorway. Eight o'clock already. I plucked Lyssa's lunch box from the armchair beside the range, then paused beside the dining table to spoon a mouthful of cereal. No time to sit and chat over breakfast.

"Mum, I'm having school lunch today remember?" said Lyssa. "It's International Book Day!"

Lyssa stood in front of the full-length wall mirror brushing her curly caramel hair and I thought, heaven help me if I ever forget something important.

True to her genes, Lyssa stood a full head above most of her classmates. Recently I'd noticed that she carried a hint of gangly awkwardness when she walked, but with no self-conscious stoop to her shoulders even when standing with her more petite pals. Her pleated skirt, bought a couple of months ago rode high above her knees, and I wondered if I could persuade her into her gingham school dress. A couple of weeks ago, when I'd suggested the weather was warm enough, she'd given me a withered look and said, 'No one wears those in Year 6.' Which just goes to show what I know.

As I watched her, the sunlight reflected in the mirror to light up her pale, velvety skin, which contrasted with determined forget-me-not blue eyes.

"What do you eat on Book Day then?" I asked.

Christmas lunch - goes without saying, Easter lunch - a chocolatey dessert, but Book Day had me baffled. Lyssa's school organised special days to get the children into eating the cooked dinners, or I conceded, reading in this case. As I tried to remember all the upcoming events at her school, I concluded it wasn't only the pupils that the teachers were challenging these days.

As always, Lyssa was on top of the finer details.

"Mrs. Wrigglesworth says the theme is James and the Giant Peach, and Charlie and the Chocolate Factory. We all voted for our favourite books, and they won. I didn't vote for either of those." Her forehead wrinkled. "Anyway, I did tell you. And you wrote it on the calendar. See." With one arm aloft, she marched across and pointed to the calendar hung beside the fridge.

This state of the art stationery item, complete with a different coloured pen for each of us, was a notable addition to the O'Donnell household and was supposed to make light work of drop-offs, pick-ups, dentist and other engagements. Sadly, it didn't fulfil its grand administrative promise. I rarely looked at it when it mattered, and Max didn't know it existed, despite it staring him in the eye each time he went to the fridge. And, I thought, why was it always my job to remember these things? Although Max was a vocal supporter of equal rights, at work, he was happy to leave me to handle all the domestic minutiae and was always ready with an excuse to avoid helping with the housework, 'Just need to alter a design, reply to this email, tweet.' For goodness sake.

Life was chaotic and there was a limit to my multitasking abilities. As I was getting ready yesterday morning Max had walked into the bathroom.

"What are you doing up there?" he said, sniggering and slapping my bottom.

Naked and balancing on the edge of the bath and still with toothbrush in my mouth, I replied. "What does it bloody look like. I'm getting the shower curtain down. You obviously haven't noticed it's thick with mould."

"I would have done that for you," he said.

"But you didn't." I said, spitting a mouthful of toothpaste into the bath.

Had I overreacted with Lyssa? A packed lunch or school dinner, it was a minor matter after all. Still, I fumed, why wasn't Max helping out more with the family and home organisation? I worked full-time now and earned a damn good salary. I made a mental note for us to sit down and have a civilized talk about sharing out the chores, such as the cleaning, laundry, and school admin, ad infinitum. I hoped it wouldn't turn into another opportunity for us to hurl vicious accusations at one another. Even Louis and Lyssa helped out, albeit financially incentivised and with a titbit or two of bribery thrown in for good measure.

Wolfstone House was so remote that it was no quick fix when we ran out of the essentials or had to ferry Louis or Lyssa to a friend's house or event. The nearest grocery store was fourteen highland miles away, and some of the kid's friends lived an hour's drive away.

I leaned on the windowsill and picked up the wicker seabird. I spotted a delicate web strung between its beak and breast and blew it away. Then I looked out at the open expanse of glens and woodland, and further still to the Assynt hills emerging from their nightly shadows.

"Mum! Are you even listening?

I stirred from my reverie to find Lyssa with brush in hand and the other propped firmly on one hip.

"Surely not everyone's having International Book Day lunch? That's a mouthful isn't it?" I said, and chuckled.

She nodded and dropped her brush with a clatter onto the table.

"Course they are. Jenny, Eve and Jules are, and if I don't, I'll be the only one." She finished with a defiant look that made it clear she wasn't about to give in. As if she ever did.

"OK, OK, Louis will eat them. I'm sure he'll emerge from his pit at some point." I made mental note number two to call him after dropping Lyssa at school.

She bounced over and rewarded my inevitable compliance with a hug.

"Thanks, Mummy. I love you."

I stroked her wild hair and relished her soft warmth. I found it impossible to argue with a daughter who had an answer for everything and a determination that reminded me of someone I knew well as a child.

"I love you too sugar."

"You look smart today Mummy. Is that your new suit?"

"Yes, thought I should wear it. There's an important meeting at work, and I want everyone to listen to what I have to say."

Her eyes narrowed. "And does a suit make people listen better?"

"I'm not sure, but sometimes we have to look smart, so people we don't know will take us seriously. Men have to dress smartly too, like Dad."

She stood back, appraising me. "I think you look super sophisticated."

"Thank you. Hopefully, I'll impress with what I have to say too," I said, and felt a flutter of nerves as I remembered what was at stake.

She ran her hand over my shoulder and added, "You should dry your hair though, it's leaving wet marks down your back."

"It'll soon dry. I reached for the towel that hung over the range and gave my hair a quick rub. "Come on Lyss." I clapped my hands. "Are you ready? Have you packed your books and water bottle?"

"Why do you always ask me? Course I have." The blatant flick of her eyes denoted her annoyance. Then she walked away and said, "I'm not Louis you know."

"Sorry, it's just habit. And can you check your blue inhaler's in the front pocket?" I said, and wondered why I had to apologise so often these days.

"Well, it was there yesterday when you checked. I know what I needed to tell you." She turned to me. Her irritation gathered momentum.

"Oh?" I replied, quite certain I didn't want to hear whatever it was she was about to complain about.

"Jules is getting a mobile for her birthday. So when she gets hers, I'll be the only one in the whole class who hasn't got one." She folded her arms. "Just so you know."

"Not again," I said, and sighed. "How many times do we have to have this conversation? Can we talk about it tonight, not now?" I turned on the tap and filled a glass. I sipped the cold spring water and wondered how much longer I could put off the inevitable.

Once more, my easy going daughter demonstrated familiar teenage characteristics. I wasn't prepared for that stage with my youngest; I would have been happy for her to stay eleven-years-old forever.

I shared such a close bond with our children but my relationship with Louis altered as he'd grown into his teenage years. At fourteen, he'd gone through an awful phase at school - fighting and being disruptive in class - and he'd gained more than his fair share of detentions. Max and I were stressed, as it was so out of character for him. Eventually, he confided that a boy in his year had bullied him. It began after Louis won first prize playing guitar in a school talent contest and he'd received a lot of attention for it, especially from the girls.

I realised that jealousy had triggered the harassment and his tormentor had called him vile names, and even taken photos of him and splashed them all over various social media with fake features and incongruous captions. Once out in the open, the school had dealt with the culprit and the persecution stopped. Louis' mood and behaviour, both at school and home, instantly improved and I was proud of the way he'd committed himself to his schoolwork, especially with his exams looming ever closer.

I knew I had put off giving Lyssa her first mobile because of the problems Louis had experienced.

At the bottom of the stairs I stopped and bent over to put on my new tan leather heels. I felt a massive head rush, the floor rotated, and my stomach lurched. I straightened up, took some slow, deep breaths and grabbed the bannister as the walls returned to their proper places. Sweat broke out on my face and my mouth filled with saliva. I recognised the sensation and hurtled across the hall to the cloakroom just in time to retch into the toilet.

Afterwards, I rinsed my mouth, splashed my face with cold water and examined my reflection in the mirror above the sink. I looked washed-out, and my lips had shrunk and faded. At least my hair appeared to be minus any muesli like vestiges. I sat on the toilet seat and tried to gather my thoughts and steady my shaking legs.

Lyssa appeared in the doorway.

"What's up Mummy?"

"I've been sick. But I'm OK." I tore off some toilet roll and blew my nose. "Came out of the blue."

She grimaced. "Eew! I hate being sick."

"At least you feel better afterwards, usually," I said, and hoped that would be the case today.

I stood up, flushed the toilet again and went through what I'd eaten yesterday. Then I put on my coat and looked at my shoes lying abandoned at the bottom of the staircase.

Lyssa watched me with a deep frown. "You could take the day off Mum."

"That's thoughtful, but I'm fine. Get your jacket and hop in the car. I'll be there in a minute."

"OK, if you're sure?" She picked up her school bag and turned to me again, her expression serious. "Eve says her mum is always being sick. She hears her screaming at her dad, doors slamming and her mum throwing up. Eve was crying at school." Lyssa chewed the inside of her cheek. "Her mum should go to the doctors shouldn't she?"

"Yes, she should." I sighed. "That does sound upsetting." And added. "Hopefully, I'll only be sick the once."

Oh dear, it looked as though the rumours about Fiona, Eve's mum, were more than mere rumours. Always fun at dinner parties, she often ramped up the atmosphere with her sparkle and joie de vivre. However, it didn't sound like she was saving her party drinking for special occasions. I made mental note number three to have a discrete word with the school counsellor and their teacher, reasoning it wouldn't be interfering, but showing concern for a child and a good friend. I felt guilty, realising I hadn't talked to Fiona in weeks. I hadn't seen her at school, and it hadn't occurred to me to ring her. I resolved to call her to arrange something.

The trouble with increasing my hours the past year meant that I'd lost touch with some of my closest friends; some made years ago through baby and toddler groups. I loved to visit friends, invite them over for lunch or go for a walk, but that had become impossible to fit into my hectic diary. Perhaps that was why so many people were hooked on Social Media. Our busy lives meant that talking in a virtual world took the place of getting together in the flesh. A poor substitution. Although I dabbled with Social Media when I had the time, it was something I could take or leave. I was so busy living my life, and I couldn't understand how people found the time for it. Our snail-paced broadband didn't help either. Maybe I could make more of an effort on-line, I thought. Mostly though, the stuff people shared either irritated me by its insignificance or bored me rigid.

I sat on the bottom stair. My stomach still groaned and I realised that I'd felt out of kilter for days. And a more immediate problem was how I was going to get through the day feeling so ropey. Of all the days. I was chairing a meeting with the government department that funded our region of the Environment Protection Agency. Funding was a huge issue, and there had been threats of job cuts and a possible merger with our sister region. I decided against my power heels, as I didn't fancy feeling ill and potentially keeling over in front of the management team, legs akimbo, knickers on display and my dignity in tatters. Flats might be just the thing to make my day that bit easier. And it wasn't as though I needed the extra inches, at five foot nine I was eye level with most of my male colleagues.

A few minutes later I headed through the front door in my unglamorous leather flatties and felt ready to face the day. I thought about Louis, still asleep. Each morning, I made a point of going in to see him, to wake him up and remind him he was off school to give him time to revise, not to catch up on sleep or the latest YouTube vlogs. Just for today I would ring him to check that, a) he was up, b) he was revising, while c) trusting he was being honest, over the phone.

Last night when I went to say goodnight to him, I sat on his bed and looked across at the colourful array of clothes tossed onto the floor. Sat there in his vest and shorts, I realised, he wasn't a boy anymore. His shoulders had broadened, his soft, boyish features had faded and instead he'd developed a strong jaw line, well-defined cheekbones, a slightly Roman nose and dark brows that framed intense blue eyes. Recently he'd gone for a trendy haircut, cropped at the sides with a thick curly quiff on top. His skin tone and hair were darker than Max's, but otherwise, they were incredibly alike. They shared similar personality traits too; the same sensitive and creative side, which joined forces with a fresh wit and a puckish sense of humour. Ever since Louis' voice had broken I often listened in on them talking, and tried to work out which of them said what, their voices were so alike in tone and resonance.

8

"I've got way too much to revise, and the exams are only a week away." He shuffled up the bed and flicked through his phone.

"Would it help if we put together another revision timetable?" I offered.

"I guess."

"It might help if you left your phone in the kitchen. You know, less to distract you?" I said, and threw a pointed look at his phone.

He shot me an affronted look. "It's the first time I've looked at it tonight."

"It's fine Lou, you've been working hard, and it's good to take the odd break." I thought back to my exams and remembered how I spent far more time taking breaks than revising.

Louis was more diligent than some of his friends, who by all accounts were spending their study leave on the latest video games. I'd denied Louis that option because I'd disconnected his games console until after his final exam.

I swung open the driver's door.

"Mum, have you seen the time? I'm gonna be late," Lyssa said. "Are you still poorly?" she asked, concerned, and fiddled with the stereo.

"I'm fine. I just swapped my shoes."

"Were you sick on your brown ones?"

I laughed. Lyssa's insatiable curiosity for all things, especially the gory details, warmed my heart.

"No, I wasn't sick on my shoes. I just fancied wearing a more comfortable pair. Which reminds me, my meeting could run on tonight, so it'll be Dad picking you up." I switched to the news channel. "Come on, in your seat."

"Hey, I was listening. Can't we have Radio One?" She clambered into the back and fastened her seatbelt.

I reversed. "Don't you want the news?" I peered at her through the mirror. "Find out what's happening out there."

We often went through this routine, where we wrangled over who chose what we listened to. It rarely resulted in my choice of station or music.

"Why don't you listen to it after you've dropped me off, then you can tell me if there's anything important I should know about?" she kindly offered.

Resigned as always, I switched to Radio One, midway through Bastille's *Overjoyed*. I turned up the volume, and we sang along at the top of our voices.

Generally, I loved the morning drive to school, but as we set off down the snaky lane, I felt my stomach gurgle in protest at the jostles and jolts of the weather worn tarmac. I tried to distract myself by admiring the heather clad and wooded hillside of Applecross that sprang up like a gleaming emerald before us.

It looked as though it would be a glorious day. The sun's generous spring rays beamed down between Applecross and Fairy Glen of Balnaknock and illuminated the burn that wound its way towards the village of Daxters a few miles further east. The rich variety of trees that rose from the banks of the stream up the side of Balnaknock had emerged from their long, unadorned hibernation. A lustrous green shimmered and rose from the valley floor like a great wave. Our side of Applecross and Balnaknock lay swathed in deciduous woodland with a flourish of birch and beech trees. In contrast, a few miles up the valley lay large areas of pine forest and rolling heather clad glens.

The fourteen-mile drive to Lochinver took thirty minutes unless it had snowed or we got held up behind a tractor or scatterings of sheep, in which case it could take considerably longer. As we rounded a bend in the road and hit the bottom of the hill, my face grew hot, my head began to swim, and I felt a flood of nausea. I had to stop, and damn quickly too.

"Sorry, I need some air."

I swung into a layby on the edge of Loch Dubh, and the car shuddered to a halt. I pushed the door open and ran down the embankment. I leaned against a boulder and retched until my ribs ached and the back of my throat burned.

My thoughts raced as I considered what was making me ill.

It's morning, and I've been sick. Even so, our marriage hadn't been a hotbed of unbridled desire and spontaneous sex recently. I cast my mind back. Max had been distracted, moody and often tired the past few months. Several times I'd tried to get him to open up, talk things through, but he hadn't been forthcoming. Rather, he had responded by snapping at me and arguing over the slightest thing. Still, now wasn't the time to deliberate our relationship or the state of my sexual health. I needed to get a grip, get Lyssa to school and myself to work.

Stirred from my thoughts by a sharp screech of brakes, I spun around to see the roof of a white van as it pulled up behind my car. I heard a door slam and remembering Lyssa was alone in the car I felt a spark of adrenaline and sprinted back up the bank. As I reached the top I heard my car start. I watched helplessly as it shot forwards and tore down the road at a startling speed.

CHAPTER THREE

I sprinted into the road. "Wait!" I screamed and watched my car disappear around the bend. "Lyssa!"

I ran to the van. The door remained open, but it was empty. My heart sank – the keys had gone. I could barely breathe, let alone think straight. My head spiralled. Lyssa was in the car with a lunatic, a psychotic killer, a paedophile for all I knew. My bag and phone were in there so I couldn't call the police or anyone.

"Lyssa!" I fell to my knees, my vision flashed white and I vomited.

I ran after the car, but the futility overwhelmed me. Perhaps when he saw Lyssa in the back he would let her out or run away himself. I imagined Lyssa screaming and opening the car door as they moved. And what about her asthma? She'd be petrified and panicking. My mind reeled with gruesome scenarios and I couldn't figure out what to do.

I slowed to catch my breath. Where was the traffic? This road could never be considered busy, but there was usually a steady run of cars, especially in the morning. As I jogged, I was sweating on the outside and freaking out on the inside, and the road in front appeared weirdly distorted. For the next hundred yards or so, I heard only the soft rhythmic thud of my rubber soles on the tarmac and my breath which came in recurring, heavy gasps. Then over that I heard the distant rumble of a car.

I spun around.

"Hurry up," I cried and willed it to appear.

A black Jag flew over the brow of the hill. I stood in the middle of the road and waved my arms like a demented air traffic controller. The car's wheels juddered and the window slid down.

"Help me. Someone's got my daughter... my car."

The man and woman looked at me, their faces wide with alarm.

"Get in." The man urged.

As I climbed in the back, the woman turned round in her seat.

"Which way?" she said.

"Straight on. We might catch up." I wanted to offer to drive so I could put my foot down. "I need to get to the police, in Lochinver?" I sat forwards and scanned ahead. "Can I use your phone?"

I couldn't get reception and I dialled 999 over and over again. "Bloody hills. For Christ's sake."

"Can you pull over at the top of the hill?" I said.

I got out of the car and raised the phone in the air. It caught a glimmer of a signal and I got through to an emergency operator.

"I'm putting out an immediate alert. Make your way to Lochinver police station."

"We're going now," I said, as I shook and sobbed.

I left a frantic message on Max's phone and knew it would scare the life out of him. I hoped it would. I needed him. Why wasn't he picking up?

I tried his office. His PA, Carla, told me he was visiting a client.

"Oh God," she said. "I'll get hold of him."

The woman drove quickly. The car hugged the bends and picked up speed on the straights. I explained what had happened and frantically looked down every road, gap in the trees and track that we passed.

The woman's eyes remained on the road ahead, but I saw her exchange a harried look with her partner. I tried Max, but again he didn't answer. I figured he had no signal; blocked by the hills and mountains.

I remembered Louis at home, but I didn't want to scare him, especially as I wasn't with him. No, better for him to remain in blissful ignorance, at least for now.

I felt the bile scorch up my throat. I clenched my teeth, breathed hard in and out, but I refused to yield to yet another wave of nausea.

I tried Max again, and his phone went straight to answerphone. "Jesus Max. Where the hell are you?"

CHAPTER FOUR

Absent Without Leave

We raced over the arched stone bridge that spanned the river Inver, headed into town and disregarded the flashing 30mph warning sign. I directed them to the police station, an unassuming red brick building next to the village hall. It sat midway down Main Street, which ran parallel to the bay with its busy fishing port and narrow shingle beach. We pulled up, I blurted 'thank you' and slammed through the doors. I saw an officer behind the front desk, and she immediately knew who I was, no doubt by the look of panic on my face.

"Katriina O'Donnell?"

I nodded once and fresh tears fell.

"Chief Inspector Christine Keir," she said, and lifted the counter panel. "I have the report."

Pete and Viv appeared beside me.

"Come with me. Does Lyssa have a mobile phone?" she said, and reached into her jacket pocket for a notebook.

"No and she's been after one for ages," I said, and followed her down a narrow corridor. "Could we track her if she did? Wait, my phone's in my handbag, in my car."

She led us into a small meeting room that overlooked Main Street, and pulled out a chair for me. "And does your phone have tracking?" she asked.

"I've never requested it," I said, and sat down.

"We'll give it a shot. I'm alerting all police within the area and further afield. They'll be searching for your car, for Lyssa. We're drafting in two helicopters to carry out an air search. Officers are heading to the van, and they'll bring it in for forensics. I'm going to speak to the Chief Commissioner about drafting in additional resources." She paused and shifted position, intense eyes searching mine. "Did you catch a glimpse of anyone, hear voices, anything at all?"

"No. No screams, nothing. Only the car starting and then it was gone." I stood up and went to the window. I parted the blinds half expecting to see my car pulling up, the driver having realised what a terrible mistake he'd made. "Where is she?"

Inspector Keir joined me at the window and touched my arm. "Please Katriina, sit down. I'll get you some tea." She guided me back to my seat. "You're shaking and in shock."

"I don't want tea. I want my daughter."

Viv put her arm around my shoulder.

Inspector Keir continued; her tone quietly controlled. "Yes, we need to find her, and we'll do all that we can and as quickly as we can."

"I have to talk to Louis, my son. He's at home."

"I'll send an officer to fetch him as soon as I can spare one."

I nodded, but felt an overwhelming sense of panic building inside of me.

"I need to try Max again," I said.

"There's a phone in the office," she offered.

I followed her through to a room behind the front desk. Two officers looked up, one was on the phone, and the other spoke into his radio. A phone rang, and Inspector Keir picked it up. My stomach lurched, was there news? But instead she organised for more officers to come here. I stood at the only free desk and dialled my mobile. It rang out then went to answerphone. The same thing happened again. Perhaps whoever had Lyssa had switched it off or thrown it out. I tried to remember if it was still on silent from how I'd left it last night.

I rang Max. Still, there was no answer.

"I need you Max. Lyssa's gone. It was a van driver." I sobbed and hung up.

I rang Carla.

"I'm so sorry Kat, I can't track him down. I left a message with his client in Penrun. They were supposed to meet at nine."

"Please Carla," I begged. "You have to find him."

I hung up and dialled Max again. I listened to it ringing over and over. I calculated that he had set off from home at seven-thirty, it was nine-forty-five now, and it couldn't have taken more than forty minutes to drive to Penrun. Perhaps he'd stopped off somewhere. It went to answerphone.

"Where the fuck are you Max?"

15

CHAPTER FIVE

Break A Leg
Oban, Scotland, May 1993

"Mum," I shouted from the bottom of the steep, narrow staircase. "Mum."

"What?" Came Mum's sleep-ridden reply.

I'd forgotten Mum had worked a night shift and I ran upstairs to my parent's bedroom. The curtains were drawn, save for a three-inch gap that allowed a rectangular block of sunlight to shine through. Miniscule specks of dust floated randomly through the light, and bounced against one another before disappearing into the ether. I stepped over to Mum's dressing table chock-full of various lotions and pots of inexpensive ethnic jewellery. I picked up a can of hairspray and slipped it into my coat pocket.

"Sorry Mum. I'm off to rehearsal. I've had lunch, packed my costumes."

Mum's strawberry blonde hair lay spread out in messy streaks across the midnight blue pillowcase, reminiscent of flames licking the night sky. She lay on her back and her heavy-lidded eyes peered up at me.

"Of course. What time will you be home?"

"Adrian said we'd be there 'til everything was perfect, so it might be late."

"OK honey. Don't walk home on your own," Mum said, and turned over. "Good luck. I mean, break a leg."

"I think you're supposed to save that 'til the first performance." I knelt on the bed and planted a kiss on her head.

Now that I'd reached the golden age of sixteen, my parents had given me almost complete freedom to come and go as I pleased, and I took full advantage of this liberty. I glanced at the bedside clock. Adrian had been most insistent on us starting at two on the dot.

"Howdy girls. Everyone ready?" Adrian leaned a thick, muscular arm against the door to the dressing room. "Come on ladies. Leave your make-up. Katriina, where's your dress?"

"Isn't it customary to knock before you come into the girls' dressing room?" I called, and slipped behind the near-empty clothes rail.

"I shouldn't think that includes me. I am the Director, and I've seen plenty of naked women before."

I watched him shift position to give himself a better view.

"Not me though." I crouched down, and cursed that I'd forgotten my robe.

The other girls shrieked with laughter.

"Has he gone?" I peeped out from behind a silver sequinned jacket that hung on the back of a chair.

"Aye, not that he was in much of a hurry. Come on Kat, you're first on," said Polly. She flung my white strappy dress at me.

As Polly zipped me up, I whispered, "Adrian's giving me the creeps."

"Oh but he's cute. Those biceps and those eyes. He definitely fancies you," she said. "Don't you like him, even a bit?"

"No I don't, he's ancient. And I don't think Hal would be too happy to know he's been perving around," I said, and stepped into a pair of six inch glittery stilettoes.

"Anyway, the show will be over soon," Polly said. She stood in front of the full-length mirror, then turned sideways on to continue her assessment. "Think you'll do the next?"

"Maybe. Depends on the play." I sat on the stool in front of the dressing mirror and applied the ruby red lipstick I'd been instructed to wear. "And who's directing it." I caught Polly's eye in the mirror.

Adrian's best RADA voice came over the intercom.

"Please will all cast members make their way to their starting positions? Curtain up in five minutes. I repeat, five minutes

CHAPTER SIX

The McNalty Clan - 1993

"Here's Johnny!" called Gordon McNalty, and banged the front door shut. He hung up his black woollen work jacket on the old wooden coat stand in the corner of the hallway.

"In the kitchen, my love," called Anna.

"Hiya Dad," said Allannah, as he walked into the kitchen.

"Hello my beauties." Gordon brushed a calloused palm down Alannah's cheek as he passed, then kissed Anna on the mouth.

"Where's Kat? Upstairs revising or over at Hal's?" he asked.

"Neither, it's dress rehearsal day." Anna served up the evening meal. "She's been at the theatre all afternoon."

"Aye, of course. What night do we see it?" he asked.

Anna placed a heaped plate of spaghetti onto the kitchen table. "Saturday, the grand finale. Should be nice and slick by then."

Gordon washed his hands in the sink full of warm soapy water. "Blinking-well hope so, or they'll have missed the boat. Any parmesan?"

"In the fridge," said Anna, and set a bottle of homemade lemonade at the centre of the table. "I'm sure it'll be wonderful. I know Katriina will be. She's spent endless hours practicing her lines. And she's got so many."

"You've got me a ticket haven't you Mum?"

"Of course my love. Front row seats."

"Have you seen the shoes she's got to wear? Seriously, Kat in stilettoes," said Allannah, giggling. "I bet she can't even walk in them, let alone do the Can-Can."

"Aye, that'll be, how shall I put it - entertaining? Reckon I'd be OK in them though," said Gordon. He performed a clumsy high-kick and staggered across the kitchen lino.

18

"Oh stop it, Gordon. She'll blow everyone away with her Oscar-winning performance, and you two will have to eat your words."

"How was the sea today Daddy?" said Allannah, as part of her welcome home to Dad routine.

"Rough, again. Far too many sick passengers."

Allannah pulled a face. "Aww Dad, don't. I'm eating."

Gordon guffawed before grating parmesan over his dinner. "You did ask," he said. "Hope it's OK Anna, I said I'd meet a few of the lads later at The Angel."

"Course, I might join you. But it'll have to be after Pride and Prejudice, final episode tonight. Oh, I know what I meant to tell you. I've booked the flights to Oslo. I rang Mum, and she's so excited about seeing us again."

"Och heck. I'll have to brush up on my Norwegian," he said, and managed a poor impersonation of Anna's accent while he twisted spaghetti around his fork. "Give me the dates, and I'll book the time off. How was your shift? You weren't back when I left."

"Busy as ever. But, I stayed on because I wanted to sit with young Frances until her mum arrived." Anna glanced at Allannah. "I don't think she's got long. The poor lass is asleep more than awake now, bless her heart." Anna rested her spoon and fork against the bowl. "It's breaking her parents' hearts, and they haven't begun to come to terms with what's happening. Don't expect they ever will." Anna's eyes brimmed with tears.

Gordon chewed slowly. "Life can be so cruel. It's hard to believe I watched Frances compete against Katriina at sports day only last year. I remember Kat saying how pleased she was to have beaten her, as if she was the one to beat."

Allannah fiddled with a strand of her curly auburn hair. "Tom wasn't in school last week. I wondered if it was because of Frances."

"It might be better if the boys were in school, help take their mind off things." Anna reached across the table and gave her daughter's hand a gentle squeeze. "Gordon, could you drop round and see Michael when you get a chance? He can't be at Frances' bedside as much as Pearl. Someone has to look after the boys." Anna's tears rolled freely down her cheeks as her food grew cold.

"Aye, I'll go tomorrow. I can stay with the boys while he visits. And I'll take him some bottles of homebrew too," he added as an afterthought.

As their evening turned to night, the McNalty family, minus one Katriina McNalty, continued talking with ease around the kitchen table, of both the significant things going on in their lives, as well as the day's trivialities. The lampposts began to light up in turn around the harbour, sending shimmering flickers across the gentle ripples of the sheltered water as the last of the fishing boats returned to their moorings beside the harbour walls. Outside, the melodic clinking of the flagpole sounded in the wind, and the occasional call of a gull still scavenging for any fish discarded by the fishermen.

CHAPTER SEVEN

Temptation
The Swan Theatre, Oban

Late that evening, after one diabolical dress rehearsal was followed by another marginally less diabolical dress rehearsal, we changed out of our costumes and made our way, somewhat dispiritedly, into the auditorium. Adrian sat alongside Pat the stage manager with several sheets of notes spread out on the table in front of them. They talked in undertones, with solemn expressions.

I slumped into the seat next to Polly and awaited the dressing down I knew was about to hit us. We'd been rehearsing for hours, I was shattered and just wanted to go home, soak in a hot bubble bath then collapse into my warm bed.

"Here we go," I said to Polly, and looked at my watch.

"Hey guys, settle down. Shhh!" Adrian stood and waved his arms melodramatically until the talking died down. "Listen guys. I realise you're all here for the love of your art, but we have to make this production the best we can. We want good reviews in the press don't we?" He paused for emphasis. "And I was thinking, if we pull it off we could take it to the Edinburgh Fringe Fest'. Rent a flat on Princes Street. We'll *wow* a more cultured, slash, international audience." He drew a breath. "But some of you are still making slip-ups on your lines. Steve, Kim." Adrian consulted his notes, "Polly, Ricky. I'm sorry, but that cannot happen on Tuesday. It's not fair to the rest of the cast, and it'll be humiliating. Get 'em right, yah?"

Adrian talked, no wittered on, for another fifteen minutes, each and every one of us instructed where we had gone wrong.

I sat next to Polly on Row G, and rested my Doc Martens on the seat in front. I raised my hand.

"Yes, Katriina." Adrian plucked off his reading glasses and sucked the end of an earpiece as though he were deep in intellectual thought.

I tilted my head and smiled sweetly. "Did any of it go OK?"

"Of course it did." He nodded, enthused. "It's just I don't want to keep you here all night. There were plenty of fantastic performances, and some of the scenes were quite moving." He paused briefly. "Right, thanks people. Any questions?" He skimmed the auditorium. "Great. I'll see you all tomorrow for the technical rehearsal, OK? Change into costumes if you want to get into character, but otherwise come as you are. Six on the dot."

We all got up to leave. As I reached the bottom step, Adrian put a heavy hand on my shoulder.

"Katriina, a quick word?"

I glanced at Polly. "Yeah sure."

"It's OK Polly." He nodded. "You get off. I won't keep her long."

"Oh right. Are you sure you don't want me to wait Kat?"

Before I got a chance to say, 'Yes. Please don't leave me alone.'

Adrian stepped in. "No need. I'll see Katriina safely home."

"See you at school then." Polly gave a cheerful wave and followed the other young thespians out through the auditorium doors.

I watched the doors swing shut behind her.

"I want to run through the scene where you meet Kav for the first time, OK?"

"I'm sure you said that one went well," I replied, and felt annoyed at being kept later than the others.

"It did go reasonably well. I just think you can bring out the, how can I put it, the tension a bit more."

"You should have asked Ricky to stay. Surely it's a two-way thing?"

"He had to get off, and I can play Kav. Come on. It'll only take five minutes."

Full of reluctance, I followed him to the rehearsal room and wondered why we couldn't run through it on the main stage.

"So, as Kav walks in, you clock him, take a sip of your drink then look back at him. You can't take your eyes off him. Your gaze drifts up and down his taut muscular body, and you imagine what it would be like to be with him. Try it from there." Adrian pulled out a table

22

and indicated for me to lean up against it like it was a bar. Adrian stepped out of the room, then when he walked back in I saw him flick the light switch. The door clicked shut and plunged the room into darkness.

My voice rose. "Hey, what's happening?"

"Stay where you are Katriina. I'll find you."

Feeling panicky, I grabbed the edge of the table, ducked down, and slipped underneath.

As he neared, he spoke in a deep, gravelly voice. "I never resist temptation, because I have found things that are bad for me do not tempt me."

What was he on about? That wasn't a line from our play. Instinctively, I knew I had every reason to be frightened and I crawled out from between the table legs and headed for the crack of light beneath the door.

I heard him bang into the table.

"Katriina, I want us to get to know one another better. You want it too don't you?"

I made a bolt for the door.

He grabbed my leather jacket and swung me around. "Don't go. I won't hurt you." He forced himself up hard against me, his hands all over my backside.

"Get off me," I hissed, and kicked out.

"Katriina! Katriina, are you here?"

I heard Mum's distinctive Norwegian accent echoing through the auditorium.

"Mum!" I screamed. "Mummy."

Adrian shoved me away and opened the door wide. The fluorescent light from the corridor poured in. I bolted down the passageway and through to the auditorium, straight into Mum's arms.

"Katriina, whatever's the matter?" Mum's eyes were wide.

Adrian appeared behind me.

"Hi, Mrs McNalty. We were just practising one of Katriina's scenes, and the light bulb went in the middle of it. Think it frightened you, didn't it Katriina?" He forced a phoney smile, but looked straight through me.

Mum took my hand. "You're shaking my love. Are you OK?"

23

"I'm all right, I think," I said, and edged behind her.

"It's a good job I turned up by the look of things." Mum's eyes locked on Adrian's. "I don't know what's been going on, but I'm taking Katriina home. Trust me, young man, it had better not be anything you might live to regret."

Our white, pebble-dashed terraced cottage on the harbour front was just a short walk from the theatre. Mum sat me down in our small but warm living room and switched on the television.

"Try to relax Katriina. I'm going to make us some hot chocolate."

I nodded and turned to the TV. A wildlife documentary about ants. I watched as a beautiful, raven-haired scientist guided a microscopic camera into the depths of an ant's nest, revealing its crazy inner workings, with its tunnels, clusters of shiny white eggs and myriads of ants that scurried about in manic streams.

Mum soon returned with two large mugs and a serious expression. She placed one in my hand and sank onto the sofa next to me. "What went on in there my love? It's important you tell me. And I want you to remember that nothing, and I mean nothing ever shocks me."

I lifted my cup, sipped some of the creamy froth and swallowed. "Adrian said the rehearsal was over and we could leave. Then he stopped me and said I had to rehearse one of the scenes again. All I remember is him switching off the light in the rehearsal room and shutting the door. And he started talking about never resisting temptation. It was horrible."

I cried and tears spilled across my cheeks. I drew a deep breath. "I don't know what would have happened if you hadn't come."

Mum mulled it over. "Did he touch you anywhere?" she said evenly.

"In that room when it went dark, he grabbed me tight. Then you shouted, and he pushed me away. And he's been creeping me out the past few days. Especially today when we were getting changed."

"He came into the girls changing room?"

"And I wasn't wearing much."

She placed her mug on the coffee table. She turned to me and took both of my hands.

"Why did you come?" I asked. "You never pick me up."

Mum shook her head lightly. "I'm not sure. I only remember having an intensely strong feeling, more of a sensation really, that I must find you. I can't explain it."

"I'm so glad Mum. I was scared. And he turned that light off. It wasn't the bulb going."

"OK my love, leave it with me. Are you still going to do the play?"

"I'm not missing out because of him."

"That's fine. I'll have to tell Dad, and we'll decide what's to be done."

"Thank you, Mum. And thank you for coming to find me." I kissed her cheek, and we held one another.

The following evening, I arrived at the theatre with Mum firmly in tow. Adrian greeted us somewhat less heartily than usual. He acted as though nothing untoward had happened the previous night, but I noticed him cast a nervous glance at Mum.

"Right people, we're almost there. One final push to get us ready for opening night."

"Hey Adrian, how did you get the black eye," asked Polly, with a grimace. "It looks sore."

I looked at Mum with a lift of the eyebrows, and she gave the tiniest wink back.

"Umm, I tripped on the stairs, fell face first into the banister," came his chipper reply. "And yes Polly, it is extremely sore."

CHAPTER EIGHT

Cupid's Arrow - 1997

It was Freshers week and I was working behind the bar of the packed out Student Union, a much sought after position at Strathclyde University. Drinks promotions, combined with an air of youthful exuberance made for a vibrant atmosphere. I noticed there were also a fair number of students in their second or third years that had come along to join in the fun. As I was working, I had a legitimate excuse to check out all the new faces. Oasis' hit *Wonderwall*, blasted out.

My friend, Rosie - pretty, blonde and uber confident with the opposite sex, tapped me on the shoulder. "Hey, Kat. See the super tall Greek god with the cheekbones to your right."

I glanced over, but feigned only slight interest.

"Yes, he's gorgeous, but I bet he knows it. And if he isn't taken I don't reckon it'll take him long to hook up here," I shouted. "Anyway, looks like Pippa's first in line." I noticed my pint was overflowing and flicked the tap up.

"Like hell she is," said Rosie.

And with all the grace of a rugby left back, Rosie elbowed Pippa aside. Pippa looked over at me, her face an absolute picture.

As I poured a pint of snakebite and black for a fresher with an unfortunate case of acne, I noticed Rosie all but snogging her Greek god. She leaned across the bar and pretended she couldn't hear him, then with a coquettish smile, she took his money. He grinned and lapped up the attention like a hypnotised puppy. A noticeable nudge from Jess, the manager, meant Rosie had to move on to serve some of the less attractive students.

Rosie sidled up to me and with a smug smile said, "Guess who's off to see *Max* as soon as we finish here?"

She pronounced his name in a bewildering accent that I couldn't place with her overriding Yorkshire accent.

"You've got a date?" I said.

"Well, not exactly, but I asked if he wanted to hang out later, and he said, 'yeah that'd be grand'." Cue strange accent. "Max is from Dublin, and his voice is soo fucking sexy. Just like him." She laughed and darted away.

How did she do it? She couldn't resist the urge to seduce every man she took a shine to, and most of them fell for her in a nanosecond. Not that I was in the least bit jealous. I'd recently finished with my first real love of eighteen months, David, and while I had initiated the split, I was still feeling raw and nowhere near ready to start seeing anyone else. Despite that, I'd already had three tolerable offers from eager Freshers, and that was just in the past hour. I felt rather like a seasoned undergraduate, more motherly figure than girlfriend material. I also got the impression that some of them struggled to handle being away from home for the first time, with access to unlimited cheap alcohol. I had a decent view of the room, and I figured Cupid must have been firing his arrows left, right and every which way, as the place seemed to be full of beautiful young things in search of love. Either that or everyone was intoxicated.

By eleven o'clock I realised what a fantastic job I had. It allowed me to socialise with friends and bag several free drinks in the process. What a result. But it was hard work too, and I was relieved when the bar closed, and I'd done my fair share of collecting and washing glasses. Lots of students still milled around, although they listed in various directions and swayed when they walked.

"Kat. Over here."

I spun around and saw Rosie waving. I headed over to the orange plastic sofas, and as promised, she was sitting up close to Mr-I'm-a-hunk-and-don't-I-know-it.

"Katriina, meet Max, he's from Dublin." Cue accent. "He's doing …what was it?" she said, gazing into his eyes and placing a well-manicured hand on his thigh.

"Hi there Katriina, great to meet you. Have a seat. You look all done in." He extended his hand and shifted over to make room.

I shook his hand. Great, I thought, I look knackered. Students didn't generally shake hands. Still, he didn't look like your average Strathclyde student. More mature I guessed and better dressed. He wore a green shirt under a black woollen jumper, slim fitting stonewashed jeans and brown leather Jodhpur boots. A stylish look, I thought. I looked down at the gaping rip in the knee of my baggy jeans and hastily crossed my legs.

"I've just finished my degree at Dublin Uni, and I'm doing a Postgrad in Sustainable Architectural Design. Think I made the right choice coming here," he said, and smiled.

With his warm Southern Irish accent and humorous eyes, he was becoming more attractive by the second.

"How about you," he asked me. "What's your subject? Wait, let me guess." He paused, wrinkled his nose, tilted his head and said, "Drama?"

"Actually, no," I said, and laughed "I'm doing Environmental Science, final year. Which means I'm going to have to knuckle down to some serious study." Then I realised this made me sound like a signed up member of the geek squad, and quickly added. "But I'll be making the most of the social side of things."

The three of us chatted for a while, and I soon realised he wasn't anywhere near as shallow as his good looks might have suggested. He seemed super intelligent, mature and genuinely interested in what we had to tell him about Glasgow and the University.

"Kat, I promised to show Max around campus. Do you want to come or would you rather go home and sleep?" She followed this with a non-too-subtle wink, which meant I had little option but to decline her kind offer.

"Ah, a tour of the campus... at midnight." I resisted the urge to wink back. "No, I'll get back." In fact, I felt revived. Still, I thought, all's fair in love and war.

Despite my tired legs and alcohol consumed I slept fitfully. I had a couple of vivid dreams, one of which involved Max. I dreamed that he gave me a piggyback up the steps of a steep lecture theatre and as he climbed he squeezed my bottom while I nibbled his earlobe. It felt exquisitely erotic and my insides pulsed with pleasure. I decided not to share that dream with Rosie.

I felt sure Rosie would have spent the night at Max's digs and I resigned myself to a quiet morning alone. She might have brought him back to the flat, but that wasn't usually her style. But as I padded barefoot and bleary-eyed into the kitchen, the aroma of fresh coffee greeted me and I saw Rosie with a mug in her hand. She gazed wistfully out of the window.

I rinsed a mug under the tap. "I didn't expect to see you this morning."

"No, me neither." She regarded me sideways on for a moment then took a sip of her coffee. "Max and I had such a lovely stroll across campus. Then he made up an excuse about having to go home, alone, something to do with a flatmate."

Clearly, Rosie wasn't pleased to have been rebuffed, and it certainly wasn't something she experienced often. Men tended to swarm around her like bees around honeysuckle, drawn by her flirtatious self-confidence and beauty.

She leaned against the storage heater, sipped her coffee and looked at me. "In fact, if I'm honest, what irked me was he wanted to talk about you. Though I'll give him his due, he tried to be subtle."

"Oh, I'm sure you imagined it." I poured some coffee. "Why, what did he say?"

"You know, dropping your name into the conversation. Asking when we'd met, where you were from, blah blah blah." Her eyes narrowed. "It's OK Kat. I wouldn't mind if you did fancy him." She sauntered over and placed her cup in the sink. "I could hardly blame you. I did kinda dump you didn't I?" Her voice became sheepish. "Sorry about that."

"Well, you looked like you were getting on, and anyway, I'm not ready to start dating again." I sat at the breakfast bar and thought she looked a bit down, which was quite out of character. One of the things I loved about Rosie was her upbeat personality, and how she bounced back from any setbacks.

In truth, I had found Max attractive and felt envious of Rosie. However, I decided she'd imagined his interest in me, and I knew I wouldn't be doing anything to bring about a chance meeting. More importantly, I was starting my final year, and while achieving a first was probably too hopeful, I knew if I worked hard I could get a 2.1, the next best thing.

CHAPTER NINE

Ancestry

When I was a child we were often short of money. However, I looked back fondly on my childhood. My parents loved one another and enjoyed spending time with my sister and me, whether we were away camping, exploring the coastline or playing epic games of Monopoly on a rainy afternoon.

My parents had met in Oban when my Norwegian mum travelled with her two best friends and visited the Western Isles.

Dad sometimes regaled us with his version of how they met, and delighted in the memory every time.

"The moment your mum stepped on that ferry I was spellbound. She wore her long, golden hair in a shiny side plait, she was tall and tanned, and when she beamed her gorgeous smile right at me, I just knew she was the one." Dad often looked wistful and dewy-eyed.

"What your dad's forgotten to mention is that it was me who asked him out. He was far too shy. Admittedly he didn't take much persuading." Mum used to tell us. "If I hadn't asked him I'm not sure we'd be here today and neither would you two girls."

I never tired of hearing them talk about it and in my over romanticised mind I pictured them hand in hand on the deck of the ferry as they leaned against the rails and gazed into the sunset on the horizon.

"Once I'd returned to Norway, being apart was such torture that one day your dad turned up in Bergen and that was it," Mum said, and smiled like the cat that got the largest share of the cream.

After I came along, and two years later my sister Alannah, we moved back to Oban where Dad resumed work on the ferries like he had never been away. I had a few vivid but imprecise memories of life as a young child in Norway, but I wondered if it had been the photograph albums that Mum had lovingly put together that had planted such recollections.

Every so often, I tried to imagine what my life might have been like if they had chosen to stay in Norway. I had found it incredibly beautiful whenever we visited relatives; though, I conceded, no more beautiful than Scotland, and just as rainy.

CHAPTER TEN

Local Constabulary

After another interminably long hour sitting and waiting, a stomach-churning pain continued to curve and coil through me like a surgeon's needle had threaded its way around my every nerve and fibre. Viv laid a light hand on my arm, and as I turned to her, it occurred to me it was unfair for them to be involved.

"Shall I try ringing Max?" she said.

"There's no point. I've left enough messages," I said, and then added, "You don't have to stay."

"But we can't leave you on your own. And we want to know Lyssa is all right," she said.

As I looked into her eyes, I realised they were already emotionally involved, despite it being mere chance they were here with me at all.

"If you swap numbers you can keep in touch," Inspector Keir suggested. "I'm sure Mr O'Donnell will arrive soon."

Even though we'd only met a few hours ago, we hugged like close friends.

"Please call if we can do anything to help. Even if only to drive you somewhere, or to look after Louis." Pete said, and wrote down his number.

"You've been so kind," I said.

"I only wish we could do more." Viv clasped my hands, and tried to smile through the tears that threatened to unveil her composure. "Have hope and faith, Katriina."

I stood at the window and watched Viv turn to me with the faintest of smiles and a small nod before getting into the car.

"The incident room is up and running, and forensics are out back going over the van," said Inspector Keir.

I felt increasingly bewildered as officers passed the open doorway. They talked with urgency and gave the impression of making strenuous efforts to pinpoint Lyssa's whereabouts. A couple of them introduced themselves and explained what they were doing to help. If they were trying to reassure me, it wasn't working.

An officer walked in. "I'm Constable Lynne Pearce. Inspector Keir has asked me to sit with you until your husband arrives." She closed the door behind her.

I would have preferred the door remained open, but I didn't have the presence of mind to object. As she drew up a chair, I wanted to tell her she was wasting her time and should be out there doing her job. She shot me a sympathetic smile and talked to me, no doubt to divert my thoughts.

I had seen her a few times around Lochinver, but not in uniform. She was instantly recognisable with her pretty, chocolate-box face and jet-black hair, tied back neatly. I assumed Inspector Keir didn't dare leave me on my own, fearing I might succumb to full-blown hysterics. Her upbeat words did nothing to reassure me.

"So my Danny's at school with Louis, year above." She nodded. "Has Louis got a girlfriend?"

"No," I said. I didn't add that if he had I would probably be the last person to know.

"My Danny's been seeing Jo for over a year. She might as well live with us. They're never apart. No matter how often I tell him he needs to focus on his studies, all he's interested in is seeing her. That won't help him get into University will it?" She tutted and pursed her lips.

"No," I mumbled, and was curious as to why she kept referring to him as my Danny. I wondered if she'd had a custody wrangle with his father.

"She's a lovely girl though."

"Who is?" I asked, in a tone that I hoped would deter further conversation.

"Jo, my Danny's girlfriend."

Why wasn't she asking about Lyssa? Hadn't she been trained to investigate a crime?

Shrouded by morbid thoughts, I abandoned the small talk and zoned out from her nervous chatter. My stomach made peculiar noises, and I felt queasy again, although now I wasn't sure if it was down to stress or a continuation of what I'd felt earlier.

Word must have got out about Lyssa, and I noticed a couple of reporters with cameras and microphones hovering outside. I watched as one of them, a young woman, tried to get into the station, presumably to better suss out the gory details, and when that failed, she commandeered anyone willing to stop and join in the drama. They prowled around like wild dogs, ready to pounce on any unsuspecting victim. The sight of them sickened me, and I wanted to scream at them all to bugger off.

Finally, three hours after I had first rung him, Max's Range Rover screeched to a halt in front of the station. Constable Pearce hurried through to the lobby and brought him in.

"Is it true, you've lost Lyssa?" His look of disbelief showed that my messages hadn't sunk in.

I cried again, but felt a hint of relief to see him. I reached out to hold him; I wanted him to tell me everything would be fine.

He stepped away.

"Someone's taken her Max. Got in my car, there was a van. It drove off. I don't know where she is." I was shaking and babbling incoherently.

"You're not making sense."

"OK. OK." I took a breath. "I stopped in a layby because I felt sick and dizzy. And when I was down the bank a white van pulled up. They've taken my car and Lyssa was in the back." I took Max's hand, but he yanked it away.

"You left the door unlocked and the keys in the ignition, with Lyssa inside?" His eyes sharpened.

Max blamed me. Was it my fault?

"But I wouldn't put her in danger, and you know it."

"But you did."

I saw a muscle twitch at the corner of his mouth. His face was bitter, his features suddenly ugly and unfamiliar.

Constable Pearce tried to diffuse the argument brewing in front of her. "Max, I understand you're upset. Inspector Keir wants to speak to you to see if you know anything that could help."

Furious, Max turned on her. "I wasn't there was I? What the hell do I know? You're wasting time when you should be out there looking for her."

As he protested, Inspector Keir walked in and closed the door behind her.

"Chief Inspector Keir," she said, and extended her hand.

Max's hands remained firmly at his side.

I thought it was the shock that made Max behave rudely.

"It'll only take a few minutes, and rest assured, I have no intention of wasting anyone's time. I've already questioned Katriina. We often find out vital information where no one expects to, so if you'll come with me we won't be delaying the investigation one bit."

Max scowled and nodded once, signalling his reluctant but unavoidable compliance.

I moved to follow them, but Constable Pearce took my arm.

"He won't be long, and sometimes it's useful to talk to family members on their own." She sat down, swept up a strand of black hair and tucked it back into her ponytail.

"I don't know what he can tell her," I said, and shrugged "He's right, he wasn't anywhere near us."

I slumped back onto my seat and felt helpless. Surely it was better if the police were out driving around and searching for her? Anything was better than sitting at the station and wasting precious time. I felt as if I was going mad with fear. Maybe whoever had stolen my car didn't want a terrified eleven-year-old girl with no idea what would happen to her. Perhaps they'd already let her go; left her alone at the side of the road.

Please let that be it, please.

Then I thought, what if - what if he did want an eleven-year-old girl?

My mind raced from one horrific scenario to the next, and I cast my thoughts back to cases of missing children. I remembered a child abduction in Cornwall. A seven-year-old girl was snatched as she walked to a friend's house a few doors away. It took the police two days to find her small, bruised and broken body lying in a ditch only a few miles away. The accused man awaited trial.

I recalled several more heart-breaking cases and I couldn't remember a single one of them that ended well. The only instances I remembered that hadn't turned into murder investigations, happened where teenage girls had run away with older men. Most of them had been paedophiles, but in their twisted minds they justified their actions because the girl had gone of her own accord. Perhaps my distrust of online social media, particularly concerning the potential dangers for young people, was justified. I thought, at least there was sometimes a better outcome for the child in these circumstances, though they would always live with the long-term psychological and physical effects.

Where did that leave Lyssa? So young and innocent, so entirely naïve when it came to anything relating to men and sex. At school, they'd had a few carefully placed lessons on sex and the dangers of grooming, and I had contrived a few discussions with her myself to introduce the world of womanhood and relationships, still several years away. Even so, such discussions couldn't have prepared her pre-teen mind for anything of that nature.

Another monumental tidal wave of anxiety rose up in me, and I hoped to God such pessimistic thoughts weren't warranted.

Max returned. Without a word he sat down, hung his head and sobbed – loud and rasping.

I pushed my chair back and knelt down in front of him.

What could I say? Words were futile.

CHAPTER ELEVEN

The Sly Fox - 1997

Exactly a fortnight after that first night in the Student Union bar, I saw Max again. I'd been a member of the University hiking club since my first year, and for our first weekend expedition of the year, fourteen of us would head up to Loch Lomond and the Trossachs National Park. James, our club chairperson, had planned a route up Benn Arum on the edge of Loch Leven, one Benn amongst a spectacular range of ancient volcanic mountains.

We loaded our rucksacks and camping gear onto the minibus, took our seats and, full with excitement, chatted about the trip.

James stood at the front looking official with clipboard and pen. "Welcome everyone. It's great to see such a fantastic turnout, and some new members too. We're gonna get going in a minute, but does anyone know Max O'Donnell?"

"I think I know who you mean, but I don't have his number or anything, sorry," I offered.

"OK, we'll give him a few minutes. I've not heard anything to say he's backing out."

As James finished speaking a white mini pulled up, exhaust blowing, and a painted Irish flag across the roof. The door swung open, and Max stumbled out with an enormous rucksack the size of an African elephant.

He staggered onto the minibus. "Sorry I'm late guys. Couldn't get my rucksack in the car."

"Really?" James smiled warmly. "Max is it?"

"Yup, that's me." Sheepish, he looked down at his rucksack and with a chortle said, "I guess I've over-packed. I was a bit unsure of what to bring."

"Or what to leave behind?" James said. "No worries mate. Bring it to the back . . . if you can."

We tried, without success, to suppress our amusement. Max could barely lift it, let alone carry it on tomorrow's fifteen-mile mountain route.

Tactful, James tried to alleviate Max's embarrassment. "You know Katriina don't you?"

Max looked over and smiled. "Yeah. Hi Katriina."

He took a seat in front of me and twisted round as the minibus moved off.

"Settling into your course OK?" I asked.

"Yeah, it's grand. Pretty full on, but exactly what I was looking for. The profs are truly amazing."

It felt wonderful to catch up with the club members, most of whom I hadn't seen since before the long summer break. Georgina, a petite, fitness obsessed redhead and one of my favourite walking buddies, was desperate to find out all of my news, especially about my split with David over the summer. By all accounts David had complained about me, and I felt relief that he'd given the hike a miss. Max slipped into the conversations going on around him. He had a gentle way about him, was unpretentious, at times self-effacing and very funny.

As we drove into the hills, the sun sank, unhurried, behind Benn Arum and the sight of the magnificent mountain, with great dark shadows that fell in-between the scarps and wide ravines caused me to sigh in admiration at the natural beauty.

Max interrupted my gaze. "It was the promise of views like this that made Strathclyde a natural choice."

"Isn't it incredible? And that peak there is our target tomorrow," I said, and pointed to the summit, currently clear of cloud and sharply radiant beneath the setting pomegranate sun.

Max let out a long low whistle. "That's one mammoth mamma."

I smiled. "And as we're taking our camping gear, we're in for a tough climb. I'm gonna leave what I can behind, and I think maybe you should do the same?" I lifted an eyebrow.

He laughed. "Maybe you could help whittle my bag down?" he asked.

His smile broadened; full of humour and sincerity and I thought he had attractive features. His smoky eyes and thick wavy hair, combined with a dark stubble, made for a striking appearance overall. He didn't look like the rugby-playing type, but his long nose had a slight kink in it as though he'd broken it at some point.

"Sure, happy to help." And I felt a spark of energy flicker deep within me.

Max was easy to talk to, and I relaxed in his company. I realised I'd flirted with him, which took me by surprise.

We were staying at a hostel near Benn Arum, which made it the ideal starting point for our first day's hike. We clambered off the minibus and lugged our rucksacks up the gravelled path. I thought how the hostel looked like one of the finest I'd stayed in. It was a large old grey stone building set back from the road and had beautiful original sash windows. It was functional inside, freshly painted, clean with well-lit rooms and high ceilings.

After we dumped our rucksacks, we headed down to the village pub, The Sly Fox. The well-stocked wood burning stove, made the atmosphere warm and inviting. We bought drinks and ordered food, then settled ourselves on a rustic arrangement of wooden stools and beer barrels around some tables. Locals filtered in, and as we were in the heart of prime hiking country, there were plenty of healthy-looking outdoorsy types. I looked around and admired the gnarled, unpainted beams and stone floor. I also noted the absence of any pretentious pub décor and wondered why we hadn't visited the pub or area before.

James vied to be heard above the raucous chatter and shouted to me across the table. "Another drink, Kat?"

"Umm, go on then. Just a half thanks."

As we all drank more than we should the night before a long hike, Max's accent grew more pronounced, and a sharp sense of humour came to the fore.

Richard, a new club member urged. "Hey Max, you must know a few good jokes."

"I do indeed," Max said, and cleared his throat. "An Irishman is struggling to find a parking space.

'Lord,' he prayed. 'I can't stand this. If you open up a space for me, I swear I'll give up the Guinness and go to mass every Sunday.' Then suddenly, the clouds parted, and the sun shone on an empty parking spot. Without hesitation the Irishman said: 'Never mind, I found one.'"

I'm sure I wasn't the only one to have heard the joke before, but fuelled by high spirits and alcohol we all shrieked with laughter.

"Another!" Georgina cried.

"One more. The beer's strong and my brain's gone fuzzy," said Max, resting his pint on his knee. "A sobbing Mrs Murphy approached Father O'Grady after mass. He said: 'So what's bothering you, Mrs Murphy?'

She replied: 'Oh, Father, I have terrible news. My husband passed away last night.'

The priest said: 'Oh, Mary, that's terrible. Did he have any last requests?'

'Indeed, he did, father. He said, 'Please Mary, put down that damn gun.'''

Max looked across the table at me, grinned and lifted his glass. "Slainte!" And downed the rest of his pint.

More ear-splitting laughter followed, and we continued to share Scottish, English and Irish jokes until the landlady kicked us out.

"I can't for one minute see how you lot are going to get up Benn Arum tomorrow. You'll never even manage to get out of your beds. Now leave," she said, and ushered us through the door.

After many goodbyes, thankyous and hugs, we staggered back to our hostel as instructed.

At 7 am prompt, James rapped on our bunk room door.

"Get up you lazy louses if you don't want to be left behind."

Minutes later, we stumbled downstairs, all worse for wear. Georgina and I took a seat at the end of a long trestle table.

"There's nothing like a few drinks to give me the munchies the morning after. I'm ravenous," I said, and tipped a heaped spoon of brown sugar onto my porridge.

"Me too . . . I think. If this doesn't revive me I'm in trouble," said Georgina. She contemplated her bacon, eggs and black pudding but looked decidedly peaky.

I glanced to the far end of the table where James and Max ate breakfast, apparently hangover free.

Max caught my eye and gave a little wave. "Mornin'. Are you still up for the rucksack challenge?"

"There's nothing I'd like more," I said, and gave a silly wave back.

After I'd spent a few frantic minutes helping Max with his rucksack, we were out of the front door and on our way. We clutched our water bottles, desperate to rehydrate for the long climb ahead.

A sunny and pleasantly mild October morning greeted us and despite our heavy night we felt excited. We headed up the narrow lane, sunken and hemmed in by drystone walls and after a few hundred yards turned up a rough but dry farm track. After a mile or so the track ran steeply up to a large run-down farmhouse. We drew closer. It was silent and still, and I thought it must be unoccupied. But then, without warning, two sheep dogs charged from an outbuilding, and barked frenziedly. One of them stopped in front of me; it snarled and bared its teeth, while the other circled us, growling and sniffing the air.

"Keep walking and don't make eye contact, they don't like it," Max suggested.

"I think they're wolves," I said, and tried not to look at either of them.

"Walk behind me, and they'll get me first," said Max. He laughed nervously and positioned himself between the dogs and me.

They barked and prowled as we hurried onwards. Then just as I thought we were safely away, I heard a terrifying snarl and a pounding of paws close by. I swung around to see one of the dog's rush headlong towards us, the hairs raised along its back, its eyes ablaze and intent on me or Max.

"Holy shit," I cried.

"Kai! Kai, get back."

Immediately, the dog skidded to a halt, and its tail dropped down between its legs. It whimpered, turned about and slunk back to the doorway of the outhouse. I looked up and saw a man in the upstairs window with a pale naked torso and shaggy grey hair that looked matted and dishevelled. But I was far more frightened by the shotgun propped under his arm.

He glowered down at us. "What the fuck are you lot doing? The footpath goes through the woods, not my fucking farm. Now get off my land, or I'll set them on the lot of you."

James started to jog. "Christ. He's deranged. Let's get out of here."

None of us needed any encouragement to get a move on.

I stole a swift glance over my shoulder and was relieved to see both dogs had sat down and were watching us with suspicion, but without any intention of threat.

"There we go, just protecting their territory," said Max, trying to make light of it.

"Let's find the proper path. Don't want that mad bastard coming after us with his gun," said Georgina, and jogged to catch up with James, her rucksack bumping up and down on her back.

"That dog was coming right at you Max. Did you see its eyes?" I said.

"You're not kiddin'. I'll be seeing them in my sleep. Do you think it was me it was coming for?" he added.

"It was after one of us."

We hurried past the out buildings then continued along a stony path that rose sharply beside a narrow, fast-flowing burn skirting the edge of the woods. Well out of earshot we talked again, though less light-heartedly.

"They should be chained up," said Nick. "I love dogs, but they must have had one shit life to make them crazy like that."

"I can't imagine him treating any of his animals well," I said.

"Red sky at night, shepherd's delight. Red sky in the mornin', get off my fuckin' land," boomed Max, in a surprisingly good West Country accent.

Relieved to be well away, we roared with laughter, and the mood of the group lightened.

We walked hard for around fifteen minutes until I stopped and gazed back down and took a photo. Max hung back too. From our position the farm looked picture postcard and snug, nestled amongst the drystone walls, trees, and heather, and it reminded me of the model farm my sister and I used to play with. I knew the scene belied the hard, unforgiving existence for the farmer and his family, especially during the dark and freezing winter months.

"These farms are no architect's dream, but they can't half withstand the weather," said Max, and then peering through his camera lens took a couple of photos. "It'd be amazing to design a home for a setting like this." He pulled a new film canister from his pocket and turned to face me. "Designing Eco homes is what I want to do."

"What about renovating old run-down houses or barns?" I said. "There're a few nowadays, either in disrepair because of the massive costs of maintaining them or sold on by families wanting an easier way of life."

During previous hikes we had come across farmhouses and crofts, carefully renovated and given a thoroughly modern look, resulting in stunning homes.

Max leaned against a pine tree, one side of its trunk cushioned with pea green moss.

"It's expensive conserving and repairing the old wood and stonework and making it into something people can afford." He took a long swig from his water bottle. "But nowadays so many of these old farm buildings have preservation orders so that's the only option. It's not just a case of knocking them down and rebuilding something new, though realistically, that would be a lot easier."

"But the farms and crofts are so integral to our landscapes. It would be a tragedy if we lost them all to modern buildings, even if they were designed to fit with their surroundings."

"Yeah, I guess," said Max.

I turned my camera on him and took a photo. "Would you live somewhere this remote?"

"As long as I could escape to civilisation once in a while then I can't think of anything better. My Uncle Melvin married a Scot, Auntie Joan, and they moved near here I think. Mum and Dad brought me to visit when I was younger . . ." his words trailed away.

"Oh," I said. "Better catch up with the others. I've got my map, but I don't know the route. Can you read a map?"

"Are you kiddin'? Nah, hopeless." Max marched off, then he turned to me with a grin and said, "Come on Katriina, you're holding me back."

By the time we reached the upper boundary of the woods, my heart pounded and I felt roasting hot.

"Good, they're waiting for us." Max pointed to the others, rucksacks off and sitting down in the middle of the path.

I drank a few gulps of water. "Thank heavens for that breakfast," I said, breathing hard.

As we progressed, the path became steeper and rockier and I tried not to sound breathless as I matched Max's unrelenting pace. We caught up and were allowed a welcome respite, and I flopped backwards using my rucksack like a reclining seat. I gazed up at the sky, still with the odd spot of blue peeking out between the ballooning clouds.

"OK gang, let's get going," James instructed. He looked comical standing with one leg propped up on a rock.

Max held out his hand. "Here, want a haul up?"

I gripped his hand, but as he started to pull me up his feet slipped from under him and he fell forwards, almost in slow motion, and landed face first between my breasts.

He lay there for a moment then peered up at me. "Oh my God! I am so sorry."

I looked at his blushing cheeks and realised how absurd we looked. I giggled. Max joined in, as did the rest of the group, and it took several minutes of uncontrolled hysterics for us to compose ourselves.

"Hey Max, I think you're being a bit forward," James managed to splutter.

"I just slipped. I swear."

"Didn't look like it, mate."

Georgie chuckled as she walked alongside me. "Blimey Katriina, if you and Max carry on at this rate, you'll have met his parents before we get to the campsite."

I cringed. "How embarrassing was that? I am such a clunk."

"Any other bloke and I'd think they'd done it on purpose, but Max, no, a total accident. It was the funniest thing I've seen in a long time and such a wasted photo opportunity."

Benn Arum was a steep mountain with two false summits and it lulled climbers into a false sense of achievement. At one point I wondered if I would make it to the top; my leg muscles burned and my back hurt, but finally we found ourselves on a long narrow ridge with a crinkled skyline and jagged summit within sight. I felt vertiginous up on the exposed ridge as clouds swelled and rolled overhead, and the bitter wind jabbed at our uncovered skin. As was usual on these walks we were entirely focused on reaching the summit, and I felt delighted when we overtook a couple of serious looking walkers.

The wind groaned and intensified as we scrambled up the last few metres to the peak. We stopped and gazed at the spectacular views and took group photographs. I tried not to look too eager when Max asked me to stand for a photo on my own, and I hastily pulled my flapping hair off my face.

"Come on guys, we need to move," shouted James, above the roar of the gale-force wind. He pointed theatrically to the skyline behind us. Dense, black clouds drifted towards us at a dramatic speed, and I knew it would be risky to be up on the exposed peak when they passed overhead. Lunch would have to wait, so I grabbed a bag of jelly babies from my pocket and handed them round as we searched for the track to take us back down.

"Guys, this way," yelled James.

The storm gathered momentum and the clouds released an ice cold torrent. The path soon became treacherous. Loose stones shifted beneath my feet and with my rucksack unstable in the wind, I almost lost my footing time and time again.

Max gripped my arm. "What's that?"

I looked through the low-lying cloud and sheeting rain to an unnatural bright green shape, barely visible, fifty or so metres away.

"I don't know," I yelled, as the wind whipped my back and the rain sliced into me.

"I think it's a person," said Max. And without further hesitation he clambered over the rocks.

I shouted a warning to the other's backs. I realised they couldn't hear me above the storm, and I knew I had to follow Max. If somebody was injured, then he or she needed help. I climbed over the rocks, and boulders, convinced it was a body. Max reached the figure. He removed his rucksack and squatted down. He turned to me, and I saw the look of fear on his face.

The stranger lay face down over a boulder. I noticed a dark, rain-soaked patch of blood on the back of the skull and when I moved a few strands of long hair I saw a deep wound, with loose skin and exposed bone. We turned him over and carefully lowered his head back onto my rucksack. I placed my palm against his cheek and to my relief I felt some warmth, despite his deathly pale skin. Not dead, at least not yet. He looked young, early thirties, his hair long and loose, and he had a neat goatee beard. Oddly, he wore a jumper, jeans, and casual trainers, but no coat or rucksack. I felt down his neck and searched for a pulse. It was discernible but fast and weak.

"What shall we do? Where are the others?" asked Max, and looked back.

"They didn't stop. One of us should go for help."

Max took my hand. "Please Katriina, you go. You map read, and hopefully the storm will soon pass over."

Torrential rain seeped through my coat and clothes, and dripped between my breasts and shoulder blades, but as it hadn't been forecast I hoped he was right and it might soon move on.

Max still had hold of my hand.

"If you're sure you'll be all right?" I said.

He nodded. "I'll be fine. It's him I'm worried about."

"Thank God you spotted him," I said, and withdrew my hand.

I removed my woolly hat and eased it onto the man's head. "I know, use your tent to protect you both. If he freezes, he'll die of hypothermia let alone from that wound. And you'll be no good to him if you get too cold." Although I put on a brave face, I was terrified he'd die before we found help.

Max unstrapped his tent. He delved into his rucksack and pulled out a T-shirt. He placed it under the hat and against the wound. "It might stem the bleeding."

As Max opened the tent it filled with air and flapped wildly in the wind. Between us we secured it over the injured man. Max sat close to him and tucked the canvas beneath his legs.

"Talk to him Max, about anything. He might be able to hear you, and it might help him to hang on."

When I crouched down and hugged Max, I thought I felt his fingers stroke the back of my head.

"I'll be back soon." I turned away and set off to find the path.

Relieved of my rucksack, I picked my way over the rocks and jogged down the track as fast as was physically possible in the conditions.

Two hundred yards down, the path narrowed and cut steeply below a rocky outcrop that hung above me. The path was obvious, and I felt sure I was going the right way. Rainwater poured off the rocks above me in miniature waterfalls and a small stream flowed down the path and filled my boots with water. I figured I would catch up with the others soon. I felt wet, cold and uneasy, and annoyed with James that he hadn't even noticed we were missing.

The path emerged through a steep sided gully and widened out, although the mist and driving rain meant I couldn't see more than a few yards in front of me. I reached a fork in the track and stopped. Neither way looked more obvious, and so I consulted my sodden map. I estimated my location and turned left, and hoped it led down to the road that ran between Glassford and Kilberry. Once there I could flag down a driver to help us, or hitch a ride.

As the rain began to ease and I was no longer blinking the rain from my eyes, I drew back my sodden hood. I gasped as a rush of ice-cold water tipped down my back. I heard the familiar clatter of shifting rocks, stopped and spun around. I felt a shot of adrenaline when a few yards back up the track a dark figure emerged from the swirling gloom. With long straggled hair and green jumper, I thought he must be the injured man but miraculously recovered. He moved rapidly towards me, running despite the slippery surface underfoot. As he neared there was nothing in his features to acknowledge he had seen me and afraid we were going to collide I quickly stepped aside.

"Hello," I said, as he drew alongside. I thought I detected the tiniest of nods before he had hurried on past. My gaze flew to the back of his head, but I could see neither a wound nor patch of blood to identify him as the man I'd left fighting for his life. I knew he couldn't be the same man but thought he must be a brother or a close relation.

"Wait! I need to speak to you," I shouted.

I set off running after him, but stumbled and fell and landed heavily on my hands and knees.

"Bloody, fucking hell!" I cursed. I leaped back up and rubbed mud and grit from my hands. I scanned the way ahead and all around me, but the figure had disappeared despite there being nothing nearby to conceal him. Maybe I was going nuts because of the situation and I'd only imagined seeing him. I was wasting time. What if he had already died? Max would still be awaiting help, cold and alone, possibly succumbing to hypothermia.

It felt like an eternity since I'd left them and I still hadn't reached the road. I pushed on down a rock-strewn track that zigzagged steeply through rain-laden bracken and heather. Then finally through the haze and still some distance downhill, I spotted headlights and knew the road was near.

I felt relieved and looked up. "Thank you, God."

"Where the hell have you been and where's Max?" Georgina fired as I reached them.

They were sheltering from the wind against the drystone wall.

I described what had happened but noticed James was missing.

"We were worried. The storm hadn't let up so James doubled back. Didn't you see him?" Georgina got out her mobile, stood on tiptoes and held it up. "Why isn't there any reception?".

"Cus we're about fifty miles from the nearest mobile mast," replied Nick, with a wry smile.

"I did see someone… not James though, he must have taken a different route. Haven't you asked anyone for help?"

"We knew something must have happened. We flagged down a woman. She said she'd get hold of mountain rescue," explained Nick.

"He'll need air rescue," I said.

"Did he have any ID, a wallet or anything?" asked Nick.

"Nothing at all. He didn't even have a jacket or rucksack," I said.

The minutes dragged on as we huddled together and awaited help.

"It's been too long. No one's coming," I said. "Let's stop a car."

"I agree. Come on," offered Georgina.

Nick looked up the hillside. "Is that James?"

James had emerged from the low-lying mist and was hurtling down the track. He walked the last few yards and leaned over, breathing so hard he could barely speak.

"So what you're telling me is… Max is back up the mountain with a critically injured man… potentially a dead man?" James' face

48

drained of all colour, feeling the full weight of responsibility for the group.

"Fraid so." I didn't soften the truth.

The distant yet distinct rumble of a helicopter silenced us. Moments later it appeared out of the cloud cover and followed the line of the road. We all waved our arms. The helicopter slowed and circled overhead. The only safe place it could land was the road, and we ran out and stopped the approaching cars.

The rumble of the engine and blades thundered through me and the force of the airstream whipped at my skin and hair. Instinctively, I stepped back from the machine's roar and power as it lowered and landed. The door slid open and a man jumped out and ran across to us.

"I was with the injured man," I said. "He's got a deep head wound. Max stayed with him, short of the summit this side," I added. My legs felt hollow.

"Are you OK coming up, point us in the right direction?" he said, with a nod to the helicopter.

"Of course," I replied, sounding far keener than I felt.

On-board, and with seatbelt tightly fastened, I felt the engine growl as the pilot powered it up. We lifted off the ground and hovered above the road briefly before it surged forwards and forced me back in my seat. The three-man crew talked back and forth to one another through their headsets. I shut my eyes as we banked at an alarming angle around the crags I'd passed through earlier and when I opened them again my stomach rocked at the terrifying proximity of the mountainside and the rising and falling sensations.

"Poor visibility approaching the peak, the pilot warned.

I pressed my forehead to the window. We flew out over the far side of the summit and circled back round again.

"Got them. Three o'clock," called one of the crew.

The helicopter lowered and hovered. I caught sight of Max waving something above his head. It was impossible to land, and instead they lowered the winch and stretcher, along with one of the crew. The helicopter swayed back and forth as the pilot fought against the wind that gusted around the peak. I peered down through the mist and glimpsed some activity. The crew radioed messages back and forth, but much of what they said sounded like code. My stomach churned and I reached for a sick bag and prayed I wouldn't need it.

After what seemed like forever the wire spooled back in, and the laden stretcher reappeared alongside the open doorway. The crew pulled them inside, unhooked the stretcher and lowered the winch again. My entire body sickened when I realised the poor soul had breathed his last. Wide eyes stared out from a vacant and lifeless blue face. Then like a flash of sheet lightning I saw the lone figure that had passed by me on the mountainside, the exact same face.

I caught the eye of one of the men who was securing the body.

He shook his head and drew the sheet over the man's face.

My insides turned over, and I heaved into the bag. My body trembled, my teeth clattered, and my eyes couldn't focus.

Within a couple of minutes, a soaked and silent Max had been brought safely aboard, our rucksacks in tow. His face looked almost as pale as the corpse but thankfully he shivered violently and appeared very much alive. As he strapped himself into the seat beside me, I put my hand on his arm and searched his eyes.

"Are you OK?" I said.

He turned to me and burst into tears. I rummaged in my coat pockets for a tissue, but only found two soggy jelly babies.

Max rubbed his eyes. "I didn't know what to do..." he wept, unable to go on.

The helicopter flew through the gloom and layers of cloud and I held onto Max. We clung to one another, silent, drawn together by the tragedy that had unfurled around us.

"You need to get checked over mate," the pilot said to Max when we were back on terra-firma.

"There's nothing wrong with me," he said. "I don't want to waste anyone's time."

"No arguments Max," the pilot insisted.

We stood aside, helpless, as they stretchered the body away.

"You don't look fine," I said. "It won't do any harm, and I'll be with you."

"Don't spose I've got much choice," said Max, and set off behind the crew.

A young nurse led us to a treatment room. Max shivered violently as she took his pulse and temperature.

"Your temperature's normal so just a case changing out of your wet clothes. Have you got any?" she asked, and eyed our rucksacks.

"They should be dry," I replied.

"Off with those wet clothes, or you'll end up with nasty chills. I'll make some tea," she said briskly.

I took hold of Max's hand. It was smooth, firm and surprisingly warm. "Better do as we're told." I grinned at Max, but he didn't return my smile.

We removed our wet coats and jumpers and I draped them over the hot radiator. Max went to the window and split the blinds. He stood and stared out, silent.

The nurse returned with two cups of tea. "Here we go, nice and sweet. It's the best thing for shock." She placed them on the cabinet by the window. "I hear an officer is on his way to take your statements." She tried to catch Max's eye but he remained unmoving.

"Of course," I said.

She closed the door as she left.

I found a dry shirt for myself then delved into Max's rucksack. When I turned around, I saw he'd been watching me. I handed him jeans and a T-shirt.

"Come on Max, you have to get out of your wet clothes. Promise I won't look." I faced the other way and took off my T-shirt and slipped into a cotton blouse. I turned back and saw Max look away quickly, which reassured me he wasn't too traumatised.

"Your turn unless you want me to fetch nursey to help?" I said and smiled. I turned a chair to face the wall and plumped down.

"Sure," he mumbled.

My eyes came to rest on a dent in the wall where the door handle had repeatedly knocked against it. It was then that I saw Max from a different perspective, and recognised he was less robust than he appeared on the surface and far from immune to the impacts of life's shocks and blows.

"Not sure about the T-shirt," he said. "A bit wide of the mark under the circumstances."

I twisted around in my chair.

Max pulled on the bottom hem of his Superman T-shirt.

"Well, I think it's very apt and that shade of blue matches your eyes perfectly."

Moments later there was a knock at the door and an elderly police officer walked in.

"Afternoon. Inspector Harlow," he said and extended a hand. "Max O'Donnell and Katriina McNalty?"

"Yes, hello." I picked up our cups of tea and passed one to Max. I took a sip, grateful for its warmth and sweetness.

He pulled up a chair and settled down then placed his briefcase on his knees. He smoothed a hand over his hair, flipped up the catches of his briefcase and brought out a pad of paper. As he rolled his biro between his fingers, I noticed they were heavily nicotine stained. He forced a thin smile. "You came in with the man who died on Benn Arum?"

"Yes," we said in unison.

"Do you know who he is...was?" I leaned forwards, my hands wrapped around my cup.

"Not yet, but I don't expect it'll take long for someone to report him missing. He was wearing a wedding ring." As he spoke, he rubbed two middle fingers along his furrowed brow as though trying to rub the lines away.

Inspector Harlow asked questions and took notes as we described the chain of events that led to the man's death. I knew we were innocent, but I felt guilty and wondered if we could have done things differently.

"Did he regain consciousness, open his eyes, say anything at all?"

Max nor I spoke.

"You see until his autopsy results come through we have no idea what caused his injuries, and we may never know why he was off the track, and so inappropriately dressed."

Max stared into his lap.

"I think Max is in shock," I said.

"Max?" Inspector Harlow shifted his gaze to gain Max's attention.

Max pulled on each of his fingers in turn. His voice trembled as he spoke. "I talked to him, but he didn't wake up apart from just before he fitted. Then he stopped moving, and I think that was when he died."

Tears spilled down Max's face and I leaned over and touched his hand. "It's all right Max, we couldn't have done more. At least you found him and stayed with him until the end. If it weren't for you he'd probably still be lying there with no one any the wiser."

Inspector Harlow finished writing, closed his notebook, and nodded. "Quite. And I'm sure his wife and family will be grateful for the support you gave him." He slotted his pen into his breast pocket. "That will do for now." He glanced from me to Max. "Can I ask you both to write your statements, read them through, and if you're happy, sign and date them. We'll see what the autopsy report comes back with and I'll need to speak to one or two in your walking group. I've got your details should I need to ask any more questions."

"Wasn't a great deal I could put on my statement," Georgina said.

"Me neither," said James. "It's ticking boxes, I imagine. Come on, I want to get my tent up in daylight."

As we gathered our belongings I watched as a petite young woman with blonde curly hair and a child hurried through the automatic doors and up to the reception desk. On impulse, I stopped to listen.

"I think my husband Roy Simpson could be here," she said. "He's been missing since yesterday, and when I rang they said a man came in and it might be Roy."

"I'll find a doctor," replied the receptionist, and looked to the nurse beside her.

"What's the matter with him? Is he unconscious?" she asked, her face and voice distraught.

The nurse spoke quietly to the woman then led her away down the corridor.

I thought she looked too young to be a widow and the boy far too young to be fatherless.

I grabbed Max's arm. "I think that's his wife."

"I can't," said Max. "I couldn't speak to her if she was." He pulled his arm away and walked out.

"Let him go. You two stay, and we'll meet you outside," said James, and followed Max out.

53

"Oh dear. Poor Max," I said.

We put down our rucksacks, and Georgina bought two coffees from the machine.

Georgina handed me my cup. "I'm going to wash that blood off your rucksack."

"Thanks, Georgie," I said. "Check your hands for any cuts, you can't be too careful."

"Ah yes. I'll get some rubber gloves," she said, and headed over to the reception desk.

People filtered through the foyer and I realised it was already visiting time. The small kiosk was doing a roaring trade in chrysanthemums and boxes of chocolates. Just as I thought I should enquire about the blonde woman, she returned with Inspector Harlow. She wept and the boy clung to her side. I felt my stomach churn.

The Inspector saw me watching them and spoke to the woman before he led them across.

"This is Katriina, Mrs Simpson. She was one of the students who found your husband. Where's Max?" He looked around. "Max stayed with your husband while Katriina went for help."

"Max is really upset. He's gone for some air." I searched for the right thing to say. "I'm really sorry for your loss." I knew my words sounded woefully inadequate.

She held my hand. "Thank you… for being with Roy. And your friend Max." Then almost to herself, she said, "I don't know what Roy was doing up there, he's always hated that mountain."

I looked at the boy's pale face and held back the urge to hug him. I shuddered. I tried to imagine how I might feel if either of my parents died, but the thought alone unsettled me.

The Inspector led them both away.

"Oh Georgie," I said, and burst into tears.

Georgina wrapped her arms around me. "Come on," she said. "We need to find the boys."

CHAPTER TWELVE

Hunger

By the time we arrived at the campsite the other students had pitched their tents in a circle, and a small fire burned invitingly at the centre. They'd already bought food and alcohol from the village store, and stew and burgers cooked over the fire. The meaty aromas wafting my way reminded me how much I needed to eat.

In contrast to the storm on Benn Arum the sheltered valley was warm and tranquil. I looked around the beautiful campsite and felt the tension slip away. A mixture of birch, oak, and Scots pine trees lined one side of the field, interspersed with bright thickets of juniper and blackthorn. At the bottom of a gentle slope, a small loch sat serenely amongst the peaty grassland like a dazzling charm, and the setting sun danced across the rippling surface of the water. To the far end of the campsite, a burn glistened and meandered gracefully through the glen.

Max's tent had been ruined, but he helped to put up my small ridge tent.

"Looks like it's had plenty of use," said Max, and straightened out another tent peg.

"I bought it for my first Duke of Edinburgh award."

"I only did the bronze level," Max said. "Still, I'm making up for it now."

We ate burgers and sipped cheap plonk. The others gathered around, eager to hear the gory details.

As the autumn light began to fade, the campsite owner came over.

"I hope you're not planning on having any parties or playing loud music. We don't permit any noise after eleven. And no wacky backy - I know what you students are like," he said.

"No problem sir," James replied with a salute. "We had the rave last night. All out of drugs and recovering tonight, eh guys?"

The owner regarded us all, his eyes narrowed and unsmiling. "And make sure you put that fire out!" With that, he left us to it.

"We might want to come back here you great pillock," Georgina said, and launched a chocolate digestive at James.

The burgers and stew tasted divine, and afterwards, we sat around the fire, drank more wine and reflected on the day's events. Without saying a word, Max got up and walked across to the burn.

"Will you shut up about the bloody dead man, can't you see it's upsetting Max," said Richard.

I was concerned about Max, and I got up and followed him. Sitting on the bank, he gazed into the peat-stained water that flowed over smooth pale stones. I sat down beside him and looked at the dark wooded hillside beyond the burn, and in silence we listened to the last of the birds evening song. Although I wanted to talk, I was reluctant to speak first.

I was about to get up and leave him to his thoughts when he breathed a heavy sigh.

"You know you were amazing today, Katriina."

I felt Max's hand on my cheek, and he leaned in and kissed me. His lips were warm and soft, and I responded. We kissed long and deeply, and everything else fell away. It felt natural, and yet at the same time I was shocked. The intensity of the feelings that emerged from deep within me felt overwhelming.

Sometime later, reluctant, we pulled apart and gazed intently at one another. I think we both knew that today had been both terrible, and yet incredible at the same time. I touched his face and took in his features in the half-light. His mouth was wide with perfect teeth, but for one front incisor that overlapped another slightly. His eyes shone with a shared anticipation.

We walked back to the camp, our hands joined, without a hint of awkwardness. I noticed the others exchange knowing looks as we settled down and nestled together by the fire. I felt excited and happy, and despite the tragic death of the man earlier, I felt no shame for it.

As the others drifted away to their tents I stood up, took Max's hand and pulled him to his feet.

"Are you tired?" Max asked, with an expectant smile.

"I should be," I said, and tucked a strand of hair behind an ear and smiled back. "We can maybe talk for a bit?"

We crawled into my tent, Max zipped it up, and shut out the chilly evening air. Without speaking, we zipped our sleeping bags together. Any remaining daylight had vanished. A full moon had risen, and a share of its luminosity shone through the tent walls and allowed us subtle glimpses and silhouettes as we unhurriedly undressed one another. Our fingers touched and caressed at every movement. His breathing quickened as his hands moved softly upwards over my stomach and ribs, and sent flickers of desire shooting through me. He rested his hands over the curve of my breasts, holding their fullness, and traced his fingers over my nipples which stiffened with anticipation at his touch. I trembled, and my whole body burned and ached with a hunger I had never experienced before. Max was lean and muscular, wiry, and I ran my hands over his shoulders and down through his soft, curly chest hair.

He didn't hide his desire. "Katriina, you're blowing my mind," Max said, breathless. "I'm not sure we should...you know, go all the way, though you know I want to." He inhaled slowly. "You're incredible Katriina and you don't even know it." He grabbed a handful of my hair and we kissed slowly, his tongue feeling, probing.

I traced my fingers up his back and neck and through his silky hair.

Eventually, he drew back and looked at me, then took a few strands of hair that had fallen across my face, and coiled them between his fingers. "Sweet Jesus," he whispered, "you don't give much away with your clothes, but you've the body of an angel, you know?"

"You have too," I said, hardly daring to speak. His words echoed around my head, soft, like the lure of a whisper, and I felt sensations in my abdomen reach down through my thighs. I was charged with hunger.

We kissed again and the touch of his fingers as they moved down my spine and the curve of my buttocks, felt like falling silk. He lowered his mouth to my breasts, kissing, exploring, his breath hot and urgent. He slipped his hand between my thighs and I gasped.

"I want it to be as incredible as I know it will be if we can wait, just a bit. Let's get to know one another properly," he murmured, and then grinned at me.

I felt pleasantly surprised. Although in my current state I would have given my all to him in an instant. "You're right," I said. "Besides, we should take precautions." I laughed softly, and recalled my paranoia with previous boyfriends, but tonight hadn't even entered my head.

He took hold of my hand, lifted it to his lips and planted the most delicate kisses on the inside of my wrist and palm. It felt as though a beautiful butterfly fluttered across my skin. We fell, intertwined onto the sleeping bags and began to discover who each of us were and what we could be together, our bodies connecting, our lives starting to bind and link.

That night we proved safe sex didn't mean holding back, and we discovered the depth of our feelings and the power of our mutual desire. Max was tender and knew intuitively how to please me, and I relished every delicious moment and pinnacle. We drifted into sleep for an hour or so until at some point we awoke. We kissed and touched and aroused our senses once more.

The first watery wisp of daybreak crept cross the loch, then overhead and in-between the scattered tents. We lay naked and held one another, blissfully fulfilled, having all but forgotten our experiences of the day before.

We packed away our camping gear in the stark, honest daylight, and we remembered and talked.

"I don't know what else would have helped him. And it's not like you or I have any medical experience is it?" I said.

"Exactly," agreed Max. "And it was pure chance we found him. The others just kept their heads down in the storm."

I took his hand and in return he gave me a lingering kiss.

"The only positive is that he didn't die alone. Thanks to you Max."

"Come on you two," Georgina called over. "Only twelve miles to get through today."

CHAPTER THIRTEEN

Siblings
Lochinver Police Station

The ticking of the clock seemed louder, yet the passage of time remained hidden as we anxiously awaited news. Every so often Inspector Keir came in to update us on the search plans, but there had been no worthy news. I felt as though I was sinking ever deeper into a dark emptiness as the shock of the situation tightened its cruel clasp on me.

Once again Inspector Keir walked through the door. Her radio buzzed into life, and I watched her turn it down as she sat opposite me.

"I believe the sooner we make a televised appeal, the better. It's the most effective way of alerting the public and to appeal to her abductor. It may open up communication with him." She paused and her forehead wrinkled. "The sheer scale of the search is a challenge. It's not the easiest environment to find someone who is determined to hide. If we have the public looking out it could make all the difference."

I didn't need her to tell me why time was of the essence and I knew full well that the longer Lyssa was missing, the chances of finding her alive diminished.

"What do you think?" said Inspector Keir. "Could you speak in front of a camera and journalists? I'll be there to guide you."

"Yes, when?" I replied, without hesitation, grateful to have something, anything to do that could help.

"A crew from BBC Scotland are en-route. They'll be here in a couple of hours. Other press agencies will want to be present too. Have you got another recent photograph of Lyssa, it's useful to have a couple?"

"On my phone and in my purse, both in my car," I said, with a sigh. "I've got a couple on Facebook, but they're old, and she's changed so much this past year." I turned to Max. "You've got some."

Max flicked through his phone. He studied the screen before he handed it to me. "I took this in Northumberland at Easter."

Lyssa stood with Louis on the beach, with Bamburgh Castle up on the cliffs behind them. Their arms were linked and they were laughing. Hit by a rush of emotion, I stifled a moan.

Inspector Keir leaned in. "That's lovely. Is Lyssa wearing her hair loose today?"

I nodded, unable to speak.

Max's phone pinged, but before I saw who it was he snatched it from my hand. Taken aback at this gesture, I watched him check his phone.

"Sorry, it's work." He slotted it back into his pocket.

"Max, are you going to send me the photo of Lyssa?" asked Inspector Keir, and eyed him keenly.

"Oh yes." He dug back in his pocket.

"Email it straight away," said Inspector Keir, and jotted down her email.

"We've got a picture of your car model Katriina. Also," she paused, "I'm sending Constable Pearce to fetch Louis."

I nodded. "Thank you."

When Louis walked into the room I jumped up and held him close. We cried, and reluctantly I drew away.

"We will find her Louis, I promise you," I said, to reassure him as well as myself.

Louis sat beside me, took my hand and stroked it over and over. Fresh tears fell unchecked.

Like most siblings, Louis and Lyssa were at times a complete nightmare together. They would argue and bicker over the slightest thing, and often drove me crazy with their incessant squabbles. However, in equal measure they were great mates. For a moment I recalled one of their pastimes when housebound due to bad weather. They would take it in turns to sit on Lyssa's skateboard, propel one another at full speed down the long hallway and crash into a padded barricade of beanbags and cushions. They'd wear Lyssa's floral helmet, which made the game all the more comical to watch. Louis was so at ease playing the big kid with Lyssa, and she adored him for it. Living where we did, we had little choice but to enjoy one another's company, or we would go crazy from isolation and boredom, especially during the long winter months when the weather often kept us cocooned indoors.

They scheduled the TV appeal for half-past five in the village hall next door, in time for the national and evening news. I noticed the small car parks at the front and rear of the station were virtually full. The sound of intermittent police sirens reminded me of the calling out of gulls that circled the fishing boats in the harbour from dawn until dusk.

Again, I wondered why all of these vehicles weren't out further afield searching for Lyssa.

"We're ready in the hall. The reporters may want to ask questions, but I'll answer them. What we're aiming for is to make an appeal to her abductor's better nature to return her safely, to urge the public to be vigilant about anything they see or hear, and to share any information they might have." Inspector Keir looked from Max to me. "I know this is going to be incredibly hard, but if you can try to remain calm, it'll help you to get through it, and will give it more impact."

She opened the door, and we followed her out.

CHAPTER FOURTEEN

University Bubble

In the days and weeks that followed our return from Benn Arum, Max and I spent every spare moment together. Each incredible and dreamlike night that we lay in one another's arms led me far beyond anything I could have believed possible. Sometimes, instead of making love, we held one another and talked. We got to know and understand one another better and to revel in our new feelings. The depth of Max's love, and the intense workings of his mind made me so grateful that we had found one another, that I had found him. At odd moments, if I awoke in the small hours or was alone by myself at home, the all-consuming love I felt for him troubled me. Within a matter of days, our relationship had become such a huge part of me, and I was afraid something might happen to alter or end it. It wasn't so much I was worried he would meet someone else, and I didn't feel overly jealous when pretty girls flirted with him - which they often did - it was more that our relationship seemed so perfect that I wondered if it was too good to continue in the same intense way.

One evening, as Max prepared for an exam at his flat, I voiced my concerns to Rosie.

"Rosie, I know it will sound silly, but when you look at Max and me do you think our relationship looks strong enough to last?"

She put down her textbook, came over and sat on the leather footstool. "It's hard for me to say. My longest relationship was five months. You remember Christopher? I thought that was the real thing. You know, true love, mind-blowing sex - a lot of mind-blowing sex. He was attentive, blah, blah, blah. But that went pear-shaped when I started fancying Kahil." She crossed her legs. "How long has it been with Max?"

"Three months. And I haven't fancied anyone else before you ask."

"I wasn't going to. You and Max seem like the real thing. And I know the sex is good," she said, and winked.

I felt my face burn. "How do you know?"

"Because there's a squeaky spring in your bed that resonates through the walls each time you do it. Sometimes wakes me up. What was it, twice last night?"

I thought for a moment. "Oh my god Rosie Dickens, you're right. Fancy not saying anything." I bit my lip and giggled. "I'm so sorry."

"I'll admit to feeling a bit jealous when I'm on my own with only Paddington to cuddle up to. But mostly I think it's nice for you. If you do ever fancy a night off though, send him through to me."

"Rosie! Anyway, I never fancy a night off."

After spending our nights together, Max and I went to our lectures, and I would count down the hours and minutes until we met for lunch, usually in the Union bar or the University gardens. At other times we studied in the library or pushed a trolley around the supermarket together. Sometimes, when we lay in bed for hours, I felt that I had deserted Rosie, but she proved just why she was my best mate. She'd been gracious that I'd fallen in love with Max and held no grudge. She even brought us cups of tea in bed, and only wandered around the flat in her underwear when she forgot Max was there.

Occasionally, I felt guilty that we hadn't hung out more with our friends. We'd become too self-contained and didn't feel the need to be with other people. Rosie was our only exception, neither of us tired of her company. Max was reluctant to continue with the walking group, but as I insisted I was carrying on, he agreed to go, but I felt his reluctance. I asked him if it was because of the shock he'd experienced that first weekend, but he insisted it was because he preferred walking with me alone. Despite his hesitancy, everyone adored him; his energy and humour. Everyone that is, except David.

Early one Sunday morning, a few weeks after the Benn Arum hike, we took a short minibus drive to Clyde Muirshiel for a charity sponsored walk. We all piled out of the bus and David finally realised I was 'with' Max, and couldn't hide his feelings.

He pulled me aside. "Do you know Kat, I believed you when you said there wasn't anyone else. How naïve was I?" The bitterness in his voice was palpable. "No one even bothered to tell me." He glared at the others.

"But I only met Max last month. There was no one else. I just didn't want to see you anymore," I insisted, and felt annoyed by his petulance.

"Is everything OK Kat?" Max marched up and positioned himself between David and me. "Who's this then?"

"I'm David, and I was with Kat well before you, matey. My sheets are practically still warm. Now, why don't you bugger off back to Ireland, or wherever it is you've crawled out from?"

"Come on Kat. I'm not having this bell-end speak to you or me like that. Just do one," said Max, and thumped David hard in the chest.

David staggered, fell and landed on his backside. He leaped up, face coloured with humiliation and squared up ready to repay Max. "Can't we be mature about this guys?" I said, and stepped in-between them. "I'm perfectly capable of choosing who I want to be with without you locking horns like rutting stags for Christ's sake."

Furious with the ridiculous display of machismo, I turned away and left them there, speechless. I marched over to Georgina who discreetly stood a few feet away, but was nonetheless listening in to the confab.

"I knew David would be upset when he found out. Hope there isn't a full on fight," she said, excitedly. Her eyes literally shone with anticipation.

To Georgina's disappointment, there was no fight, and the two men maintained a civilised distance for the rest of the day. David skulked moodily at the rear, and slagged off Max and I to anyone who was prepared to listen. But it became David's final walk with the group and I felt relieved when he also failed to turn up to the social events.

As we neared our finals, Max and I hibernated together for days on end in my flat, books strewn across the dining table. Life with Max was blissful, and I worried what would happen once we relinquished our sheltered, student lives. I'd seen many relationships quickly disintegrate after University if one-half of the couple had moved elsewhere for work. It made it impossible to maintain the relationship, or that glistening University bubble just seemed to burst and there was nothing left to hold the relationship together.

On graduation day, my parents drove up from Oban, and I felt excited when I introduced Max to them. From the outset, I could see in Mum's eyes how much she liked him, and they chatted together effortlessly, and laughed at funny anecdotes from my childhood that Mum shared. Following the graduation ceremony, we went to the drinks reception in the Union Bar.

"I expect you'd like to hear about Katriina and the boating lake, wouldn't you, Max?" Mum asked with a smile, and the dimples in her cheeks deepened.

"Yeah, I reckon so." Max looked at me and raised a brow in question.

"I don't spose I have a say in the matter do I?"

Mum drew a breath and continued regardless. "We were on the lake with Katriina, Alannah, and her Uncle Pat. Katriina, about six at the time, decided she should do the rowing. After going round and round in circles for what seemed like forever, and Katriina getting more and more frustrated, Uncle Pat insisted he was taking over. Well, Katriina was not happy, and the resulting tantrum was something Beelzebub himself would have been proud of."

"Hey! Earth calling Mum. I am here you know," I said, and waved my arms. "What Mum hasn't told you, Max, is I might've only been six, but I distinctly remember it was Uncle Pat throwing the wobbler when I took the oars. Mature, eh Mum?"

"You might be right, but Uncle Pat isn't here, is he?"

That evening the four of us went for dinner at Guy's Bistro, and I regretted that Max's parents hadn't made it over from Dublin for his graduation. I hadn't met them, and Max hadn't told me a great deal about his family. I meant to rectify that soon one way or another.

I noticed that Max was a touch too well-mannered towards Dad – he insisted on buying the drinks, hinted that we'd never slept together and virtually tipped his graduation cap at him. It was as if he wanted to win Dad's approval, or perhaps I had read too much into it.

I took Max's hand and whispered, "Relax, they think you're great."

He smiled and afterwards did seem to relax. In truth, I had found it reassuring and sweet. Even though University had ended, he didn't think our relationship was over and any worries I might have harboured soon disappeared when we waved goodbye to my parents the next morning.

"We're going out tonight, my angel, so put on your poshest dress and meet me at the Cow and Calf at seven."

"Where're we going?" I sidled up to him and tried to wheedle it out of him with him a lingering kiss.

"It's a surprise, so don't think you can be charming it out of me." He kissed me on the lips and squeezed my bottom before we went our separate ways.

I was intrigued. These past nine months I was always money conscious. 'Tight' Max called it, and whenever he suggested we go to a nice restaurant, I argued that I couldn't afford it, and I wouldn't allow him to spend his grant on me. Consequently, we rarely ate out unless we went for a cheap curry at one of the many cheap curry houses around campus.

Back at the flat, Rosie was in high spirits, having just been offered a graduate job with a top marketing agency in Edinburgh. She was in the process of packing her things into suitcases and bin liners and the living room looked like a massive jumble sale with clothes piled high on the sofa and chairs.

"Good grief. I didn't realise you had so many clothes," I said, picking up a slinky dress.

"And I'll be needing a whole new wardrobe now I'm going to be hanging out with some swanky business types."

She was deadly serious too.

"I'm having a sort out if you see anything you fancy. Got to downsize to make room," she said, and launched a full bin liner into the hallway.

I put down the dress and suddenly felt miserable. I flopped onto a bit of free sofa. "Don't go Rosie. What'll I do without you? Who will I share my problems with?"

She stepped into a pair of glittery sandals, then tottered over and hugged me. "What problems?" she said. "Anyway, you won't be on

66

your own when you and Max get a place." She picked up a pink jumper, sniffed it and wrinkled her nose before she stuffed it into a bin liner. "I'm surprised he's been paying his own rent - he's here most of the time."

She was being flippant, but I knew she would miss me as much as I'd miss her. "But I'll have problems if you're not around to share your words of wisdom. I'm going to miss you. We have to meet up…a lot."

"Stop, please. I was feeling grown up, my first proper job, a flat." Her eyes welled with tears.

I took her hand. "We'll just have to take it in turns to visit. Your place first for the housewarming party."

Rosie was the sort of girl who appeared to have it all - intelligence, beauty, self-assurance, plus wealthy parents who'd paid for her private education. It gave her a certain poise and confidence.

"I knew you'd get a first Rosie. Didn't I tell you?" I said. "Guess you worked hard too."

"There's no guessing about it. I was down on my knees and wrung out like a wet rag after those finals," she said, and lightly pinched my arm.

I was pleased with my 2.1. But I hadn't managed to get a graduate job in the environment sector, where I wanted to work, and I thought perhaps a first might have smoothed the way. I possessed little patience. But Max had been the other reason I hadn't found a job. The few applications I'd completed were for roles in and around Glasgow as I wasn't sure where Max wanted to live and we hadn't yet had that conversation. I knew it was the wrong way to launch my career, but I couldn't risk him not upping sticks and coming with me if I found a job further afield. Although we talked about so many things, we were becoming experts at skirting around the things that mattered.

That evening at the Cow and Calf, I found Max at the bar talking to the barman, drinks at the ready.

"I hope you haven't cheated. You need to eat your money's worth tonight at, drum roll please," he slapped his thighs. "Sebastian's."

"Seriously? What will that cost?"

"Don't think about the cost. It's called celebrating." Max replied.

"Have you got a job then?" I jumped up and down like an excited child and played the game like an expert.

He handed me a glass of chilled white wine. "No clues and no guessing."

Sebastian's – a Michelin Star restaurant that students rarely visited unless their wealthy parents were in town, and owned by TV chef Sebastian Mackay – was always fully booked for weeks, if not months in advance. I found out because Rosie's parents had treated her after graduation and they'd booked their table months ago.

After the waiter had taken our dinner plates away, I took Max's hand and kissed him lightly. "I could get used to this, my love." We sat in a cosy alcove with ambient lighting. Enya's voice serenaded us. I picked up a dessert menu and wondered if I had room.

"Kat," he said, and coughed.

I found his eyes with a sharp look.

"You know I love you, far more than is good for me. And now we're officially full-blown adults, I want to make this, us, permanent."

He delved into his jacket pocket and produced a small black box. He opened it, placed it reverently in my hand and said, "Please Katriina, marry me?"

I leaned over, kissed him once and said, "Oh Max. Of course I will."

The next morning, I stood on the doorstep in my silk kimono and kissed Max goodbye. I remained there, watched him and hugged my arms. From behind, Max was almost as gorgeous – tight little buttocks in Levi jeans, slightly bowed long legs, fine-knit jumper that revealed broad shoulders and a golden head of wavy hair tousled by the breeze.

Even the way he walked gave me little butterflies that quivered deep within me. At each step, he'd spring ever so slightly off the balls of his feet. He reached the corner, turned around and waved before he disappeared.

Back in the kitchen I sat down opposite Rosie and nonchalantly rested my chin in my left hand.

She looked up from her newspaper and it took her all of three seconds to notice the ring.

"Are you frigging kidding me? Oh my God!"

She took my hand and touched the ring. "That's one valuable ring." She was still admiring it, her eyes wide.

"Oh, the value isn't important. It's probably only a copy or something," I said.

"That's no fake. It's pure genuine diamond and a bloody big one at that. It must have cost Max five grand," she said, speaking as though she were an experienced diamond dealer.

I laughed and said, "He doesn't have that sort of money. I know that for a fact."

"Are you sure, because that's one expensive diamond? Maybe he's taken a loan out, or his parents subbed him. That or he's won the lottery." She let go of my hand. "Oh, and by the way I'm happy for you, in case I didn't say." She walked around and kissed me. "You're amazing together, and I'm completely green with envy."

I knew Rosie was pleased for me, but she hadn't been able to hide her shock at the value of the ring on my finger.

Max came over that evening, and I knew I should have asked how he'd paid for such a valuable ring. But it was one of those things, those things that despite being important, too significant to ignore, was in fact expertly overlooked by both of us. I convinced myself he must have saved up for it and that it wasn't anywhere near as expensive as Rosie had made out.

We began to plan our future together and broached the subject of where we could live. I suggested Edinburgh as my second favourite City and by no coincidence, where Rosie had relocated to.

"I dunno, Kat," said Max. "I'd prefer somewhere more out of the way."

I decided to leave it to chance for a bit, wait until one of us could find a job, and take things from there.

A couple of weeks later as we sat in Max's living room, drinking tea and listening to the breakfast news, Max rolled out some drawings onto the coffee table.

"Will you take a look at these and tell me what you think?" he asked. He lifted his mug and flattened the edges of the paper.

I saw they were designs of a sizeable five-bedroom upside down house. There was a vast amount of external glazing, an enormous arched roof and a section in the middle that looked like an open hallway.

"Are the bedrooms downstairs?" I asked, pointing to a large bedroom with an en-suite.

He nodded. "They are. It means the living areas upstairs can take advantage of the views."

"That's going to make someone a beautiful home, Max. Is it a commission?" I said, and picked up a different drawing to take a closer look.

"Yes, kind of. Do you want to know who's going to be living in it?" Max put down his mug, leaned back on the sofa and linked his hands behind his head.

"Someone with plenty of money I imagine. It's enormous." I pictured what it would look like when completed. It had a fair number of sustainable energy features; solar roof panels, a wind turbine, water collection tanks and a grass roof.

"Why don't we take a drive up north and find the perfect plot of land to build this house, or should I say our house."

I stared at him, and the drawing fell from my hands.

"A house we might live in?" I said. It hadn't entered my head it could be for us. How could it? I didn't have a job, and neither did Max. Between us, we had no money.

I racked my brains for the right thing to say. "It's amazing to think we might own something like that one day. But you can't mean we could build it now? Where would the money come from?"

"Don't you want to live somewhere beautiful? All you need to know is I've come into my not insignificant inheritance, left by my generous, but sadly deceased Uncle Sean." Max took my hand. "Which means I ... we, can afford to build our dream home and I can build my business." He plucked a pencil from behind his ear and wrote on one of the drawings. "A house like this will be one heck of a showpiece for prospective clients."

I saw his face light up, and I didn't want to dampen his fire with awkward questions or doubt his word.

I didn't know how to respond so I fell silent and studied the drawings as I considered what he'd told me. Enthused and oblivious to my unease, he showed me different features of the house. I thought we'd grown to know one another inside out. Max hadn't once mentioned any inheritance even when we'd discussed paying off our overdrafts. I thought he must have only just found out and that would explain the obvious omission. Now we were engaged, I reasoned, we had our whole lives ahead of us to get to know and understand one another.

CHAPTER FIFTEEN

Home

Making the televised appeal felt surreal and the moment it ended I felt strangely disconnected from everything, as though I had looked down on the whole proceedings from above. Furthermore, I couldn't recall a single word of what either of us had said. I felt angry with Max, but why? My mind churned and nothing made sense.

Inspector Keir led us through to the kitchen at the back of the hall, and explained that there was a door through which we could leave discretely.

"You did so well. I know it's difficult, but what you did out there is precisely what we need to get the nation looking for Lyssa. It's also possible that whoever has taken her will see it and make contact."

She opened the door to the rear car park and turned back to me.

"It might be wise for you to go home. He… or she may contact you tonight."

"And we can't stay here all night." Max turned to me and his brows pinched together.

"But what if you find her?" I looked from Max to Inspector Keir.

"If we hear anything," she said, "and I mean anything, we will ring you."

An officer came through from the hall, his expression serious. "Excuse me, Inspector," he said. "Can I have a word?" He gestured to the door.

Inspector Keir glanced at me briefly before she disappeared into the hall. I grasped Max's hand. My head whirled. He gave my hand a quick squeeze. Had the officer told her that Lyssa had been found alive or…? The room turned around me suddenly and I clutched Max's arm for support. I couldn't contemplate the other possibility.

When Inspector Keir returned, her face gave nothing away until she had shut the door. "At last, news on the van. It was stolen yesterday from a warehouse near the port in Ullapool. We know it's low on diesel, so it's possible whoever took your car was worried about refuelling and wanted a car with fuel. We can only speculate. There are items for forensics to work on - hairs, cigarette butts, a can. With DNA we might have him."

But not Lyssa, I thought.

I didn't want to go home, but we couldn't do any more here. I figured Inspector Keir was right to anticipate that her abductor could contact us in some way.

If he'd only wanted the car, which was plausible, he might have let Lyssa go, and she'd soon be found safe. I had to think positively, or risk falling apart. I had to hold it together for my beautiful daughter and for Louis too. Max kept control of his emotions, although he'd distanced himself and withdrawn from me. He barely spoke to me unless I asked him something, and then he could hardly ignore me. Every time I looked at him - I'd see his eyes narrow in disgust before looking away. I had never needed Max more than I did right now, and yet I had never felt so alone.

CHAPTER SIXTEEN

Bridging the Divide

As soon as I arrived home I checked the phone for messages and missed calls. There were messages from work and Lyssa's school asking why we'd been absent. I paced the corridors, checked every room and shouted her name. I half expected to find her reading or drawing as she waited for us to arrive home.

I returned to her room and sat on her unmade bed. I stared at the indented pillow where she had lain. Her favourite teddy bear lay nearby and forgotten on the floor. I lowered my head onto her pillow and breathed in little by little, and inhaled her scent. My eyes fell on one of Lyssa's recent drawings of the four of us standing on a hillside. Lyssa held mine and Max's hands and Louis stood to my other side. I'd admired this picture before, with the colourful clothes and outlandish hairstyles, set beneath a rare blue sky and radiant sun. It captured her joyful nature and made my heart ache even more. But I could see that something wasn't right with Lyssa, her expression, and when I realised what it was, I gasped. Max, Louis and I had wide blue eyes and lipstick red smiles, but not only was Lyssa not smiling, she didn't have eyes. I moved closer and smoothed a fingertip over the paper to see if they had been rubbed out, yet it was as if they had never been added.

"Oh my baby. Where are you?" I sobbed, as terror clawed at my heart. I pulled the duvet over my face as dread overwhelmed me.

"Lyssa," I shouted. "Lyssa it's Mummy."

She gazed out towards me but I could tell by her expression that she couldn't see me. She was sitting on a bed and hugging her knees to warm herself. The bed rocked back and forth, as if it was afloat; an abandoned boat cast adrift on the ocean.

"Wait!" I cried.

A man stood nearby, but he faced out to the horizon.

"Lyssa, don't go."

As she retreated, her features faded until I was no longer sure that it was her.

Someone called to me.

"Mum."

I spun around.

"Mum!"

The voice drew nearer.

"Mum, wake up."

I opened my eyes and saw Louis, standing over me, his face concerned.

"Mum you need to get up."

As I sat up I felt dizzy and disoriented. I tried to rationalise what I'd seen. I might have been asleep, but it had been no dream.

"The news is on any minute," Louis said.

I took his hand.

Max stood at the living room window and nervously drummed his fingers against the window frame. The programme titles started, and Louis sat with me on the sofa, our hands still tightly gripped. Max came to sit on the footstool.

The newsreader revealed what we already knew, delivered in a deeply solemn tone, as though she already knew it wasn't going to end well. They showed the layby at Loch Dubh, and Inspector Keir appealed to the public for any information. Then Lyssa's picture appeared, windswept curly hair, a carefree smile during happier times. An image of my car. Then the camera was on Max and me, with Inspector Keir.

It zoomed in. I could still feel the same gut-wrenching pain scrabbling at my insides. I thought back to Inspector Keir's advice, 'try to keep calm.' Some hope.

In contrast, Max looked remarkably unruffled.

"We need Lyssa home. I beg you, whoever you are, let her go."

Where was the emotion? His mouth opened then closed, and it was clear he didn't know what to say. He turned to me, and so did the camera.

I looked out across the hall. Cameras clicked and flashed. I nodded at someone or something, and braced myself.

"Listen to me. You've made a mistake, that's it, a terrible mistake. You may not have meant to take Lyssa, that's possible. But you have, and you can still make it all right. Lyssa is only eleven years old." I spoke slowly. "We love her, and she loves us. She needs to be home - with us."

The camera panned across to Max, who stared at me. A deep frown had formed.

I continued, and the camera zoomed back. "And Lyssa has asthma, and her inhaler is in her school bag, which is in the car. Please let her hold it. If you release her everything will be OK. Lyssa, remember we love you, and you'll be home with us soon. We will find you."

There followed a telephone number to ring and an email address for anyone with information.

The newsreader moved onto the next item, and I breathed again. Is that it, I thought, is that all Max could manage?

Louis spoke first and cut through the silence.

"If he hears it, it'll make him stop and think about what he's doing."

"Yes, it might." Max eyed me briefly and got up.

The house phone rang. We all froze and looked at one another.

I leapt up and ran to the phone. "Hello, Katriina O'Donnell."

"Katriina my love, it's Dad. We're driving up tonight."

"Oh, Dad. I need you here." I felt mortified. It hadn't entered my head to ring my parents, such was my madness. It seemed the clearest sign yet that I had lost my mind.

Louis took my hand again, and I watched his pale, frightened face. His expression mirrored my thoughts and I had a sudden moment of lucidity. I knew what I needed to do first thing in the morning. There would be no more sitting around waiting for bad news, I was going to help search for Lyssa.

Louis took himself to bed after making me promise to wake him if we heard anything. Shortly afterwards I followed him downstairs and found him sitting up in bed, on his phone, as he flicked through Facebook.

"I've posted something about Lyssa and asked people to share it. Look." He handed the phone to me. "It could help us find her."

Seeing Lyssa's beautiful, rosy-cheeked face beaming at the camera, I could see that Facebook was the perfect vehicle to publicise crimes and find criminals. So many people used it and checked it throughout the day.

"That's inspired, Louis. You're such a smart and thoughtful brother." Unable to take my eyes off Lyssa's photo, my stomach turned somersaults. "I'm proud of how you're handling this. I'll share it too. Something might come from it mightn't it?" Tears ran down my cheeks and I felt woozy again.

"We have to try," Louis replied and placed his phone on the bedside table.

I sat down at Louis' desk and took in his piles of textbooks and revision notes, no longer his primary focus. "I don't imagine we'll sleep tonight." I sat down on the edge of the bed. "But we have to try and rest so we can help tomorrow. And I want you to help too, Louis. Lyssa may be miles away, but even so, I have the strongest feeling we'll be able to find her."

"Do you think so?" Louis said, biting his thumbnail. "What makes you think that?"

"I don't know," I said. "I have a gut feeling. Call it a mother's intuition." I moved and smoothed out his duvet. "Sweetheart, if you need me in the night, shout or come in. Don't lie there worrying. I'll be awake."

I heard footsteps and turned to see Max standing in the doorway. I hugged Louis, planted a kiss on his cheek and left them alone. Louis idolised his dad, and I felt certain that if anyone could reassure him, it would be Max.

I got ready for bed, splashed my face with cold water, and changed into a pair of loose leggings and vest, ready to leave instantly if necessary. I remembered my herbal sleep remedy in the bathroom cabinet. During stressful periods and worries about work or the children, the drops worked well, but not so that they'd knock me out. I didn't expect them to make tonight any easier, but since falling asleep on Lyssa's bed, for some unfathomable reason, I didn't feel in the same heightened state of panic that had gripped me all day.

Max walked in and shut the door behind him. He turned to me and his eyes drilled mine. "Why did you tell Louis you were going to find Lyssa, and that he could help?"

"Because," I paused, unsure how to continue. "I need – no, we need to feel like we're doing something. Don't you?"

"You know I do, but she could be anywhere. Don't you think the police are more likely to be looking in the right places, with all the officers and help they have?" Agitated, he rubbed a hand across the back of his neck. "We should call them first thing and see if there are any leads before setting off on a wild goose chase."

"I'd hardly call hunting for our missing daughter a wild goose chase. Jesus Christ Max. What the hell is the matter with you?"

"What?" he barked. "Only that my daughter has been kidnapped after you left her sitting in the car with the door wide open and the keys in the fucking ignition."

For the first time in our twenty years together I felt like hitting him.

"You rotten bastard. You can't keep throwing that in my face. And of course I'm going to speak to the police. Do you think I'm an idiot?"

He snorted, turned abruptly and walked into the bathroom. He slammed the door behind him. How dare he try and blame me for Lyssa's abduction, and tell me what I could or couldn't do to help find her.

I turned on my iPad to check my emails and social media and saw messages from work and friends, but I didn't read them properly or reply. I was only looking for or a message from an address I didn't recognise.

Max came out of the bathroom, but avoided catching my eye.

"Are you checking for messages?" I said.

He tutted. "You really have to ask? Are you checking yours?" He snarled and unbuttoned his shirt. "I've had messages from our friends. They're thinking about us, asking what they can do to help. We'd be doing the same if it was happening to any of them." He scrunched his shirt into a ball and threw it at the foot of the bed.

Guilt washed over me as I wished that it had happened to one of them instead.

In bed, with my head on the pillow, I imagined Lyssa's face, her eyes wide, as her hair spilled across her cheeks. I shivered and thought about who had her and what he might do to her. I tried to picture her surroundings, just as I'd dreamed as I slept on her bed. Perhaps if I concentrated I'd visualise her, see something to identify her location – somewhere that I recognised. I pictured her with my eyes closed, and when that didn't work I stared at the ceiling. Sill I saw nothing but shadows that flickered from the tree outside our window as the branches wafted in the breeze. My hands rested on my stomach. I clenched my fists and imagined what I would do if I got hold of the sick freak that had taken her.

I reached for Max's hand and squeezed lightly. I waited for him to return the gesture as always, but it didn't come.

"Why Max?" I turned to him and studied his shadowy profile. "I can't bear to think about what she could be going through and how terrified she must be."

In silence, he put his arm around me, and I clung tightly onto him. Although I could touch his skin, feel his warmth, the distance between us seemed vast, as though a crevasse had opened up beneath our feet, and had left us on opposite sides, looking across at one another, unable to connect. Even though I felt gripped by fear, I wished we could kiss, touch one another honestly and openly. I knew he blamed me for leaving Lyssa alone, and I felt a sudden, desperate need for his love. Plagued with black thoughts I tried to remain on the right side of a panic attack. I wondered if I should tell Max about my dream, ask him if he knew what it meant. No, I was being irrational. It couldn't have any connection with reality. It was only my mind trying to untangle the whole heap of mess plaguing it. I closed my eyes and lay enfolded by sadness; sleep a distant possibility.

CHAPTER SEVENTEEN

Connection

"Mummy, where are you?"

I awoke, and sat bolt upright? I remained still in the darkness, and listened to the silence.

"Mummy, I'm here." Lyssa's voice whispered to me like an echo, and yet she sounded so near.

I flew out of bed and ran into the darkened hallway. Light from Lyssa's bedroom cast into the corridor, and beckoned me like a beacon. Was she home? I walked closer with a rising sense of trepidation.

I stood in the doorway and whispered, "Lyssa is it you?"

I knew she was nearby – perhaps she waited for me to go to her. I ran in and grabbed the wardrobe door handles, swung them open, and ripped apart the hangers. I crawled on hands and knees and checked under her bed. I half expected to find her there, grinning at me like in a game of hide and seek. I stood up. I felt a strange sensation, as though being dragged by invisible fingers that tore at my skin and pulled me towards the rear of the house.

I turned the back door key and pulled the handle, but it stuck as though someone had hold of it on the other side. I gripped, wrenched harder and the door flew open and scraped over my bare feet. Outside it rained. No, it wasn't just rain – it battered the ground with torrential force, rattled against the windowpanes and heavy droplets bounced high off the floor.

I stepped into the deluge.

The torrent pounded against my skin and I looked into the darkness beyond it.

"Lyssa, it's Mummy," I called. "Can you hear me?"

Then I heard her.

"Yes, Mummy . . . I."

But her voice sounded distant.

I looked for any movement, or a sign that she had returned home.

In a few seconds the downpour ceased. Rainwater poured from the roof and down the drainpipes, and trickled in rivulets down the path. The wind turned gentle as it caressed and curved its way over the roof and coiled around the walls of the house. My eyes adjusted and I made out the dark hillside that rose steadily before me.

Then a hand fell like a cloak on my shoulder. I spun around.

I looked at Max, confused.

"What is it? What's out there?" He held out his hand to me. "You're wet through."

"I heard her Max. I think Lyssa's home," I cried.

But, I knew I was mistaken. My legs felt weak and I leaned against the doorframe.

Max pulled me upright and closed the door. "There's no one there. It was a dream," he said, trying to rationalise my crazed behaviour. "Perhaps your parents have arrived." His eyes continued searching mine.

"No, Max. You don't understand," I said, and looked into the darkness again. "I heard her. It was real. Lyssa was real."

Max tried to take my hand, but I pushed him away. I left a trail of water as I ran through to the front of the house. But the sensation I felt earlier had gone, and there was no one out there either.

A few minutes later, I found Max at the kitchen table with two hot drinks in front of him.

"You were dreaming Kat. And it's hardly surprising given the strain you're under, we're both under."

He pulled out the chair next to him and placed a cup in front of me. "Drink your tea, and then we'll see if we can rest. Tomorrow's going to be... well who knows, but we have to be ready."

"Why can't you understand? Lyssa called me."

It had been more than my imagination playing tricks on me, and I felt frustrated by Max's patronising response. As I sipped my tea I realised that if I was in his place, I might well have said the same platitudes.

Back in bed, I turned away from Max and cried into my pillow.

CHAPTER EIGHTEEN

Intuition

I lingered on the edge of sleep until eventually I fell into a dark and restless slumber. I dreamed that a throng of cloaked demons carried me towards a great burning pyre like a sacrificial offering. As we drew closer I looked into the flames and knew I would soon be devoured by them, but rather than resist, I submitted and accepted the inescapability of my fate.

Max woke me a few minutes after seven to say that my parents had arrived.

I was dripping with sweat and I began to cry the second that reality hit me. "Have there been any calls?"

"Nothing," he said. "I'll ring now, and I'll let your parents know you're up. Your mum said I should let you sleep, but I knew you'd want to be up. At least you slept a bit." He sat on the edge of the bed and tied his shoelaces.

Despite everything, I had slept, and that was the strangest thing. Then I remembered last night – my premonition as I slept on Lyssa's bed and then the early hours, when she had called out to me.

Why though? And how? Had Lyssa spoken to me through some deeply buried channel or mind mechanism? Now that it was daylight, I knew they were revelations of some kind; something much more than dreams that remained at the forefront of my mind when I awoke.

My parents sat at the kitchen table with Louis, talking quietly. Mum stood up and held out her arms.

"Come here my poor, poor girl."

I fell into her embrace and clung to her as I wept.

Eventually she drew back and held me at arm's length. "No need to explain what happened, Max has told me everything. I'll make you a tea, and you should try and eat."

My hand trembled as I wiped my tears. "I'm so glad you're here." Mum pulled a tissue from her jacket pocket and gave it to me. I blew my nose, and Dad hugged me.

"We will find her, Katriina. Whatever it takes... wherever she is." As he enfolded me, I felt saved in some small way.

Max strode into the kitchen with such a serious expression that my entire body stiffened. I breathed in sharply and braced myself.

"The police have received some calls from people who believe they've seen your car. They're checking them out. Inspector Keir recommended we stay put. She believes he could still get in touch."

"Does she think it's a planned kidnap then, did she say?" I asked.

"No, and we explored that possibility, didn't we?"

"But there might be someone one of us has upset through work, an unpaid debt, a job gone wrong."

"Well it's not me," Max shot in reply.

"I wasn't accusing you. Where were the sightings?"

"She can't confirm yet."

"Why not?" I said. "And she can recommend we stay here, but there's no bloody way I'm sitting doing nothing again all day. I'll take Mum and Dad's car. OK, Dad?"

Dad nodded.

"And you've got yours Max. We can pick two separate routes."

They all regarded me with various degrees of incredulity.

"But that's like looking for a needle in a haystack," said Max. "You can't think we'll just happen to bump into them. We need some idea surely, it's way too random otherwise?"

"I cannot sit here while my daughter is missing," I said.

Louis pushed back his chair and came to stand with me. "I'm coming with you Mum. You said I could help, and I know the area well, especially off the main roads. You're right, there's no point staying here."

"Thank you, Louis," I said, and took his hand.

"That's settled then. I'll sort out breakfast while you get yourselves ready." Mum opened the fridge, pulled out various packets and placed them on the worktop.

83

"What a waste of time. Louis, you're staying here, and Kat, you're in no fit state to drive anywhere. You might have an accident," Max said.

"Honestly, Max, I don't care what you think. I need to do something, and I'm perfectly capable of driving. It wasn't me who was driving so recklessly that I skidded off the road, writing off my car and almost killing myself in the process. Perhaps you need to think about how fit you are to drive." I shot back at him, then turned to Louis. "It would be helpful if you want to come with me, but I'll understand if you'd rather stay here."

A few minutes later, I had checked my iPad for messages, and then I was forced to sit at the table. Mum placed a full cooked breakfast in front of me.

I said feebly, "I could manage some toast." Yesterday's tummy upset, stress or whatever, had returned, and that uneasy feeling bubbled again.

"Just eat what you want and leave the rest," Mum said.

Mum had never been one to force-feed us, but I knew she only wanted to feel useful, in a situation where we all felt so utterly useless.

"I'll try." I looked down at the eggs, beans, and mushrooms, picked up a piece of toast, and took a small bite. I swallowed and felt it lodge at the back of my throat. I mumbled an excuse, sprinted down the stairs to our bathroom and knelt down in front of the toilet. Now I didn't have to wonder what was making me sick; I'd barely eaten in the last twenty-four hours. Could this be happening? Of all the years, months, and days to find out I was pregnant, why now? It hadn't been planned or even talked about. At forty I enjoyed a proper career again, and until yesterday life had been wonderful and full, let alone the matter of a missing daughter. If I was pregnant, and I felt sure of it, then I had neither the time nor the inclination to think about it. I needed to channel all the energy I could muster into finding Lyssa.

And then another thing occurred to me. Something started buzzing and reverberating right through me. Was this a warning, or a terrible omen? One child had gone missing, but in some cold-blooded way another child would replace her. The chances of Lyssa disappearing, and finding out I was pregnant seemed surreal. I wondered whether it had been a cruel coincidence – one precious life to replace another.

I knew the new life slowly taking form within me wasn't something I could share with anyone, not even Max. I could barely get my head around the idea, and talking about it was impossible.

"Katriina, are you in there?" said Mum, from the other side of the door.

I drank some water from the tap, and opened the door to see her troubled face.

"You dashed off. Are you all right?" She asked and smiled to try to soften her concern. I looked at her puffy eyes and realised she hadn't slept either. Her long hair, threaded through with streaks of silver, and usually so neatly tied back looked messy and uncombed.

"How can I be all right?" I flushed the toilet and washed my hands. "I want to get out there and start looking. Being here is driving me mad." I sat on the bed, pulled my hair back and tied it into a knot. "Can I borrow your phone? The police said they might be able to trace my phone, which could lead us to Lyssa, but nothing's come of it."

"It might do yet. Take Dad's phone, his has fairly good coverage up here." She sat beside me and looked at me before speaking. "Sweetheart, I can see Max is going crazy with worry, but I can't help thinking he's acting strangely. I'm not trying to frighten you more than you are already," she paused. "Have you noticed anything unusual about his behaviour?"

My heart pounded in an unnatural rhythm, like heavy raindrops against my skin.

"I don't think so. Why?"

"He's on his phone constantly, looking at things, probably messages -"

"But I'd be on my phone if it was here," I said, and felt annoyed.

"Well yes, and I'm not trying to be alarmist, but when Max was in the living room, and I walked in, he was talking on his phone, but not in a normal way, more whispering. When he saw me he said he had to go, and hung up. I asked him if it was the police and he didn't even reply. It seemed out of character and…" Mum stopped mid-sentence as Max appeared in the doorway.

"Kat, I'm going to the police station. I want to know about those car sightings, and as long as someone is here," he looked at Mum, "I think that would be more helpful, don't you?"

"Definitely. It's pointless being here. I'm using Dad's phone so call me if you hear anything. I'm heading off with Louis, not sure where yet." I looked Max in the eye. "If I'm out of range leave a message, and I'll call you back."

Max looked vulnerable, and it made me feel protective of him despite our disagreements. "We have to get her back." I said. "This can't go on, can it?"

Max pulled me up and held me close. "This will test us Kat, beyond anything we've ever faced before." He kissed me on the cheek, turned away, and moments later I heard the front door slam.

His small gesture gave me renewed hope. Yes, it felt like a test, and I wasn't going to let it break me, at least not yet.

Like every other morning I drew back the blinds and inspected the sky. The weather looked disappointing; it wouldn't help the search. Swollen clouds hung over the house, with Applecross barely visible on the far side of the glen. It hadn't rained yet, but I watched the mist rolling down the hill and around the house and knew that rain was imminent. Blast it, poor visibility was going to be a real hindrance.

I felt drained suddenly and sat on the bed. My stomach complained, my eyes felt heavy, and every part of me ached. Mum stared out of the window, and I reflected on her words. She was right, she had noticed something about Max, and I couldn't ignore it. Mum had detected an underlying change that I'd hardly dared to admit to myself, to avoid confrontation with Max. There was something odd about his secretive behaviour.

CHAPTER NINETEEN

Foundations - 1999

A mountain of cardboard boxes, bin liners, and carrier bags stretched the length of the hallway, and left only a thin strip of tiled floor through which to enter and leave the flat. Unlike Rosie, I hadn't got rid of much as I didn't own anywhere near as many clothes as she did. I'd even held onto some of my baggy old jumpers that had seen better days. I reasoned that I'd need them even more now that the middle of winter had set in, and anticipating the much harsher conditions I was about to find myself in.

"That's it, the sum total of my worldly possessions packed, meter readings taken, toilet flushed," I said, as I surveyed the heap from the kitchen doorway.

I had no regrets to be leaving behind my digs of three years and my beloved Strathclyde University to start a new life with Max way up north.

Six days previously, we had signed the contract and purchased a two-acre plot of land on the stunning lower slopes of Benn Cady, way up in the Highlands, and a few miles inland of the North West coast. Max must have done his research as it was only the second plot we'd looked at. The first plot – located in an incredible setting at the foot of a hill, was on the edge of a loch. We quickly discovered the marshy land was often flooded, and we knew that would be a step too far for his first building project.

"Besides, being so close to the water, the midges will drive us crazy and keep us caged up indoors," Max said, and swiped madly at the thousands of tiny critters that amassed around us.

Ten weeks ago, late in October, we journeyed into the Highlands, and turned onto a steep and bumpy track at the base of Benn Cady. I gazed out of the car window in awe at the beauty that surrounded us.

As I stepped out of the car, I heard the haunting call of a bird of prey and I looked up and spotted an eagle that circled the air above us.

I tugged Max's coat sleeve and pointed. The eagle then spotted something and it dived and came to land on a rock a short distance away. The bird remained there for several minutes and boldly eyed us, unafraid, before it unfurled its huge, beautiful wings and soared in silence back up the mountain. We watched it until it became a tiny black smudge that vanished into a cloud and out of sight.

Max took my hand and gave it a gentle squeeze as we walked along a sheep path through the bracken and heather. I had never been a stranger to the stunning landscapes of the north, but I saw it anew with the possibility that this could be our view every day. The seasons had transitioned - Autumn russets and buttery yellows mingled with olive greens and emerald shades that lingered and created the most amazing kaleidoscopic spectacle.

The plot, despite being on an incline, looked sufficiently even, and Max, with his architect's eye said a recent ground survey showed it was devoid of too many invasive rocks that could make laying the foundations difficult. I noticed the track was solid enough for vehicle access and appeared adequate to accommodate the trucks needed to deliver the wood for the all-important frame and other building materials.

I gazed out across the glen and wondered why such a beautiful plot hadn't already been snapped up. "Is it really for sale? And there's planning permission to build?"

"It is," he said. "Apparently, the owner has secured planning for a five-bed house. Got some plans drawn up but then decided to sell the land on. I couldn't find out why, but I've checked it all out, and there's definitely building permission. I'll need to submit my designs, but as we'll be using local labour and materials as much as we can, and it's got so many renewable energy features, I honestly can't see it being a problem. Plus, the guy I spoke to in the planning department seemed pretty confident." He grabbed me around the waist, pulled me to him, and our breaths merged to form one cloud.

"So whaddya reckon?" He gazed at me, his face alive with excitement.

"I can't believe it, Max. And I can't imagine a more idyllic place for us to live. Let's do it."

And we kissed long and slowly, our chilly lips warming. I marvelled at the speed my life had changed and I felt excited. Finally, we drew back, and I saw that his eyes brimmed with tears. My gaze ran over his face, taking in the smooth skin, yet strongly defined features. With my thumb, I brushed away a solitary tear that slid down his cheek. The moment felt like a new beginning. The beginning of an incredible dream.

In the New Year we loaded all of our possessions into Max's Volvo Estate, bought to tow the enormous caravan that would double up as our home and site office. We'd spent the past few weeks talking late into the night as we planned the build; what materials to use and which building contractors to hire, but most of all we romanticised about the things we would do when we were not busy working.

The budget for the build appeared to be less of a matter for debate as Max assured me he had it all under control, and was happy to see to that side of things.

"Both our names are on the deeds," he reassured me.

It was his money, so I didn't feel I had grounds to push for too many details. Max wanted to build his business, and I wanted to apply for jobs up there. I had compiled a list of environmental concern companies and agencies in the area, posted out letters and CV's, and made numerous phone calls in my bid to find the right job.

"You needn't worry about finding a job straightaway Kat, you can always help me with the business and the build, and it's not like we're desperate for the money is it?" Max drummed his fingers on the steering wheel. "And don't take any old job. You want decent hours and not too much driving."

"I know, but I want a career too, and I haven't done my degree for nothing. I've dreamed about conserving our environment, especially Scotland's environment. You know how important it is to me."

The car radio blared out some hideous heavy metal garbage, and I switched channels. I knew I'd sounded harsh, but I'd found his comments condescending. Max didn't bite back, and I found another radio channel. *Psycho Killer* by Talking Heads filled the car.

I started to sing along and tap my feet.

"Psycho killer, qu'est-ce que c'est,
Fa fa fa fa fa fa fa fa fa far better
Run run run run run run run away."
"I get that," he said. "I just don't want you to feel under any pressure, at least not from me." He reached over for my hand, lifted it to his lips and planted soft kisses, which made me feel guilty for sounding ungrateful and selfish.

When we arrived on our exposed plot of land, I quickly realised mid-winter wasn't the best time of year to start the build. At times I worried that in the fierce winds the caravan might roll down the hill with us asleep in it. As the days passed we realised the building wouldn't be anywhere near as straightforward as we had imagined, and for the first few weeks the ground remained frozen or snow covered for days on end, which left the hired digger out of a job, and progress on the build non-existent.

But we took advantage of it and lazed in bed. Sometimes we listened as the snow whispered to us as it fell on the caravan roof.

"He says it's Katriina's turn to be on top," said Max.

"Actually, she's saying Max will have to kiss Katrina from lips to toes first." I laughed and tweaked his nipple.

One evening, towards the end of February, fresh snow had fallen, and although it was no more than a few inches deep, we'd had to leave the car down on the road, as the track was impassable. We'd bought in provisions, were all set to hide away for the weekend, and with plenty of time on our hands, we discussed wedding dates and possible venues.

"We should find out when your parents can come over Max. I know it's harder for them, and we can't set a date until we know when is good for them."

I still hadn't met his parents, and again I'd sensed resistance from Max when I'd suggested we go over to Dublin to visit. His excuse seemed just that, an excuse. I couldn't imagine not wanting Max to meet my parents, and I felt frustrated with him, but became increasingly curious.

The next morning, he went to fetch some drawings from the car. I jumped at the opportunity, turned on his phone and looked in his contacts for his parent's number. I soon found it, jotted it down, and resolved to ring them soon. I assumed Max had told them about me and they were curious to meet me. After all, we were engaged to be married.

On this occasion the snow didn't last for more than a couple of days. The builders returned to site, Max directed them, and I pursued job opportunities.

One afternoon I felt upbeat as I'd set up a meeting with the Director of Highlands Protection who needed a management trainee for the region. The fresh burst of confidence persuaded me to call Max's parents. Parked up in the middle of town I dialled the number. It rang for a good thirty seconds, and I was about to hang up when someone answered.

"Hello," a woman spoke with a soft Irish accent.

"Hello, is that Mrs O'Donnell?"

"Yes, it is." Her voice sounded warm.

"I'm Katriina, Max's girlfriend... I mean fiancé." I paused. "I've been feeling bad that I haven't managed to meet up with you yet."

"How lovely to speak to you, Katriina. Max has told me so much about you. Not that you'd got engaged though, or I'd have insisted that he bring you over to see me. When did you get engaged?"

"Oh, a little while ago. We've been talking about dates for the wedding, but I said we must check with you both first." I heard shouting and looked out of the window to see two teenage boys kicking a football.

A long pause followed.

"Are you still there, Mrs O'Donnell?"

"Yes my dear. I can come anytime. I wouldn't dream of missing the wedding. You go ahead and set the date."

"What about Max's dad, will he be OK for any date too?"

"I'm sorry, but hasn't Max told you? His daddy won't be able to come to the wedding."

"No, he hasn't," I said.

"I'm afraid Brian's unable to leave Dublin right now. But I know he'll be thrilled about the wedding. Set the date. I'll be there, and Max's cousins would love to come too."

It would have been logical for me to ask her why Brian couldn't leave Dublin, but I detected her hesitant voice and held back. As this was the first time we had spoken, I wanted to make a good impression, which didn't include being nosey or insensitive. So instead I said how good it was to have spoken and that we'd be in touch soon with a date for the wedding.

After I'd hung up, I wondered why Max hadn't mentioned his dad couldn't leave Ireland. Was he housebound, or ill? I also felt upset that she hadn't known about the engagement. My entire family knew all about it within hours of Max's proposal.

That evening as we tucked into paella and were onto our second bottle of Pinot Noir, I spoke up.

"Oh, I know what I meant to tell you. I rang your parents to talk about wedding dates as I know it's not that easy for them to come over."

His body instantly tensed and he blinked several times in succession.

"Where did you get their number?" He snapped a langoustine in half, and visibly struggled to remain composed.

"I phoned Directory Enquiries," I said, and crossed my legs under the foldout table.

He put the langoustine in his mouth and chewed slowly. A deep frown formed.

The wind batted the caravan, and now and then it shuddered and rattled in the stronger gusts.

"Anyway, I spoke to your mum, she sounds lovely by the way, and she said she could come over anytime."

Max glowered at me, and breathed in sharply.

"Though she did say your dad wouldn't be able to come. Is he OK Max, you didn't tell me he couldn't travel?" I chewed my lip and suddenly regretted making the call.

He carefully placed his fork onto his plate. "Didn't I? If you must know, he's agoraphobic, has been for a couple of years. It came on after he was made redundant." He flicked a speck of something off his sleeve.

"That's awful. We should go and see him if he can't travel here." I felt uncomfortable, and Max squirmed in his seat.

Max fell silent and his eyes closed for a few moments.

"Max, why didn't you tell her we were engaged? She didn't know." I went in for the kill. "I hope you're not going to tell me she's got a memory like a bloody goldfish."

He stood up quickly; his long legs knocked the table, and his dinner plate hurtled across and crashed into mine.

"What the bloody hell do you think you were doing ringing Mam without asking me first?" His face and neck flushed red.

I'd never seen Max lose his temper and my heart raced.

I slid off the bench and backed away. "You kept saying I would meet your parents but you didn't arrange anything, and I thought it was too important to ignore. So rather than keep going on about it I thought I'd save you the trouble."

"Oh you did, did you?" His voice became vicious. "And how would you feel if I rang your parents out of the blue without bothering to mention it first?"

"To be honest, I wouldn't have a problem with it, and I can't see why you have. Mum and Dad would love it if you rang them unexpectedly." I moved to stand by the door. "Perhaps you should be asking yourself why I called them in the first place. If you weren't so cagey about your family, I wouldn't have needed to."

"I've never been cagey," he barked. "I just don't feel the need to tell you every detail about them, unlike you who can never shut up about how wonderful your parents are. It's not even bloody normal. Most people I know never stop moaning about their parents. I get sick of hearing about your feckin' perfect mam and dad, it makes me wanna puke." His mouth was screwed up, full with anger.

His face looked unrecognisable.

"You should have told me before. And I'm so sorry, I had no idea that being nice about my parents was something that would piss you off so much. I probably go on about them hoping you might be a bit more open about yours. Clearly, that hasn't worked, and I've resorted to sneaking about behind your back."

Max looked straight past me, his anger faded and his face fell. He looked suddenly sad and deflated. "I don't know who you are," he said. "I thought we loved one another."

He snatched his coat from the sofa, barged past me and stormed out of the caravan. The door banged behind him.

I flung the door open, but a gust of icy wind slammed it back in my face. I grabbed my coat and ran outside. I rounded the end of the caravan and heard the car engine revving, and then he was away down the track. As I pulled my coat tightly about me I watched the Volvo's rear lights until they disappeared into the night.

I knew he'd tried to make me feel guilty, and it had worked. And saying he didn't know me, that was ironic given the argument had arisen because I wanted to get to know him and his family better. I had always shared stuff with him, how I felt and telling him little snippets of things that happened to me during my day when we were apart. He was often quiet and evasive or simply announced things rather than talking stuff through with me first.

My appetite had vanished, so I cleared away the dinner plates and mopped up the mess. This had been our first proper argument, and it made me sick with worry. Anxiety fired piercing daggers through me, and I was terrified that I'd pushed him too far, that he might end all of this... us. I knew he was angry, but why run away rather than sort it out? I felt progressively more miserable as the minutes passed, but I had no option other than to wait. Daylight had departed - so had the car.

After an hour, I rang his mobile, but he didn't answer. I flopped back onto the sofa bench and picked up my book The Catcher in the Rye, but after only a couple of paragraphs I realised now wasn't the best time to read it. I turned on the stereo and put on our favourite Stone Roses CD, but as I listened the music only made me miss him more. As one hour became two and two hours became three, fear crept back in. I didn't mind being stuck in the middle of nowhere, alone, but instead I worried about Max and where he had disappeared to. I imagined what he would say or do when he got back, assuming he would be back. Later I figured time would pass more quickly if I went to bed and slept. I left the lamp on for company.

I lay back, eyes wide and staring at the dimly lit plastic panels, and ran through our argument for the umpteenth time. The sound of a car drifted from outside. I knew it was Max, and I turned over and closed my eyes to show him that his paddy hadn't bothered me enough to keep me awake.

When he came in he didn't speak, and I heard him brush his teeth and get undressed, a lot louder than was necessary I noted. He slipped into bed, and I felt his hot breath on my neck. When a freezing hand brushed my back, I just about managed to suppress a shriek.

After a minute or so he said, "You awake?"

I counted slowly to five before answering. "I might be."

"I'm sorry, Kat. I probably overreacted. Forgive me?"

"Umm, probably overreacted?"

"OK, definitely overreacted."

"That's better. And of course I forgive you," I said, and turned around.

I pushed him onto his back and sat astride him, then squeezed his hips tightly between my thighs. "But I might have to punish you first."

He grinned, and in surrender put his hands behind his head. I leaned over, bit his lips lightly, then kissed his neck, nipped his nipples and kissed my way further down.

He moaned in response and guiding my head, urged me to take him deeper.

"Mmmm. I'll have to run away more often if this is how I get reprimanded."

I lifted my head. "Don't even think about it. I won't be so nice next time."

He laughed. "Don't tempt me."

His breath came faster, and I relaxed my hold.

The next morning, we awoke fully reconciled and wrapped together, my head laid on his warm chest. I listened to the calm and rhythmic drumbeat of his heart, and as I breathed in and out slowly, it felt as though his heartbeat was mine and my breath his.

Later, as we sat opposite one another eating our sausage sandwiches, we talked about our plans for the day, but not what triggered the row. I felt relief that we'd made up and our lovemaking became even more intense and all-consuming, and in the days and weeks that followed, I came to understand that it was this pure physical connection that held us together, and would continue to do so whatever life threw at us.

I grew reluctant to raise the idea of visiting his parents again for fear of creating any tension, and Max seemed content to let it go, or at least I figured he didn't want to risk being asked further questions about them. We set our wedding date, and I was satisfied I would meet his mum and other family members then, even if it couldn't be before. Life carried on in that vein. We were in love, happy together in the pursuit of our dreams, and ultimately neither of us wanted that to change.

The harsh frosts and snowfalls of winter had, at last, retreated up the hillside and nearby mountains, and the lower slopes came alive around us. A sweet-scented display of grasses erupted from the peaty soil and with them came the delicate pinks, blues, and yellows of wild flowers and plant life: blue sow thistle, buttercup, alpine catchfly, thrift and Scottish primrose.

We treasured the simple joy of walking up the hillside together, then gazing back down, first at the foundations, and then the wooden frame and walls as they began to expand and take shape. It was exciting to see Max's drawings and vision become a reality. He insisted that it was our vision, but in truth, while we discussed all of its parts, shared ideas, suggested improvements, I saw it as his project, and I was happy for it to be that way. There were many complications, delivery delays, disagreements about prices, but Max had such a persuasive and charismatic manner that the builders and suppliers seemed eager to please him. He quickly became a great manager, and with his wry, Irish humour, and joining in with the site craic, he soon earned respect from the builders and contractors alike.

Max would invariably slip out of bed at sun-up, leaving me still hiding under the duvet to shut out the cold, and he would stay out all day long until the final lilac blush of sundown deserted the hillside.

Towards the end of May, I got an interview with The Scottish Environment Organisation for a trainee project manager. On paper it looked like my ideal job, and because I so desperately wanted it, I suggested Max be the interviewer and pose possible questions.

"So tell me, Ms O'Donnell," he said, "which would you say you preferred - giving fellatio or receiving cunnilingus?"

"Oh that's not fair," I protested, "now you're just trying to throw me off track with big words."

"We do expect our graduate trainees to have a wide vocabulary, and be able to form opinions based on learning and experience. However, perhaps that particular question is a little unfair."

"Uhh, given you've just met me, hypothetically speaking?"

"OK," he paused. "Katriina, you've told me all about what you're good at, but what do you struggle with?"

I stared out of the window and thought for a moment.

"What I struggle with is seeing man pollute our beautiful planet and destroy its natural habitats, the wildlife and ecosystems. I see our planet being skinned of resources because man thinks only about short term gain, selfish ambition and making money here and now and giving no thought to what will remain for future generations, for our children, our grandchildren, their grandchildren."

All my meticulous preparation paid off and I was thrilled to have found employment doing something that would allow me to have a positive influence on the Scottish environment, with the potential for real career progression, and just as importantly, a decent starting salary.

"That's grand Kat, you'll be amazing. They obviously recognise a damn smart woman when they see one." Max kissed me. "I know it's what you've been working for, for so long, but I'm gonna to miss you being here with me." He took my hand. "Do you think you'll have to work late a lot or stay away much?"

"It depends how warm the offices or hotels are," I said, re-reading my offer letter. "I think I've developed chilblains living in this fridge."

He peered over my shoulder. "What are the hours?"

"It doesn't say. But I won't be quibbling about that. Good grief Max, it's taken ages for me to get an opportunity like this, and I'll do whatever's expected of me, and more if I feel like it." I folded the letter up and tucked it into my trouser pocket.

I wouldn't have called Max needy. If he was, I wouldn't have found him anywhere near as attractive, but as time went on, his physical need for me and the sheer intensity of his outlook on our relationship and life, made me love him even more.

Max leaned against the small kitchen worktop. His hair brushed against the panelled ceiling. "Do you think you belong here, Kat? Not this dump of a caravan, I mean here, our hillside and what will soon be our home?"

"You know I do." I turned to the sink and refilled the kettle. "And it isn't only the sheer beauty of the place, though it's more beautiful than anywhere I've ever been. It's because I'm here with you, seeing it through your eyes, as well as my own." I lay my palm against his cheek. "Have I told you recently that I adore you?"

He squeezed my bottom. "Only once today. You are so beautiful Kat, have I told you that recently?"

"Aye, but I never tire of hearing it," I replied, and slid my hand down beneath the waistband of his jeans.

CHAPTER TWENTY

A Sketch

Louis' knees pressed against the glove box. He reached down, pulled the lever and slid the seat back a few inches. "Where shall we start Mum?"

"Let me think." I closed my eyes and hoped for divine inspiration.

Louis did his best to sound positive. "We could start in the layby at Loch Dubh, and head in the direction they went? Seems logical, and we have to start somewhere."

"Good idea. It's a long shot, but we might see something mightn't we?" I fastened my seatbelt and adjusted the mirrors.

"Drive carefully," he said. "I can look, but you've got to keep your eyes on the road too. There are some steep drops, and you're not used to the car."

"Don't worry, I'll be careful." I tried to sound optimistic. "You're so sensible Lou. All my back seat driving with Dad must have rubbed off."

"Look, Gran's packed us a flask and snacks so we don't have to stop." Louis opened up the bag at his feet. "I'm glad they've come up, aren't you Mum? They love Lyssa so much."

"They love you both, and they couldn't have stayed away." I turned on the radio and found the news.

"The weather won't help," I said. "And it was so clear yesterday."

We turned onto the Lochinver Road. The dense cloud cover had already descended, and it felt oppressive as the mist closed around the car, and somehow separated us from our surroundings.

"Perhaps it'll lift further down," I said, and looked for the fog light.

"Mum!" Louis shouted." Watch out!"

I slammed my foot on the brake as the car thumped and shuddered against something in the road.

"Holy shit! What is it?" I yanked the handbrake.

"Sheep," said Louis, unfastening his seatbelt and throwing open the door.

A newly sheared ewe and its lamb lay lifeless beneath the bumper. I felt a massive rush of blood to my head, and for a few moments my vision staggered. I climbed back into the car and reversed. Then crouching down, I stroked the lamb's warm ruched fleece, and rested my hand on its chest to see if it was still breathing. Its ears quivered, then it shook its head and sprang up. It stood next to the ewe for a few moments on shaking legs, and then scuttled away, apparently unhurt. The ewe's grey eyes continued staring out, frozen.

Louis touched my shoulder. "We should move her."

"I didn't see them Louis. Did they run out?"

"They were just standing there. You must have been distracted."

I felt dizzy again, and I leaned against the bonnet and shut my eyes until the sensation passed.

"Come on, poor wee thing," I said, crying. "I'll have to ring the farms. It's the first sheep I've hit in all these years."

"Don't Mum, it wasn't your fault," he said, and his eyes welled with tears.

We lifted the ewe, its head swinging limply, and lay it down gently onto the grass. I flapped a couple of flies off the ewe's face and shut its eyes. I stepped away, and the lamb trotted up to the ewe, nudged her with its nose, then nuzzled her udders and suckled."

"It needs milk Louis," I said.

The lamb turned to me, then back at its mother and let out a long and pitiful, "Maaaaaa."

"Mum, please. You can't do anything." Louis led me back to the car.

"Everything's going wrong. I'm sorry," I cried.

"I know, but we've got to stay focussed. Nobody will blame you."

Visibility didn't improve as we set off, and intermittently, the cloud was as thick as fog, then moments later it had lifted. Just as quickly it closed in once more. I couldn't have rushed even if I'd wanted to.

I pulled up at Loch Dubh, got out, and very slowly turned a full circle. In stark contrast to the mist that swirled around us, I could clearly picture the scene from yesterday, however not through the same panic-stricken eyes.

I hear an engine start up. I run back up to the road and watch my car jolt forwards. It moves away, but this time I can see it without any interference, more clearly. Through the tinted windows I see the back of the driver's head, no more than a shadow, an outline. I'm certain it's a man, curly hair, thick on top. I also see Lyssa turn in her seat and look back at me. She is petrified, eyes are wide and mouth open, screaming. My eye line shifts sideways, and I see the driver's wing mirror. The angle of the mirror allows me to see the face of the driver – in a fraction of a second – but it's long enough. His face is as palpable as if I were gazing at my own reflection, his features as sharp as if they were dots on a dice. Don't fade.

"Quick Louis, is there pen and paper in the glove box?"

He looked confused and then realisation flashed across his face. He opened it up and pulled everything out. "Here."

I leaned on my atlas and sketched the man whose features I saw in my mind. A narrow face with severe cheekbones, thick brows, a stubble and dark curly hair. Although not especially artistic, the image bore a close resemblance.

"Who is that?" Louis said, as I added more lines to thicken the brows and lengthen the nose.

"It's him, Louis." I clasped a hand over my mouth. "I'm certain this is what he looks like. I hadn't remembered seeing anything, but standing there it came back to me so vividly." I held up the sketch. "It was as though it was happening all over again, but in slow motion. It sounds crazy, but I know it's him, and what's more, it's a good likeness. I'm taking it to Inspector Keir."

"Do you know him, or recognise him?" he asked, and examined the rough but lifelike sketch.

"No I don't," I said, knowing I had never seen him before.

CHAPTER TWENTY-ONE

Neverland

I walked into the station feeling relatively in control in comparison to my panicked state the previous morning. Constable Pearce stood behind the desk with a phone to her ear. She watched as we strode, unswerving, to the incident room. Inspector Keir sat alongside a slim, middle-aged man. They both stared at the computer and turned to me in unison.

"Katriina." Inspector Keir pushed back her chair. "This is Detective Constable Brooks."

He came over, shook my hand firmly and said, "Morning Katriina. What news?"

"I've remembered something," I said. "Yesterday you asked if I'd seen anyone. I didn't know it at the time, but I did." I handed my drawing to Inspector Keir. "I don't know him, but someone must."

Inspector Keir looked at my drawing then up at me. "You suddenly remembered?"

"Yes. It all came flooding back when we stopped at Loch Dubh. I must have been in too much of a panic yesterday."

"What about Max, has he seen this?" she asked, and gave it to Detective Brooks.

"I'll show him. Where is he?" I said.

The Inspector glanced at Detective Brooks.

"I spoke to him first thing," she said. "Filled him in on the car sightings. But he didn't say he was coming here. In fact, he said he was staying at home with you."

Louis gave me a puzzled look. "That's weird. He said he was coming here."

I grabbed Dad's phone and called Max. I experienced déjà vu as it went straight to answerphone.

I rang home.

"But he isn't here," I said to Dad. "The police haven't seen him. Can you try ringing him? I need to speak to him." I hung up.

"I'll scan this, and get it to our photo fit guy," said Inspector Keir.

"Excuse me," said Detective Brooks, and followed her out.

"Mum, that was awesome you remembering what he looked like. Maybe you'll remember more."

All of the things I'd seen and heard made me wonder if I might see more to reveal Lyssa's whereabouts. Why though? I pondered whether the location had triggered the memory, or whether it had been down to some unexplained phenomenon. My mind whirled as I tried to make sense of it, of everything.

Movement flickered in the corner of my eye and I turned and saw a house spider as it weaved an intricate web, and watched how it looped its silk round and round. Mesmerised by its quick but methodical movements and skill, I thought, what if Lyssa had hooked up with me in a way far beyond our ordinary understanding of things? What if she and I were so in tune with one another that our minds connected because of the extreme emotions we had both experienced?

And, what was going on with Max? I wondered why he had lied. I ran through what I'd tell him when he showed his face again. The only explanation I could think was that he'd lost his mind. He had lied to me and messed me about when our beloved daughter was missing. My head throbbed with confusion, and I burst into tears.

"Sit down, Mum." Louis pulled out a chair and guided me to it. "I'm sure Dad will be here soon."

"Will he, Louis, do you really think so, because I'm not so sure?"

Detective Brooks and Inspector Keir walked back in.

"Katriina," said Inspector Keir. "Is there any place Max may have gone, perhaps to look for Lyssa, or to his office?" She lifted the box of tissues from the table and placed them in front of me.

"He said he was coming here. Why's he doing this?"

"I'm sure he'll have an explanation, but in the meantime keep ringing him. I'll alert our officers, and if you do speak to him, I want him here ASAP."

Then something occurred to me. What if whoever had Lyssa had done something to Max?

"Katriina, I'm going to videoconference call our photo-fit artist. He'll go through your sketch with you, bring it to life. We'll get his image onto local and national news." She sat at the computer. "Well done for remembering his face so clearly. This is the break we need."

"I know Lyssa will be doing all she can to get away. She's determined, isn't she Louis?" I forced a smile.

"You bet, and clever too," he said.

I wouldn't allow myself to believe that Lyssa was anything but alive, and doing everything in her power to escape. "Come here Louis, my love."

He opened his arms, and I held him close. Unlike Max, Louis was my support.

The laptop began to hum and beep, and a man's voice came through.

"Katriina, I've got Charlie on," said Inspector Keir.

As Charlie graphically redrew my basic sketch, I was surprised at how vividly I could still picture him. As he made his final revisions, it struck me that I was looking at Lyssa's abductor. The likeness was disconcertingly accurate, and the mental state it triggered in me was chilling.

"We've checked out the sightings of your car, and as two were within five miles of each other and at approximately the same time, it's a concrete lead." Inspector Keir paused. "One woman was convinced it was your registration." She watched me closely and her eyes sharpened. "What puzzles me, is that these sightings were near Loch Lomond. That's a good distance from here. Do you know anyone down there, have any connections or family there?"

I thought and shook my head. "No one that comes to mind. My hometown is Oban, but that's a decent drive away." Then without warning I felt a shot of adrenaline. "In fact, Max and I met at Strathclyde Uni, and we walked there with the hiking group a few times. It was twenty years ago though, and we haven't been down much since, other than to drive through. Could it be relevant?"

"Are you in touch with anyone at Uni or in Glasgow?" asked Inspector Keir.

"Not really, but Max may be through work. I'm still in touch with Uni friends but none that live there now."

Detective Brooks readjusted his glasses. "Was there anything that may have caused someone to have a problem with either of you?"

"No. I had a serious relationship that finished before meeting Max, but he's living in Morecambe, married with children."

"Was there any resentment on his part?" he said, and tapped his pen lightly against the table.

"At first, but he soon moved on, like you do at that age. He even went out with my friend Georgie for a while."

"Are you still in touch?" he asked.

"We're friends on Facebook, but we rarely message. He only uses it to promote his business, nothing you'd look twice at. God knows what I ever saw in him. I don't think he's got anything to do with this. And, he looks nothing like the man in the car."

"I'm sure you're right, but if you can tell me his name, it would be prudent to check him out. It could be that whoever has Lyssa was only passing through the area, taking the back roads and heading elsewhere. Any other previous boyfriends or admirers down that way?"

"No, as soon as we split, I met Max. Oh, and David's surname is Harley," I said, and thought what a futile line of enquiry this was.

Detective Brooks made a note. "And what's his business?"

"Pretty sure it Harley Architectural Design," I replied.

Detective Brook's head snapped up. "He's an architect too?"

"Yes, Max and he were on the same Postgrad course."

"Do you know if Max and he have any business links?"

"I can't imagine it. They didn't exactly get on," I said, and tried to recall if Max had mentioned David recently.

"Got through to Max?" asked Inspector Keir.

"I've left him messages. Louis, could you try home again," I said.

The Inspector's radio burst into life, and she stepped into the corridor.

I listened to Louis talking. He looked relieved. "Gran's spoken to Dad. He's had a flat tyre and trouble changing it. Says he didn't hear his phone and then saw all the missed calls."

"And what's he doing now?" I asked.

"Coming here."

"He could have rung me back." I seethed and struggled to hide it.

Even if some progress had been made, I still felt as though my insides had been ripped out, and a fear that something unspeakable had happened to Lyssa hammered away inside me and pushed aside any positive thoughts I had tried to foster.

Other abductions and their outcomes returned to haunt me, and I realised that from the outside it was impossible to understand how it really felt when something like this happened. I recalled horrific stories on the news, and how I'd felt pity for the parents, for the family. I'd even shed tears. But if I was honest with myself, these tears had been false, and all I had felt was relief. Relief that it hadn't happened to us, relief that it wasn't our beloved child going through God only knows what misery and agony before they suffered the most inhumane death you could imagine. The child you nurtured inside of you, suffered pain to be with and invested every ounce of energy within you to ensure they grew up to be happy children - how could any parent possess the strength to cope with that life being so viciously cut short? A tragic accident or an unavoidable illness taking your child would be beyond heart-breaking, but for them to suffer kidnap, abuse, and brutal murder, I never wanted to experience how that would feel.

Who was I trying to kid? That was exactly what was happening.

Max walked through the doorway and looked flustered. "I had a flat tyre, and didn't hear my phone."

As he came nearer, I noticed a fine film of sweat made his face glisten.

I got up and waved a dismissive hand at him. "Don't bloody bother, Max. I've had it up to here with your lies. You set off ages before us, and funny, but I don't remember passing you stuck on the side of the road," I hissed, and wondered how he was going to wheedle his way out of this one. When he didn't reply, I continued. "Well? Where have you been and what the hell's going on? I'm not imagining it. You're being weird and secretive."

His eyes twitched, as he took in Detective Brooks and Louis.

"Even Mum's noticed. Is it to do with Lyssa?" My legs felt weak, and I grabbed the back of the chair and sat down.

"Are you serious?" He pinched the bridge of his nose and inhaled deeply. "You've lost the plot. And do you think we can have this conversation in private?" He looked pointedly at Louis who stared at his phone.

I glanced at Detective Brooks who openly watched us.

"No, I don't think there's any need for us to speak privately. Your son's been more help since this whole fucking nightmare started, so I think he's got a right to hear your pathetic excuses."

Inspector Keir walked in. She looked at Detective Brooks and me as we watched and waited for Max to respond.

"I'm not doing it here Kat, so we can discuss this alone or you can rant to yourself. And shut that filthy mouth, it's disgusting and not helping." Max turned on his heel and stormed out.

Once we were behind the closed door of the interview room, I said, "Is this private enough for you to feed me more of your sick lies? Do say if you need a moment to come up with some. I'm more than happy to sit here crying about our missing daughter for a minute or two longer." I was being vile, but I was way beyond caring about his feelings.

Max circled the room like a caged animal looking for an escape route. I guessed he knew his excuse had to be plausible.

"So, thought of anything?" I asked, my tone unchanged. "When I think about it, you've been behaving strangely for weeks. I couldn't put my finger on it before, and barely paid it any attention, but now our daughter's life is hanging in the balance, if she's still alive, I need to know right fucking now what it is that you know."

He stood in front of me, folded his arms and his eyes burned into mine. "Fine, but before I do, I'd like to point out that I wasn't the one who left Lyssa in the car with the door wide open and the keys in the ignition. So if anyone's to blame for this goddamn nightmare, it's you," he said. "I wouldn't say this but you're trying to lay the blame on me and it's not on." He leaned back on the edge of the table; arms folded. "If you must know, I drove up the lane towards Fydon to check out the disused water pump room and was unlucky enough to get a flat tyre." He held my gaze; dared me to challenge him. "I thought it might be worth heading up there. I realised it could be a waste of time, but I'm clutching at straws too. You suggested driving around to look for her, didn't you?" I heard Max's phone buzz. He

106

paused then continued. "It wasn't my fault there was no phone signal."

"Aren't you going to see who your message is from?" I asked, and noted that Max rarely waited to read new messages.

"In a minute." His voice rose. "I was going frantic when I couldn't get hold of you. Did you think of that? Take a good look at yourself, instead of throwing accusations at me."

His anger rendered me lost for words, and I suddenly felt faint.

I shut my eyes. "Can you get me some water? I feel dizzy."

"You've gone white. I'll fetch some." Max dashed out.

White spots flashed before me, and I dropped my head between my knees.

Max returned. He took my hand and rubbed his thumb back and forth. "You OK?"

I lifted my head cautiously.

"Drink this, a bit of sugar might help." He pulled the ring on a can of lemonade. "You've hardly slept or eaten, have you? I feel ill, too."

Not for the same reason, I thought, and drank a mouthful. As we shared the can the dizziness and nausea subsided. Our argument was forgotten, at least for the moment, and I told him about the man's photo-fit and the car sightings.

"It was dark when my car was spotted so no one got a look at the driver. You need to see the photo-fit, you might know him through work. They're going to show it on the news." I paused. "What if he's a... you know?"

"Fuck Jeez, Kat. I can't think like that."

"Why else would someone want to take her?"

"There could be any number of reasons. Why assume - -"

"Any number of reasons? What planet do you think we're on? It's not bloody Neverland," I said.

Max snorted. "Anyway, how did you see his face and manage to draw it? And it was when you stopped at Loch Dubh again?"

"It was surreal. His face in the wing mirror, the whole sequence of events came back to me. And, do you remember last night, how I heard Lyssa calling? I wasn't dreaming. I heard her. She's alive Max, and she's trying to connect with me."

Max frowned with disbelief.

"I know you think I've gone mad, but I'm right, and it's going to help us find her. Lyssa, our baby, she's talking to me, Max."

My tears fell, and I knew that what I said was true, and it drove away a tiny slice of despair and offered a small glimmer of hope for me to cling to.

He circled the room, and watched me with critical eyes.

"Listen to me, Kat. If you believe that will help, fine, and by all means tell the police. They can use it if they think they can," he sneered. "But don't involve Louis in this…mumbo jumbo or whatever it is. It's not fair."

"So you don't believe me?" I shoved my chair back. "Fine, your problem. I could have done with your faith in me, in our daughter, but clearly that's not going to happen."

Furious, I marched out. Why didn't he trust me? I'd created a photo-fit of the bastard. Inspector Keir had been convinced by it.

She hadn't doubted me for a second.

CHAPTER TWENTY-TWO

A Drop of Moonshine

Max nor I had wanted a huge wedding, although Max insisted I could invite as many guests as I wanted as he was happy to put some of his inheritance towards it. My little sister Alannah was bringing her latest beau, and claimed he was 'the one', my parents, both sets of grandparents, plus aunts, uncles, and cousins who had travelled from Norway. Other than that, it was relations and close friends. Neither of us were churchgoers and although Max's family were Catholic, my family were most definitely lapsed Christians, and so we compromised with a wedding at the pretty Church of Scotland, St. Cuthbert's in Lochinver.

Rosie and I spent the pre-wedding night at our reception venue, the spectacular Conival castle a few miles north of Lochinver.

Rosie got down on her knees to straighten out the skirt of my dress.

You look beautiful Katriina, a vision of gorgeousness." She got up and walked around to face me.

Rosie looked elegant in a fifties style cream and black dress, reminiscent of Audrey Hepburn, worn with the obligatory Rosie Dickens stilettoes.

"Thank you," I said. "That dress shows off your figure to perfection. Is it new?"

"Of course," she said, mildly outraged. "You don't think I'd wear an old dress to my best friend's wedding do you? I wouldn't want to look like the poor relation."

"I don't think you could ever look poor. You ooze affluence from every angle."

"Why, thank you," she said, and she held out her skirt and curtseyed.

"Anyway," I said, "you look beautiful, and I love that flower in your hair."

She looked me up and down, then getting down on her knees again, fiddled with the hem.

"I hope Max knows how lucky he is."

"Well I feel super lucky to have him too." I peered down, wishing she'd finish fussing so I could relax.

"Mmmm, can't argue with that." She sniffed. "You're making me cry." Rosie reached for the tissues on the bedside table, dabbed her eyes and blew her nose. "I should have known I'd need waterproof mascara." She sighed.

"I feel so grown up Rosie, but I know this is it. I don't think I'll ever look at another man again."

I stood before the full-length mirror and smiled. My ivory silk dress fitted as though it had been tailor made for me, and even with the bodice tightly buttoned up, I could breathe. The shoulders to ankle sheath dress was strapless, save for some embroidered lace that ran over my shoulders. Delicate beading sewn in spirals adorned the bodice and the long train. It had been the first dress I'd tried on at the wedding boutique in Ullapool and the only alteration they'd made had been to nip it in at the waist.

My chocolaty hair fell long and loose in soft curls with a few tendrils pulled lightly back and held with a white pearl hair clip. I'd borrowed a sky-blue jewelled choker from my mother and it sparkled in the sunlight that streamed through the window. My cream satin shoes had a deliberately low kitten heel, as I planned to dance all evening.

Rosie reached for her glass of sparkling wine. "Do you know who you remind me of?"

"No…who?"

"You look like a young Anni-Frid, from Abba? Your neck of the woods, well Scandia anyway."

"Thanks, I think. Not when she had the frizzy perm I hope," I said, with a frown.

"I dunno, your hair is kinda similar." She chuckled. "It's more her colouring and statuesque beauty. Trust me, it's a compliment." She downed the rest of her wine and immediately refilled our glasses.

"Hope I don't start Chquitita-ing down the aisle," I said, and giggled.

"I love that one," said Rosie. "I can be Agnetha."

"I wonder what Max will be wearing," I said. "We haven't coordinated outfits, though I did say I was going for a traditional look."

"He could turn up in his hard hat and steel capped boots, and you'd fall to your knees," then she winked and added. "Mm-mmm... maybe only his hard hat and boots."

"Pass me my wine, Rosie. I need to settle my nerves."

She handed me the glass. "Milady. You don't seem overly nervous for a girl about to sign away sex with any other men - for life."

I feigned shock. "Rosie! I'm not the slightest bit nervous about marrying Max. It's what I want more than anything." I swallowed a large mouthful of wine. "I'm more nervous about meeting his family. I haven't met his parents yet, and his poor dad can't even come today."

I didn't mention Max's resistance to me meeting them and I hoped none of that was apparent. I wanted Rosie to think the best of him. Even I held onto that impression of perfection in Max.

"I wanted to meet his mum last night, but they weren't arriving until late, and Max has put them up at the Red Lion." I picked up Rosie's designer fragrance and sprayed my cleavage. "I don't know why she couldn't stay here. It's so much nicer."

"Maybe he wanted to see her. And he couldn't stay here could he?"

"True."

"Why can't his dad come? I bet Max is gutted."

"He's agoraphobic, can't leave the house. Been that way for a couple of years." I sat down at the dressing table and watched Rosie's reflection as she lay back on the four-poster bed. "Sometimes he goes to the local shop to buy a paper, but that's it. He won't even go out in the car." I sipped my wine. "It's so sad, and apparently counselling hasn't helped." I twisted round to face her. "Max has been back to see what he could do to help but his mum doesn't want him worrying about them so she sends him back sharpish. I've offered to visit, but since I've started my job it's been full on. I didn't think I should be taking a holiday so soon, knowing I'd need time off for the wedding and honeymoon. You know how it is?"

"True, though you should try to remember what matters in life Kat. You know, family and friends should always come first," said Rosie, and stuck one long, slim leg in the air and then the other to smooth out her stockings.

"You are wise Rosie. I'll try to remember that when I'm traipsing around getting lost on some godforsaken moor."

"Is that what you do then, spend your days in the wilds?" Rosie grimaced, horrified at the thought.

"I suppose I do, especially at the moment. It's about understanding what they do at grassroots level, seeing it all, and so much of it is in remote places. On Thursday I was clearing out a channel at Loch Durness, and the day before we were a hundred miles away in Cape Wrath."

"Really? It sounds horrendous."

"Last week I slept in a bunkhouse on Skye for two nights which isn't ideal with all the house stuff going on, and Max hates it."

"I'm sure Max can entertain himself for a night or two," she said.

"Of course. Anyway, I love it. It's my dream job."

"You always were the outdoorsy type. Not one for worrying about your freshly manicured nails, huh?"

"Life's too short for that. Anyway, I'd struggle to get my nails done here, don't think there's a beauty salon for a hundred miles or so." I studied my self-varnished nails, and picked at the odd imperfection.

"There is one," she said. "Got mine done yesterday at Salon 28."

"Really, they do nails? I suppose I should have made the effort. Still, I've varnished them," I said, displaying my fingers.

Rosie jumped off the bed to take a closer look. "Is that clear nail polish? On your wedding day! You're a class act Kat," she said, and showed me her long, perfectly manicured blood red nails.

"If you must know Rosie, it's pearl, a subtle tint. Anyway, I'm supposed to look virginal aren't I?"

"Think you'll need more than a bit of pale nail polish to convince the congregation you're still virgo intacta. How many was it at the last count, eight?"

"Shush. Max thinks he's my first and only," I said, laughing.

I stepped into the back of the Rolls Royce, as Rosie guided my train from behind. Mum and Dad climbed in behind us.

Dad sat next to me and took my hand. "I'm so proud of you. You look like an angel, just like your mum did on our wedding day." He beamed at Mum sitting opposite, then pulled a tissue from his pocket and blew his nose. "I'll get my crying done here. You won't want your old dad snivelling in church."

"I don't mind if you blub Dad. I'll probably join you."

"No, no, I need to maintain a manly façade. Grrr," he said, and flexed his biceps.

Rosie laughed. "Hey, I thought weddings were supposed to be fun."

"Quite so Rosie," Mum said. "Though I think I'm allowed a tear or two. Only to keep up my ladylike façade." With fingers splayed under her chin, Mum tilted her head and fluttered her eyelashes.

Dad produced another tissue and handed it to her. "Here we are, permission to weep, my love."

The ceremony was everything I dreamed it would be, and Max looked stunning, complete with kilt, long socks and white ruffled shirt. As I walked down the aisle with Dad to the strains of *Jesu Joy of Man's Desiring*, Max turned to me, and as he did, it felt like we were doing the most natural thing in the world. I had no doubts, and I knew he didn't either. I spotted Max's mum on the front row, and she gave me a huge smile, which filled me with a warm feeling of optimism.

Afterwards, as we walked out of the church, everyone cheered and threw confetti.

"Kat, meet Mam," said Max.

"My goodness, Max, you told me she was bonny, but that doesn't do her justice. Katriina, it's wonderful to finally meet you. You're an absolute vision, you truly are." She leaned over, and with tears in her eyes, kissed me lightly on the cheek.

"I'm so happy to meet you too," I said. "It means a lot to me, Mrs O'Donnell."

"I wouldn't have missed this for the world. And what a beautiful service. I'm so proud of him - of both of you," she said, and smiled. "And please… call me Iona."

I was struck by her poise and presence. She was tall, young and attractive. She looked sophisticated in a pale lilac dress-suit and chic fascinator.

We made our way up the cobbled path, Rosie sidled up and whispered in my ear.

"Hey Kat, now we know where Max gets his looks. And I'd say you've a look of her too."

"She's beautiful isn't she, and more importantly, she seems lovely," I said, and prodded Rosie in the ribs.

After Max and I had posed for a few photographs, we climbed back into the wedding car and were driven back to Conival Castle.

I rested my hand on Max's knee, leaned in and kissed him. "Oh my God Max. You look so fucking sexy in that kilt." I slid my hand between his legs. "Can we skip the reception and head straight to our room? No one would notice."

"Don't tempt me." He parted his thighs. "When you walked into the church, I was blown away to see you looking so beautiful and natural."

I inched my hand further up his kilt and he let out a soft moan.

He drew closer and whispered in my ear, "I'd like to rip that dress off you right now."

"You know it took me two hours to look this natural and a lot of money for the frock, so there'll be no ripping." I whispered back, "At least not yet."

"Whatever the cost, it was worth every penny." Max fell silent as we headed up the sweeping castle drive. "Wow! It's even better than I remember."

The castle stood back on a high grassy cliff. It overlooked the wild northern Atlantic, and had once been the seat of a powerful Scottish baronial family. It looked impressively grand and commanding. The young receptionist had proudly informed us that certain royalty had stayed there, though she didn't say who, as though it were a huge secret.

The great stone walls and tall towers crowned with battlements and turrets gave far-reaching views across the sapphire and crystal-tipped ocean, and the spectacular mountains of Assynt rose to the east. The drive continued over a humpback bridge and continued into a large internal courtyard where our guests awaited us.

Max and I linked arms and led everyone through the large, handsomely carved wooden doors, and into the Great Hall. It felt authentic and imposing with its large gilt-framed paintings of the family's many ancestors, and an incredible assortment of weaponry displayed above and around the colossal fireplace. The long tables had been decorated with glorious arrangements of Lilies, Irises, and Gypsophila, and as the waiting staff appeared with champagne and canapés, I gazed about me, and thought how much it felt and looked like the most picture-perfect setting.

The sumptuous wedding breakfast of lamb and barley soup, followed by fillet of cod wrapped in parma ham with pesto, was enjoyed by all. And after a divine chocolate and raspberry cheesecake Max pushed back his chair and clinked his glass to announce the speeches.

Dad's somewhat lengthy speech made me cry and most of our guests too. It sounded like a classic doting dad speech, as he welcomed Max into our family and placed me on a ridiculously high pedestal, but it made me feel incredibly loved and special.

I'd drunk several glasses of champagne by this point in the proceedings and I wanted to stand up and say a few words.

Max tried to persuade me not to bother. "We don't want the speeches to go on too long, Kat. Just say a few thank you's."

"In that case make yours a bit shorter," I said, and gave him a peck on the cheek. I tapped my glass, and climbed up onto my chair. "Ladies and gentlemen, McNaltys, O'Donnells, Henriksens, and everyone else. Welcome! Those who know me will understand I couldn't miss out on saying a few words of thanks." I smiled sweetly down at Max. "I'm overwhelmed to see you all here, to witness Max and I make our lifelong vows to one another. I hope you're enjoying the food and wine - -" I hiccupped. "I certainly am. The ceilidh will start soon and I want to see you all strutting your stuff. Don't worry about getting the moves right, trust me you'll love it. Only remember not to tread on my toes. I lifted and placed my foot on the table, but anyone else's is fine." I paused and there were plenty of chuckles. "But seriously, I wanted to say to Max's family that I'm so happy to have found him, or perhaps he found me." I gazed down at Max who winked at me. "We've been living together for a few months in our caravan, in separate bunks, of course," I added with a wink back at Max. "But we're moving into our eco home at last, which my brilliant husband designed. And finally, a toast to absent family." I smiled sympathetically at Max. "In particular, two people without whom today wouldn't have been possible. First and most importantly to Max's father, who gave Max his life." I heard a few sniggers. "But sadly, through no fault of his own, can't be here today. I hope he can get over his... difficulties, so that he can visit us in our new home -"

I felt a sharp rap on my ankle and looked down to see Max discretely swirling his finger. I lifted my chin and continued. "And lastly, to Max's Uncle Sean, who regrettably I'll never meet personally, but who I must acknowledge and thank for his generous gift to Max upon his passing."

Max grasped my elbow and pulled me down to my seat. I glanced at Max's mum, and saw that she had lost her smile.

I yanked my arm back and hissed, "Hey. I wanna make a toast." I jumped back up, raised my glass and declared loudly. "To absent family, present family and friends." I pulled Max to his feet. "And to my remarkable and ever so slightly gorgeous husband, Max."

The room erupted with claps and cheers. Rosie whistled and clapped wildly; her seal of approval.

I thought perhaps Max had been worried about his speech, but it was heartfelt, full of emotion and people roared with laughter one minute, and reached for their tissues the next.

"If it weren't for my amazing mam who's been the kindness and strength, the true cement in our family, I wouldn't be here today with my beautiful and funny wife Katriina." He turned to me and grinned, then taking my hand, he said, "I feel incredibly lucky to have met her and I know she's gonna make my life, no our lives, amazing. To my extraordinary wife, Katriina O'Donnell."

He lifted me to my feet and kissed me deeply amidst whoops and cheers. I felt dizzy with love and desire. Afterwards he relaxed, and as the lead singer of the band announced the first dance, he grabbed my hand, and we ran out onto the dance floor.

"I need a drink, want one?" I said to Max, as we finished spinning about to a particularly fast number.

"Another beer would be great," Max said.

We kissed long and leisurely in the middle of the dance floor.

"Break it up you two. It's my turn to dance with the handsome groom." Rosie came and stood between us, and I left them arm in arm waiting for the band to play their next song. At the bar, Iona chatted to her sister Mary and my mum.

"Hello Katriina, I was just telling your mum that we're having a wonderful time. It's beautiful, everything is."

"Ah, thank you. My husband and I are having the best time too," I said.

"I can see you're a kind and strong woman, Katriina. Max needs someone grounded to guide him through life - keep him heading in the right direction." She glanced at her sister who nodded. "He hasn't had the easiest of lives, though he's come through it remarkably unscathed, considering. He's made a grand choice. You're smart and you've a wonderfully warm heart."

"That's kind of you Mrs O'Donnell, but you know it's more that Max guides me. He's brought us up here to start our new life. He's used his money to build our home and set up his business." Flattered by her words, I was also slightly dazed by her glowing judgement of me, considering we had only met that day. I tried to grasp what she meant by Max not having had the easiest of lives.

"Well from what Max has told me, his business is doing extraordinarily well already. How about we visit your new home tomorrow?"

"Oh, we'd love you to."

"Wonderful. I can't wait. And remember, it's Iona," she said, and touched my hand. "Now I think you'd better reclaim your husband. Rosie's beau is looking a touch, how shall I put it… emerald-eyed?"

I followed her gaze to see Will, who stood at the edge of the dance floor, arms crossed and lips pursed, as he watched Max and Rosie whirling around, surrounded by a circle of enthused guests who clapped and jigged with them.

117

Just past midnight, and slightly drunk, Max and I stumbled to our wedding suite. Exhausted, we collapsed onto the bed and I looked up at the ornate ceiling as it slowly stopped spinning.

Max turned to me with a grin. "Katriina, my love, I've been dying to see what surprises you have for me beneath that beautiful dress. Allow me to help you out of it. I expect it's pinching in all sorts of places."

"As it happens it is beginning to scratch. Too much lace for me really."

He pulled me to my feet and turned me around so that he could undo the silk buttons at the back.

"Is this my first marital test?"

"Persevere Max, I'm not helping." I reached behind, lifted his kilt and ran my hands up his firm, naked thighs.

My dress slipped over my shoulders and I wriggled my hips so that it fell to the floor in one motion.

Max let out a long whistle. "Well, that I wasn't expecting. Stark naked, just as the good Lord intended." He pulled my hair aside and planted gentle kisses on the back of my neck. "You could have told me you were bare-arsed, I'd have dragged you up to the turrets and taken you for starters."

"Not quite naked. I did splash out on stockings and garters," I said, and turned my heels.

"So I see. Then you've surpassed our good Lord's intentions. Come here my angel."

I turned around and pressed a finger on his chest, and said, "Wait a minute, fair's fair."

I undressed him, silent as I lingered over every button and fastening, and there were plenty of them. His skin quivered, ultra-sensitive to my touch.

"You're killing me," he breathed, and as his kilt fell, he pressed himself hard against me.

We remained there and held one another, and it felt as though we were no longer two separate people, but that in some otherworldly way, our minds and bodies had combined to make something altogether more powerful - more complete.

He released me and said, "Wait."

From the bedside cabinet he took out a small dark green bottle, placed it on top, and ceremoniously drew back the bedclothes. Red rose petals and gypsophila lay scattered across the sheet.

"It's beautiful Max. Thank you, my love." I rested my hand on his hip and kissed him. "What's in the bottle?"

"That's the real surprise." He lifted it and held it, protective. "It's a love tonic, or so I've been led to believe, and it's supposed to promise us a long blissful life together, blessed with beautiful children who will also live long and wonderful lives."

"Sounds intriguing. But what's in it to make it so powerful?" I asked, and took the bottle from him. I tilted it towards the light and removed the cork. "Can I try some?"

"Perhaps I should test it first." He took the bottle back and tipped a pool into the palm of his hand. He dipped his fingers into the liquid and traced them over my nipples in turn. Then he pushed me back onto the bed, and ran his tongue achingly around them.

I arched my back and exhaled. "I need you, Max."

He looked up. "Exquisite."

"The potion or me?"

"Both, my sweet love." He took a mouthful of the potion and kissed his way down my body. I lifted my knees, my hips, opened myself to him. He kissed me fully - the fluid felt warm and intense inside.

"I'm in heaven." I closed my eyes and my entire body tensed before hot sensations rolled and exploded through me again and again.

Max passed me the bottle and I sipped cautiously. As the fiery liquid bristled over my tongue, I laughed.

"Love potion! You had me going then. Any excuse for a drop of moonshine."

"Yes and it really did get you going. Let's put it to the test some more."

Even after all these months and nights together, each time we kissed and touched one another, the sensations and anticipation of what was to come set me alight and sparked my insides.

A while later, Max propped himself up on one elbow and gazed down at me. "I'm going to remember you like this, my beautiful girl, so whenever we're apart you'll still be with me, in here." He touched his temple.

I giggled and my insides melted. "I'm not going anywhere, Max. I'm yours."

"Yes, only mine."

We sipped in turns and drank the small bottle dry, then lay back in a heavenly haze of drunken love.

Late the next morning we drove in convoy to Benn Cady. The noontime sun had almost broken through the light covering of cloud, and as we drove up the gravelled track to our newly named home, Wolfstone House, I felt excited to see it again and thrilled to show it off to our families.

Now that it neared completion its modern beauty merged effortlessly with the hillside setting. The main frame rose to a great arched, seeded roof which had already nurtured a variety of grasses and native wildflowers. Large glass panels to the front and both sides ensured flawless views of the stunning panoramas from all aspects. The remainder of the exterior had been cladded with Red Cedar, all except for one full height section of wall for which we'd used local stone. The impressive wind turbine stood proudly to the far west side and the solar panels had been strategically arranged on the south-facing section of the roof.

In the design and construction of our home we'd bought in materials that enhanced and conserved the environment, it redistributed rather than depleted resources, and we felt happier with each step of the building process. We'd given equal care to the interior, with a fresh air ventilation system, natural insulation that used sheep's wool, water-based paints and water saving showers. We bought second-hand furniture or items made from recycled materials. We had considered every last detail to ensure that it fit in with our surroundings and the environment.

"Goodness Katriina, I had no idea that you were building such an enormous house. It's magnificent." Mum's face lit up with surprise.

"Will you need any mains electricity or can you rely on the energy the house generates?" Dad asked Max.

My parents asked knowledgeable questions about its energy sources and eco features, almost as though they'd researched the topic, which I suspected they had. Of course, they knew it was something we were passionate about, but I felt touched by their interest and newfound knowledge. Iona and Mary took photographs and made enthusiastic sounds as they suggested ideas for setting out furniture and fittings.

"You see, we thought that by having the living areas upstairs and large windows, we'd be able to take advantage of the views in all their glory," said Max.

I heard the way his voice lifted, its cadence more pronounced, just how proud he was as he showed his mum around our home, his creation. Iona, in turn, chatted in equally fervent tones.

She linked arms with Max and leaned into him. "Goodness Max, your business is doing well. I'm proud of you and your daddy will be too when I tell him all about it. I honestly thought you were building more of a two up two down." She ran her hand along some wooden panelling. "Plenty of room for little ones." She exchanged a look with her sister. "Daddy was so upset he couldn't come, but they wouldn't even let him out for a day. So unfair to miss all of this." She stood back and took a photo of Max at the bottom of the staircase.

Max led her away to another room so I missed the rest of the conversation. What she said struck me as odd, but I couldn't put my finger on it.

Upstairs, I said to Iona. "I'll show you the kitchen. The units aren't in, but they're on order."

Our footsteps echoed through the empty space. The glazing to the front of the kitchen rose up to the roof and the pale wooden floorboards ran right through to the back of the house. The subtle smell of freshly cut pine lingered.

"Max has promised to cook me lots of tasty dishes. He's an imaginative cook. I've been reading Nigella's latest book for when we have friends over so that Max can't take all of the culinary glory," I said, and realised how much I had wittered on.

"I was adamant Max should learn to cook, you know, with Brian not being around. I had to work full-time, and I couldn't do it all. Men should help these days. We're expected to go out to work aren't we?"

I tried to take in what she'd said about Max's dad. If he was agoraphobic, then it didn't make sense. I glanced behind to check Max wasn't nearby.

"Iona, where exactly is Brian? Is he in the forces?"

"Ah. I wondered if Max hadn't told you... everything." She shifted uncomfortably and peered over my shoulder. "I'm afraid Brian couldn't come to the wedding because...because he's in prison. For the past twelve years. I prayed he'd be granted release on parole but sadly, it wasn't to be."

"Sorry?"

"I'm sorry Katriina, but that's the plain truth of it."

"Why couldn't Max tell me?" My cheeks burned; it sounded ludicrous that I didn't already know. "He obviously doesn't trust me."

"It isn't that. He doesn't want you to think badly of his family. It's his pride."

The sun finally broke through the clouds, and lit up the room. I saw my face reflected in her pupils. "What did Brian do?"

"I hope Max won't be upset, but as you've asked." She edged closer to the window and gazed out across the valley. "It wasn't all Brian's fault, but the Law firm he worked for, he was their accountant you see, got into serious trouble financially. When the auditors looked into it, it appeared Brian had been embezzling money. The amount was substantial." She blinked away tears, delved into her handbag and pulled out a tissue. She dabbed her eyes before continuing. "I believe Brian was made a scapegoat to some extent, and he continues to insist another partner was involved, though he's always refused to give details, which hasn't helped his case."

I stole a quick glance towards the door. All seemed quiet.

"And, has he returned the money?" I asked. She must have thought me nosey, but it seemed logical to ask.

"I believe he paid back what he could, but he must have spent a lot of it, and I don't have a penny to spare. When he's released, we'll work out how to repay it. The firm has insisted the money be repaid of course. Though the Lord alone knows how we'll manage it." She shredded the tissue between her fingers, and I realised how tough it must have been for her all these years.

Her revelation shocked me. Max's father had been convicted of theft and fraud, yet I'd only discovered this a day after we'd exchanged our vows. Max had told me an inexcusable lie.

If he could lie about something so important, I wondered what other lies he'd told me. Marriage was about truth and honesty. What did it mean for our marriage, our entire future lives? Despite my emotions running out of control, I remained composed until everyone had gone. The moment the cars disappeared, and without a word to Max, I stormed back into the house.

Max ran after me. "Kat, what is it?"

I ignored him and continued upstairs. He ran up alongside me and grabbed my arm. "You've been avoiding me. Talk to me, Kat."

"Why Max? Why didn't you tell me about your dad?"

"What about Dad?"

"Forget the façade. At least your mum had the decency to tell me." I removed his hand from my arm. "I asked her where he was and she told me. What I want to know is, why? Why couldn't you be honest with me?"

"She told you what exactly?" he said, even now hiding behind a smokescreen.

"Jesus Max. What do you think? That he's in prison for fraud and she doesn't know when he's coming out." I stormed up the final few steps, turned around and shouted, "You told me he had agoraphobia, which was a downright lie."

Max gripped the bannister and stared up at me, his mouth gaped as he searched for the right words.

"Can you not even be honest with me now?" I asked, exasperated.

He climbed the last few steps, his arms limp at his sides. "I couldn't. I'm sorry, I just couldn't."

"Why, Max? I've never held back talking about my family, about anything for that matter. I thought you were honest. I've married you. Yet I don't know who you are."

"You don't get it do you? You have no idea, Kat. You've lived such a charmed, easy life," he said. "How do you think it feels to have a lying fraudster for a dad, I mean really feels? When it all kicked off, I was fourteen." He paused and swallowed. "Poor Mam was devastated. She tried to be strong, but I'd hear her crying. Dad continued protesting his innocence, despite it being proven he was responsible."

He took my hand and led me through to the living room. We sat on the wooden window seat. "I was happy at school, popular with loads of friends. And it was a good, selective public school. Then when my friends found out about Dad, what he'd done, it turned out most weren't such good friends after all. I was teased and bullied, and then to top it all, I was chucked out of school because we didn't have the money for the fees." He turned to me. "So I went to the local High School, and the bullying continued, only there it was more brutal because I was new." As Max spoke, he pulled on each of his fingers in turn, making the joints click. "I didn't fit in. The kids saw me as different, and I felt different."

"But you know I'd never judge you because of what your father has done. He isn't you. You're the person you choose to be."

He looked away.

I reached out and turned his face to mine. "I love you, Max, and that will never change, but I want to really know you. I'm not sure I do anymore."

He winced and the pain on his face was palpable.

"We have to be honest with each other, about everything," I said. "I can't be with you any other way."

He held my hand and twisted my wedding ring between his fingers. "You're right, of course you are. And I promise from now on that's what you'll get. I am sorry. It's unforgivable."

Such stark self-reflection tore at my heart and quelled my anger. "I'll try to understand. I love you Max. I've married you for Christ's sake."

Max looked lost, hunched over, not the same handsome and proud man who had stood next to me in the church. With my finger, I traced his jawline and touched his lips. We embraced, and I felt him return to me with each steady intake of breath. I knew then that I would always have to forgive him, as he would me too. Forgiveness was one thing, but I also knew I would never forget he had lied to me about something so important. As we held one another, I hoped more than anything that this hadn't created an Achilles heel in our relationship, and in our marriage.

CHAPTER TWENTY-THREE

Lochinver Police Station

I met Inspector Keir in the corridor.

"We're running the photo-fit through police files, but I'd like to show it to Max."

"He's in there," I said, and pointed to the open door. "I need to speak to Louis."

"Of course."

She knew Max and I had argued, and I sensed she thought that Max, in some unconceivable way, had something to do with Lyssa's disappearance, yet to what degree remained a mystery.

Louis sat engrossed on his phone.

"Lou, I'm sorry your Dad and I argued. It's the last thing you need. Are you all right?" I asked.

"No, but you and Dad fighting isn't going to make things any worse."

"I know, but I'm sorry anyway. It's just we're so upset."

"Forget it." His fingers moved over the screen of his phone. "My appeal has had over a hundred thousand shares. There are literally hundreds of comments coming in, so I'll keep checking them. Hey, do you think Inspector Keir would let me use the photo-fit?"

"We'll ask. The more people who see it the better, and someone has to recognise him. I'm certain it's a true likeness."

Inspector Keir held Louis' phone and flicked through the comments. "It's on Police Facebook, but yes, please put it up too. Constable Pearce will send it across. Keep me updated if anything comes back, car sightings or names." She looked at me, "Max said to tell you he's going to the shop to buy some lunch." She returned the phone to Louis. "Katriina, can I have a word?"

I followed her to the interview room, and she shut the door behind us. "Unfortunately, Max couldn't put a name to him. However, he thought his face looked familiar, but couldn't be more specific." She handed me a copy of the image. "Keep the print with you. Look at it together. If you feel it needs adjusting, we'll do it, it isn't set in stone. It's possible it will trigger something in one of you, or your parents."

I stared at the face in front of me. Was there something familiar about him? No, but someone out there would recognise him.

As promised, Max returned with lunch. The three of us sat in silence around the table and forced ourselves to eat, if only to give us the energy to wade through the chaos that held us in chains. I sensed Max was trying to close the void between us, but I was so angry that I felt ill being near to him. Not for the first time, he seemed unknown to me, like a stranger who had turned up at a funeral.

"I'm getting an update from Inspector Keir, then I'm going home," I said to Max. "Louis, do you mind staying with Dad? He needs your support."

What I meant was, Louis would be able to see if anything was going on with Max, of that I had no doubt.

"No problem Mum. We'll keep in touch."

"Wouldn't you rather go home, son? I'm not sure what good it'll do you staying here."

Immediately my hackles rose.

"I don't mind. And we might come up with some clues, somewhere for the police to search," Louis replied, emphatic.

"Fine, if we must." Max eyed me sharply and didn't bother to hide his irritation. "I'm coming to see the Inspector too."

He threw his empty sandwich wrapper at the waste paper basket, and turned away as it bounced off the rim and fell to the floor.

CHAPTER TWENTY-FOUR

A Mother's Instinct

As I walked into the kitchen I felt emotionally and physically drained. Mum washed the pots and Dad dried them. For one moment it struck me as a familiar and comfortable scene of domesticity. They turned in unison. Their eyes searched mine.

"We saw his picture on the lunchtime news," Mum said, her eyes red from crying. "I didn't think you'd seen anyone. Has he been spotted with Lyssa?"

"No-one has actually seen Lyssa, but there have been probable car sightings near Loch Lomond." I pulled out a chair. "But, I did remember seeing the van driver. It was that in all the panic I couldn't recall a thing." I pulled the print from my pocket and smoothed it onto the table. "Have you got any idea who he is?"

Mum wiped her hands on her trousers and held it up. "No, and I didn't think so earlier. Gordon?"

Dad took the picture. "I don't think so." He walked to the window and held it up. "Someone will recognise him."

"Any calls?" I asked.

"Jason Bittles from your work, and Rosie again. She wants to come over," Mum said.

"I'll ring them when I can," I said, and felt frustrated. "I thought someone might have rung by now, demanded a ransom, or even - threatened us. It's been too long, hasn't it? Anything could have happened to her by now." I burst into tears.

"Don't think like that, please Kat, it won't help." Mum hugged me and choked back her own tears. "You're exhausted. Have you eaten?"

"Yes. I only swallow because I have to." I pulled away and my heart pounded. "Why's this happening? If she's dead...."

"Please, darling," Mum said. "We should call the doctor, Gordon. They'll give her something to help her cope."

"I don't want drugs. I have to be ready if they find her. I just want to know why. Why Lyssa? Of all the roads and cars, children in cars."

Dad took my hand. "There may be no reason. It is probably a case of being in the wrong place at the wrong time. We must try and stay positive."

"It's the waiting, the not knowing." My heart raced and the walls suddenly closed in around me.

"The only thing I would say, and I realise it's a cliché, but at this stage, no news is good news," said Dad.

"I tell myself that," I said. "But you know Dad, there are missing children cases that are never solved, and the parents go on searching and torturing themselves, forever needing answers." I paused and wiped my eyes. "This will sound strange, but I've been having these sensations that Lyssa is alive, and that she's trying to talk to me. Am I losing my mind?"

Mum put her hand on my arm. "I don't think so," she said. She looked into my eyes. "I was going to say something, but decided it was unfair, not being based on any evidence." Mum continued quietly. "I have felt the same." She placed the palm of her hand on her chest. Tears rolled down her cheeks and dropped onto her hand. "I've always believed in gut instinct. I've often sensed things, and my instincts have been proved right countless times. Believe in yourself Katriina, it may lead you to Lyssa, and Lyssa to you."

"And I can vouch for that," said Dad. "Your mum knows things even before they've happened. I'm convinced she has a gift of sorts, a sixth sense. Which means I can't hide anything from her." He touched Mum's cheek tenderly.

"Indeed, and it comes in handy sometimes," she said. "I think you're like me Katriina, and Lyssa is like you. Nurture these instincts, listen out and invite them into your heart. It can't do any harm and it could make all the difference."

"Thank you," I said. "It means so much to hear that. I knew you'd understand me. You always have." Then I added. "Max doesn't."

"Sometimes we have to do what we believe is right despite what other people think." She tilted her head and a wisp of hair fell over her eyes. She tucked it behind her ear. "We never watch the ten o'clock news, but I insisted we watch it last night."

Dad took Mum's hand. "It's a mother's instinct, there's something in it."

I went to my room to check for messages on my iPad, but other than offers of help and another concerned message from Rosie, I found nothing of any importance. From my bedroom window I looked out at the valley, its splendour marred today by a mist that swirled like the turmoil within me.

"Where are you, Lyssa? Talk to me. If you can hear me – shout. Shout as loud as you can." My breath fell softly against the cold windowpane.

"Katriina."

I spun around. "What is it?"

Dad appeared in the doorway. "Will you be all right if we go to the store? There isn't much in the fridge, and I'll get some fuel. One of us can stay."

"It's OK Dad. You can both go."

The sound of the tyres crunched across the gravel and faded to nothing. The house fell silent, and I heard the faint whir of the wind turbine and the gentle whistle of the wind as it coiled its way around the house. I felt relief to be alone and to think things through with no one to have to talk to. As I walked back upstairs, each step seemed bigger and steeper. I opened the fridge, pulled out a bottle of wine and poured myself a large glass. I hoped it might take the edge off an unbearable ache that ripped through me. In the living room I sat on the window seat, lifted my knees and gazed into the mist that skulked around the house and veiled the hillside like a shroud. There were still so many missing pieces of the puzzle, but the scattered fragments had shifted and rearranged themselves so that the all-important four corners were almost in place. I sensed the outer edges as they slid towards their proper places.

My isolation was short-lived when I saw Max's car returning up the drive. Thinking they must have heard something to be home so soon, I set down my glass and shot onto the landing.

"Mum?" Louis shouted, and slammed the front door behind him.

"Up here."

He ran up two steps at a time.

My heart hammered. "What is it?"

"I wanted to know where you were. Grandad's car's gone, and I was worried."

"They've gone to the store. I thought you and Dad were staying at the station?"

"Dad wanted to come home, but then he realised he needed petrol."

"He could have filled up on your way back. Now we don't have a car if we need one."

"But you didn't have one anyway with Gran and Grandad out. Dad's coming straight back."

"Fine," I said, and felt tears sting my eyes. "Why don't you go and relax in your room? Do some revision or get your PlayStation out? It might take your mind off things."

"I doubt it." Louis kicked off his trainers. He fought back tears as he walked downstairs, his shoulders slumped.

I swallowed the last drop of wine and lay back on the window seat. I thought about Max. Why was I feeling suspicious again? Was this another of his weird disappearing acts? Rather than calm my nerves the wine only made me feel queasy and lightheaded. It occurred to me that I shouldn't be drinking at all, and I knew I had finally lost my mind. Max already thought so, he'd said as much. If I was pregnant why did it have to be now? My legs trembled as I walked to the kitchen. I poured a glass of water and sipped it slowly until the walls no longer swayed. I tried to get my head around all that had happened during the past two days, and now the sightings of my car near Loch Lomond. They were significant, but why Loch Lomond? I sobbed, knowing that all of this was my fault. If only we had left home on time. Changing my shoes had cost us precious minutes and put us in the wrong place at the wrong time. And it was stupid of me to leave her alone in the car. Now Lyssa had paid the price for my mistakes.

As a rule, I was the sunny sort; optimistic and upbeat, no doubt to the irritation of some. But I felt as though my heart and mind had been switched with a character in a black and white film noir, rocking back and forth in the furthest corner of a psychiatric ward, drugged up, a lost cause and unlikely to be leaving anytime soon. Lost in my lonely madness, my mind strayed to the pile of shoes in my wardrobe; with pairs to create longer, slimmer legs, pairs bought on impulse and still like new, as well as my favourites worn for comfort. Of all the things that could have delayed us, why did it have to be something so insignificant? I added this to the accumulating layers of guilt that weighed down on me - pressed against my chest and prised the breath from me.

My heart pounded against my ribcage like a battering ram. I gasped for air as a sickening ache stirred deep within me. Despair surged through my insides - spread through my chest and neck and jabbed at my scalp. My throat tightened and I dropped to the floor and came to rest against the range. Its warmth gave no comfort. I cried; oblivious to anything beyond my fear, my daughter's fear – our shared fear.

Sometime later, my heart stripped bare and my bones carved out and hollow, I turned to the window. Night had drawn in, and the furniture appeared vague and subdued in the halfway light. I heard voices nearby. Were they keeping secrets from me? I got up, walked from the kitchen and across the landing to the top of the stairs. Max and Louis were in the hallway, talking in undertones. They stopped abruptly and looked up. Max's face looked ashen, and I tried to read his expression.

"What is it?" I said. "Have they found her?"

He shook his head.

"Tell me," I screamed, and my nerves fired missiles.

"They've found your car…but not Lyssa."

Max sank onto the bottom stair like a rock falling silently through black water. He dropped his head into his hands and wept.

CHAPTER TWENTY-FIVE

Stargazing

Lyssa lay on a narrow bed and gazed at the small rectangle of inky-blue sky set in the opposite wall. The chilly air reeked of mould and the damp seeped beneath her clothes and clung to her skin. She longed for a warm blanket to wrap herself in, and she turned awkwardly onto her side. With her hands bound tightly behind her back, she found it impossible to lie comfortably.

When they had arrived she was blindfolded, and so had seen nothing of their approach. He'd carried her up the stairs, dropped her onto the bed, and only then allowed her to see. He'd stepped back and studied her as he ran the scarf back and forth between his fingers. He cleared phlegm from his throat, spat onto the floor then silently turned and left the room and locked the door behind him.

She hadn't heard him stomp up and down the stairs recently and wondered if he was asleep somewhere or whether he was sitting behind the door to keep guard. She twisted her arms above her head and when that proved impossible she wriggled her hands under her bottom. But again, it was hopeless. She drew her feet towards her, leaned over and chewed furiously at the string around her ankles. Finally, breathless and beaten, she fell back and wept with fear and frustration.

He knew her parents' names and he was angry with them. He swore a lot and shouted vile things, and sometimes she didn't know if he was talking to himself or to her.

She wondered what her mum had done when he'd driven away? What was she doing now? If she was here, they could hold one another and plan their escape together.

After Lyssa had screamed for him to let her out of the car, he'd pulled into a quiet woodland track, climbed onto the back seat and tied her hands and feet. When Lyssa had kicked and struggled, her chest had gone into spasm as if she were sinking deep below the water's surface and unable to swim back up for air.

"You're not getting out so quit fucking with me," he said, with black eyes and twisted brows.

Lyssa wheezed and nodded desperately at her school bag.

"A kid at school had one of these. I tried it, thought it might give me a buzz," he said, and pressed the canister.

After three successive puffs the tightness eased, and she realised she had no option but to succumb.

Lyssa needed the toilet but she wouldn't shout for him to take her; she didn't want him anywhere near her if she could avoid it. She'd heard stories about children being snatched, and when she was little her mum would usually switch off the news. More recently, her mum explained how and why bad things happened.

"It's rare for a child to be taken. One chance in a million." Her mum had reassured her.

Sometimes she used a similar phrase to describe Lyssa; that she was her 'one in a million', usually when Lyssa had done something good, or when they hugged each other good night.

Lyssa yearned for home, her mum smiling and tucking her into bed, 'Night-night Lyssa, sleep tight, sweet dreams until the morning light'.

Her mother would often leave the curtains open and when she'd turned off the light, and they saw the clear night sky, they would look up at the stars. 'See that constellation there, Lyssa? That's Cassiopeia', or 'that's Perseus just there'. Her dad knew them too, and it was something they loved to look for, to imagine what might be on distant planets. Perhaps the stars were out tonight and her mum was standing at her bedroom window, wondering where Lyssa was.

Her bladder twinged painfully. She shuffled over to the window, pressed her brow against the damp windowpane, and looked to see if there were any stars. Veiled by cloud, the moon was only an indistinct shimmer, unable to hint at what lay beyond the four walls that held her. Tomorrow she would look into the daylight and work out a way to escape before it was too late.

She leaned against the wall and warm urine ran down her legs and into her shoes.

CHAPTER TWENTY-SIX

A Wee Dram - 1999

By the third week in September the work on our house was complete, with self-generated electricity and hot water throughout. The engineers had finally connected the wind turbine and solar panels, and miraculously, everything appeared to be working. After living in the cramped and freezing caravan for months on end, running hot water and electricity felt like pure luxury. I vowed never to take either for granted again. The wind turbine had cost a small fortune, but up here on the blustery hillside we felt sure it would in time be worth every penny.

"I'm off to run myself the hottest, deepest, bubbliest bath. You're welcome to join me," I said.

"You're not taking an eco-shower then?" Without looking up, Max laughed and scrubbed a hand through his hair.

"Not a chance. After months of deprivation, I feel like indulging myself."

Max sat at his drawing table in the naturally well-lit and still sparsely furnished office, working on some designs. I hooked an arm around his waist, ran my hand teasingly down the front of his trousers and gave a lingering squeeze.

'Mm-mmm, an offer I'll struggle to refuse," said Max. "Shall I bring you a wee dram to celebrate?"

"What before the noonday sun? Go on then," I said. "I love it when you go all Scottish on me." I kissed him, and he slid his hand up my T-shirt and fondled my breasts.

"Christ! Damn these drawings. Go on you rotten wee temptress," he said, and slapped my backside as I turned to leave.

The Bosky stove was a fantastic piece of kit, making the house cosy and warm despite it feeling so cavernous. When Max walked into the en-suite a few minutes later he was carrying two tumblers of whisky and was stark naked save for my red and white spotty shower cap perched ridiculously on his head and a flannel hanging over his appendage.

Laughing, I slid up the old cast-iron roll-top bath to make room for him. "Oh my God! What heavenly vision is this? You look like a mutant Fly agaric toadstool. Pass me that glass, now I definitely need a drink." As my gaze ran down his nakedness, I decided he had the perfect, classic male physique; naturally long, lean and toned, with soft curly hair in all the right places.

He stepped into the hot bubbly water and as we sipped our whiskies, I slipped my foot in-between his legs and wriggled my big toe which made him splutter. Then taking my glass he placed it on the floor and pulled me on top of him. I pinched the shower cap off his head, flung it over my shoulder and leaned in and kissed him slowly and deeply, savouring his hot whisky laced lips. Our bodies moved together, sliding in rhythm, seeking to give pleasure to one another and receive pleasure in return as the hot water spilled unnoticed over the sides.

CHAPTER TWENTY-SEVEN

Mountainological Knowledge

With the arrival of spring once more it was clear to see that Max was becoming the successful architect and businessman, although by his own admission he still had a great deal to learn about both his art and managing a business. He was winning more clients and getting great feedback. In turn his clients were recommending him to other individuals and organisations, which again brought in more commissions. My management trainee job was going well too. I was spending most of my time out and about making new contacts and directing projects, albeit the smaller ones. Jason Bittles, our Regional Director, had been inviting me to senior managerial meetings, and after I gave a presentation on 'Reducing our Carbon Footprint' at a recent conference, Jason personally commended me in the organisation's national magazine. The double page article included my picture and a biography, along with a breakdown of what I would be doing during my training. Finally, all the time and energy I'd invested in my education was reaping the rewards. Life was fun and full, money seemed plentiful, and I honestly didn't think we could have been happier.

One Friday evening I arrived home after two full days working away. Initially, I was disappointed that Max wasn't back, but not concerned as he often visited clients or sites well into the evenings, especially now that the days were getting longer. It had been an unseasonably warm April, which was fortunate as I'd arranged for Rosie, and boyfriend, Will, to stay over Saturday night. I hoped I could persuade them to go for a walk up Benn Cady, and if the weather stayed fine they'd love the spectacular views. I stepped through the back door and looked up to the rocky outcrop Max and I often visited, even when there were gale-force winds, as was often the case. I sensed there was something special about the place, that it held a mystery of some sort. I don't think Max was totally convinced, but he always joined in with my musings. Whether there was something special about the place or not, I always felt an immense sense of calm and tranquillity there.

I had collected in the dry clothes from the washing line and turned to go back inside when I spotted a flash of movement up near the rocks - something orange, perhaps a young deer, a fox or a dog. I felt curious and put down the basket of clothes and made my way up the steep, rock-strewn path. Oddly, I hadn't seen a fox in the whole time we'd been here, and I knew there were no houses within two miles, so I figured it could have been a lost dog.

By the time I'd walked halfway up, I cursed that I'd forgotten the midge repellent. I pulled down my sleeves, buttoned my shirt right up and fanned my hands futilely at the midges.

My breath felt raw in my throat by the time I reached the rocks and I paused for a minute and gazed back down. I never tired of the view - the warm evening sun still reached over the peak of Applecross on the far side of the valley. Gentle rays branched out and lit up the rocks and they glistened across the mountainside.

"Squawk!"

Startled, I spun around and saw a bird as it darted from a nearby bush, and then it rasped its wings and flew over my head. Just a grouse. But then I heard the sudden yet distinctive sound of children's laughter and a shriek. I stopped dead and listened. I heard more shrill laughter, and although I knew the wind could redirect noises, the sounds seemed close by. I jogged uphill and scrambled over stones and rocks to reach behind the outcrop. I froze. No more than thirty feet away I saw two young children - a boy, and a girl – who giggled and laughed as they built a tower out of stones. I moved closer but they remained oblivious to me.

I called over, "Hello there." But they didn't look up and continued to lift and balance the stones. I stepped nearer. "Hello, I'm Katriina, what are your names?"

They still didn't react and continued their game amidst shrieks of laughter. I knew I must find their parents. It wasn't safe for them up here on their own among the jagged rocks and steep drops. I walked on past them to the far side of the rocky outcrop where the hillside opened out, and tried not to let them out of my sight, but I couldn't see another soul. I decided I'd persuade them to come back to the house with me. Once safely inside, I'd contact the police and locate their parents.

I turned around, but I could no longer see the children. I raced back and looked down the path, but there was no one. I wondered briefly if I'd walked too far, but in truth, I knew that wasn't the case and within a few steps I'd returned to the half tumbled pile of stones where the children had been playing. I crouched down amongst the rocky pile and glimpsed something small and yellow. I picked it up. A tiny sword that perhaps belonged to a toy soldier. I slipped it into my trouser pocket, then ran back and forth and checked every possible hiding place around the outcrop. But within the stillness, only silence gathered, except for the speckled clouds of midges that encircled me.

A feeling of alarm rose within me along with a crushing need to find the children. I stopped, took slow breaths and tried to calm my thoughts. They must have been an impression, something ethereal, or something I'd only imagined seeing. I clambered up onto the highest of the rocks and sat there for a while, as I tried to make sense of the past few minutes. The delicate radiance of the first stars appeared. The full moon bathed the hillside in moonlight and eventually I picked my way down the path, my mind emptied of rational thought, yet even though I couldn't explain it, I understood there must be a significance in what I'd seen.

I knew Max was home, by the divine cooking aromas wafting from the kitchen.

"Been for a walk? Thought you might have already cooked my dinner," Max said, laughing. He turned, and his expression became serious. "Hey, what is it, my love?"

"Nothing, I'm just tired. It's been a hectic week." I kicked off my shoes.

"Come here sexy. I've missed you badly."

We held and kissed one another, and his warmth and vigour steadied my nerves. As we held one another, I inhaled his earthy, masculine scent, a heady mix of pine and perspiration.

I pulled a bottle of red wine from the rack.

"Want a glass?" I asked, unnecessarily.

"Yep," he said. "And tonight we have something to celebrate." He scraped chopped garlic into the pan. "Remember that chap I told you about at Upland Homes and the big project for the sustainable homes in Inverness?"

"Yes."

"He's only given me the contract. Said I had the best designs, most innovative ideas and the price was competitive too. Think it's worth 30K and it'll mean taking someone on. I can't do it all myself now," he said, stirring the onions and garlic sizzling nicely. He turned back and smiled broadly. "My first employee, how cool will that be?"

I set his glass of wine on the worktop and kissed him. "That's fantastic Max. I'm so proud of you. You deserve it."

And I was proud of him. I didn't want to spoil the moment, so I didn't mention the lost children up at the rocky outcrop. In one selfish way there was an element of wanting to keep it to myself, to take some time to figure it out. Besides, I knew if I told Max he would say I'd imagined it. Even to me it sounded too absurd to be remotely plausible. Either that or he would say the obvious, that I was getting broody. How could I explain that I'd seen two unaccompanied young children half way up a remote hillside who then disappeared into thin air?

We'd discussed having children at some point, but the truth was, having a baby was definitely not on my radar. I was focussing on my career and loving our life, just the two of us. At only twenty-three, I reasoned I had plenty of fertile years ahead of me.

I tried not to dwell on the disappearing children which was made a whole lot easier by having Rosie over. My best friend was so full of life, fun, and energy, and having her to talk to always made me feel grounded, as though I were living life completely in the moment.

Just before twelve the next day I heard a car pull up on the gravel, and I sprinted to open the front door.

"Rosie Dickens," I shrieked, and ran over to embrace her.

The first thing I noticed was that her bleached blond hair was a more natural dark blond shade; a far more flattering tone for her pale Anglo-Saxon complexion.

She stepped back to appraise me.

"Oh my God, look at you. You're more beautiful than ever," said Rosie.

Knowing Rosie would be looking trendy and expensively fabulous as always I had made more of an effort with my appearance than usual. My hair was freshly washed and blow-dried, and my long brown curls bounced down my back. I was wearing my favourite pair of black skin-tight jeans, knee-high brown leather boots and a cream fitted angora cropped jumper. I'd even applied a touch of makeup, put on a pair of amber earrings and as I'd stood in front of the full-length mirror I was happy with the overall result.

"Thank you. It's so good to see you, Rosie. I haven't half missed you."

"Me too," she said. "I'm sorry I cancelled the other week. Work was flat out."

Will gathered up their bags from the boot.

"Hi Will." I kissed him on the cheek. "You well?"

"I'm great. You look lovely." As he smiled, the dimples on either side of his mouth deepened.

"It's the mountain air. I swear there's something in it. At least when it's not freezing my backside off." I laughed and felt happy to be spending time with my best friend again.

"The house is stunning. I thought Rosie was exaggerating. It truly is a thing of beauty," Will said, taking it all in. Then retrieving something from the boot, he said, "Here Rosie, you do the honours with the house gift." And he passed her a cardboard box.

She took it from Will and handed it straight to me.

"There you go Kat, Will's far too modest to give you these himself."

I opened the box. It held three large frames. "Wow. Did you take these Will? They're incredible."

"Aye, I did. I know how much you and Max love Mother Nature and I thought they'd fit perfectly with your surroundings," he said, and smiled proudly.

They were colour photographs of a single stem of bracken at three different growth stages. In the first, the shoot was newly emerging from the soil, pastel green with tiny delicate hairs, in the second the fern was tall with coiled and curling fronds, and in the final photograph, the fern was huge, richly green and abundantly flourishing.

"You are clever Will. They're perfect. And I know just where I'm going to hang them. Come on, let's find Max."

We met Max in the hallway, and after enthusiastic hugs and kisses all round, Max whisked Will away upstairs, I guessed to crack open the beers.

Rosie and I dropped their overnight bags in the guest room. She flopped back onto the bed and let out a long sigh. I lay down next to her.

Flipping onto her side and resting on one elbow, Rosie turned to me with a quizzical expression. "Kat, tell me to shut up if I'm wrong, but am I right in thinking you're *with child*?" She said, and did her funny speech marks thing.

"Are you kidding? Why - have I got a pot belly?"

"Course not yer daft clot. I know it's a cliché, it's just that you look so radiant, your skin, your hair. Honestly, you look different."

"You sound like an advert. Sure you haven't swallowed a L'Oreal promotion?" I asked.

"That's the trouble with writing adverts all day long," she replied, with a wry smile.

"Sorry," I said, "I'm being ungracious. Thank you. I'll take it as a compliment that you've noticed my skin is finally zit free and I've put conditioner on my hair. But no, I'm not preggers and no chance of being either. We will at some point, but not yet," I said. I laid back and pinched my midriff to check it hadn't thickened.

"In that case, let's get up to the kitchen and join the boys before they drink your fridge dry."

I placed a glass of wine on the table in front of Rosie.

"Shall we sit in the living room? It's lovely now we've got sofas," I said, and raised my glass.

We still hadn't bought a great deal of furniture as we were scouring antique fairs and second-hand shops to find pieces we felt would fit with the ethos of the house. Ideally, we only wanted items made from natural materials, preferably locally sourced or that could be recycled or adapted to suit us. Andy Mason, a carpenter who had been with us since we started the build had created a magnificent wall of bookshelves out of old wooden floorboards. It ran the best part of the west wall in the living room, bar the full height window through which we could view the sunsets. Max hadn't needed much persuading when I'd suggested it.

"I've always wanted a library of some sort, ever since I visited Norwegian Granny. There's a whole room devoted to her books," I explained. "She's got a huge collection of bird and wildlife books but her real passion is crime fiction. I'm amazed there are any left for her to read."

After coming to our wedding she'd sent over a couple of her favourites, and I was working my way through them using my pidgin Norwegian, but hand in hand with my dictionary. The first story wasn't exactly flowing, but I was determined to finish it, not only to find out what happened but to cultivate my Scandinavian roots.

So far, we'd only filled a couple of shelves, and these were mostly our University textbooks. After visiting my parents I'd brought back two enormous cardboard boxes of the books I'd grown up with. I'd spent several evenings flicking through them again, and they were bringing back so many happy childhood memories.

Recently, we'd bought two futons with bright orange cotton mattresses, crammed full with sheep's wool. We'd positioned them on the floorboards opposite one another and adjacent to the large ceiling to floor windows, so that we could sit and look out at the glen, lochs, and hills beyond.

Rosie flopped onto the futon and tucked her legs under her.

"I love that you've bought futons. We're still grungy students at heart aren't we?" She jigged up and down to test its firmness.

"Yes," I said. "Though I'm not sure anyone could ever have accused you of being grungy."

"Do you remember, who was it? Oh yeah, it was Phil, put his foot through the slats on mine one night, fell over and broke my stereo," she said.

"Aye I do, and I seem to remember he had to go to hospital for an X-Ray the following morning and could hardly walk for days afterwards," I added.

"Poor Phil." She gazed dreamily outside for a moment and then turned back to me. "At least his ankle recovered, which was more than could be said for my stereo."

We lounged about for most of the afternoon and caught up on one another's news, shared stories about our newfound careers and reminisced about our time at Uni.

"Will's just taken over control of the newspaper's photography, haven't you?" Rosie said, smiling up at him and stroking his thigh affectionately.

"Indeed. It's my big chance to introduce something a bit more ground breaking and artistically challenging. I boldly told the Editor-in-chief things were getting predictable and samey, and the next thing I knew, I'd been promoted."

"I'm sure it was your coverage of the festival that did it. Everyone says how much they love your style, and you're brilliant at getting something a bit different out of people." Rosie snuggled up and rested her head on his shoulder.

It was sweet to see Rosie was still serious about Will. Perhaps her days of jumping from one man to the next were over. Post University life was, it seemed, all rosy. That evening I even managed to rustle up a salmon en-croute with asparagus, albeit ever so slightly burnt at the edges. After which we played cards and drank ourselves stupid on good wine and whisky.

Next morning, after a full fat breakfast of bacon, eggs, and beans, we agreed we had sufficient energy for a hike up Benn Cady. I was filling my rucksack with water bottles and biscuits when Rosie appeared.

I looked her up and down. "You can't go like that Rosie. We can get any weather up there, and those shoes are simply not up to the job, I'm afraid." I eyed them suspiciously.

Rosie wore a trendy denim mini-skirt over black tights. She also had on a pair of gorgeous lace up, three-inch block-heeled boots.

"I'll be fine, seriously," she said, with a twirl. "I can walk all day in these."

"No you won't, seriously. They might be just the thing for shopping down Princes Street, but you'll break an ankle up the mountain. You can borrow a pair of proper walking boots, and I've got a spare waterproof." I rummaged amongst the shoe rack under the stairs. "I know it looks warm out there but the weather changes in a matter of minutes. I was up a month ago in hurricane force winds and it's dangerous if you're not dressed properly. You'll need a woolly hat and gloves too - it's freezing at the top, even in summer."

"Fine, I bow down to your superior mountainological knowledge. Go on then, dress me up like Edmund Hillary, no wait, I'll be Michaela Strachan," she said, spreading her arms out wide.

Laughing, I handed her a pair of walking boots. "Sorry, I know I'm being bossy. I can't help myself."

"Yes you are, but I'm sure you're right." She grudgingly unlaced her boots.

Max ended up lending Will some boots too, and as the four of us set off we looked as if we were about to conquer K2, minus the breathing apparatus and oxygen canisters.

Our mountain, Benn Cady, was simple in structure, with a steep stretch up to the rocky outcrop, followed by a steady climb of about 650m to the rocky scarp at the summit. The first short rise to the outcrop was a stony path that wound and curved in-between heather, gorse bushes, and a few trees of birch, hazel, and spruce. We stopped at the outcrop, and Will took photos of us and the view down to the house. From up here the grass roof merged effortlessly with the tufted grass and heather-clad stretch in front of the house and leading down to the road. As we head up from the outcrop, Rosie and I dropped behind, and chatted about our jobs.

"What's your manager like then?" I asked.

"She's OK actually. When I started, some of the team warned me about her. They said she could be a right bitch if you got on the wrong side of her or if they didn't work late when a big deadline loomed, that sort of thing. Hannah's been all right with me, and we even go out together sometimes. We're good mates."

"Wow, that's cool. Always helps to get on with the boss."

"It helps that I'm happy to work into the evenings. I often go in at weekends. I love it - it's challenging and creative." Rosie unzipped her coat, pulled off her woolly hat and stuffed it into her pocket.

"I like my time at home with Max. You know, doing the house and everything. I'm not sure I'd be up for too much evening and weekend working."

"Yeah, there's a girl in my section, Cindy, who's just come back from maternity leave and she can't stay late, has to pick up her baby from nursery. Hannah's made a few comments about Cindy not pulling her weight. I've defended her, but Hannah's so career driven I'm not sure she can see work as anything other than a religion."

I nodded. "Some people aren't great at seeing things from anyone's perspective but their own. Probably best if you don't decide to settle down and have babies yet, at least not with her as your boss."

"Good grief. No, I need to climb a few more rungs of the ladder first. Babies would hold me back. I'm not even sure I'll ever want a baby, don't think I'm the maternal sort."

"Me neither. I don't feel remotely broody. Funny though, as soon as you get married everyone expects you to start dropping sprogs left right and centre." I prodded her playfully. "Don't they? Anyway, I'm only twenty-three, I'll wait until I'm thirty-three at least. That way I get to be the boss before I have children."

As it turned out, I'd overestimated the quantity of outdoor clothing and woollies we should wear, because the weather turned out to be perfect for the climb. Of course, the temperature had dropped by several degrees by the time we reached the peak, but there was only a light wind, and the sun had broken through the few cappuccino clouds that drifted unhurriedly over us. Rosie and I parked ourselves on a large rock, telling the men we wanted to admire the view, but wanting an excuse to catch our breath after the final ascent. Max led Will further up along the ridge to take some photographs of the stunning views to the South, dominated by Stac Pollaidh, Canisp, and Suilvan.

"It's incredible Kat," Rosie said, smiling, her eyes bright in the sun. "The view is unbelievable – and right on your doorstep." She lifted her camera and took a photo of me. "Your life's so . . . sorted. And Max, he's the best. Worships you, even though you're an old married couple."

"Maybe we're still in the honeymoon period, not sure how long it's supposed to last. But yes, I do feel jammy. I hope I'll never take him for granted though." My hair flapped around my face, and I tucked it up into my woolly hat. "I want to look at him every day and feel lucky. Not like those old couples you see in restaurants with nothing to talk about other than their kids or where they're booking their next city break."

"You paint a miserable picture of a long marriage. Surely it's better than having a clandestine affair, or worse, battering him with a wet fish?"

"What are you on about?" I said, and giggled. "Are you going soft on me? You wouldn't stay with someone who didn't light your fire in bed."

"I dunno, there has to be more to a marriage than great sex," she said, her face suddenly serious. "The sex is important, but you can't expect it to be mind-blowing every time long-term, it's not realistic, is it? You should love more than one another's bodies. There has to be more to connect you. Shared interests and kids must be a big slice of that connection,"

"You are right, but I can't ever imagine not wanting to rip Max's clothes off. I honestly never tire of doing *it*." I sniggered. "Sorry, you probably didn't want to know that."

"You're just abnormally randy – a bitch on never-ending heat," she said.

"Have you heard the saying with the words pot and kettle?" I jumped up and pulled her to her feet.

Max and Will had returned and were smiling and chatting.

"What's so funny you two, care to share?" said Will.

We looked at one another and burst out laughing.

"Most definitely not," I said, and linking arms with Rosie, we set off back down the path.

CHAPTER TWENTY-EIGHT

Motherly Urges

The children from the rocky outcrop didn't make a repeat appearance, and as I was so busy with work I didn't give them much thought. However, after a couple of months I realised something about the children had sunk deeply into my subconscious. Whenever Max and I made love the two children playing up the hillside began to flash randomly into my mind. They would appear in place of the more typical things I thought about when we were having sex, which rarely strayed beyond anything fleshly or erotic.

One evening, after a particularly energetic lovemaking session, I lay exhausted and fulfilled across the bed.

Turning onto my side I ran a hand over Max's chest and lightly caressed his chest hair. "What sort of things do you think about when we're making love?"

"Ahh, let me think," he said, and his brows knitted together. "Nearly always about you and how beautiful your body is, particularly your breasts and arse, oh and your lips - both pairs," he grinned. "Unless my mind wanders to the sink of washing up you left for me."

I nudged him. "Nearly always? And, are there any other, I dunno… things you think about?"

"Why, what do you think about?" He traced a finger around my nipple.

"Honestly, you. Oh, and how many more orgasms I can have before you."

"And do you ever feel short changed?"

"I'd say you're generous in that department, but I tend to stop counting past five or six." I smiled sweetly. "Jealous?"

"Nah, don't reckon."

"Oh?"

"You see; my one orgasm is way more powerful than all of yours combined." He stroked my hip and smiled back.

"Not a chance. If mine were any more powerful I think my life would be in danger." I fell onto my back and clutched my chest.

"Katriina, you really are a show-off." He leaned over and kissed my nose, then flopped onto his back.

I decided to change the subject, as it seemed Max wasn't seeing little children playing merrily alone on a mountainside, and even to me, it did seem pretty ridiculous. Max stared at the ceiling for a few moments and then turning to me, placed his hand on my belly before trailing a finger back and forth.

"Kat, I know we've only been married a few months, but the business is going from strength-to-strength and I was wondering if you'd thought much about us starting a family. Are you feeling any motherly urges?"

I could tell by his expression that it was something he wanted and I decided I should be cautious about replying too quickly or too honestly.

"Well, I wouldn't say I hadn't thought about it, but I do think we should wait a year or two until my career is more established. My training doesn't finish for another eighteen months."

"Oh, OK." His hand fell still, and he lay back.

"But I'd like to at some point. You know that don't you?" I said, and brushed his fringe off his forehead.

"Of course, it's fine. I don't want to rush you. It's only that I think having children would make our lives even more perfect . . . if that's possible."

I knew he was suppressing some disappointment, but I simply didn't feel ready, and it was my body. I knew I wouldn't be having my coil removed any time soon.

At first I put my nausea down to a tummy bug and then when it continued I thought it must be a virus, lingering for longer than it should.

"Kat will you go and see the doctor, please? I'm worried. You haven't been yourself for weeks."

Usually, I felt so fit and healthy and I rarely saw a doctor. But Max's concern bothered me, and so I booked an appointment.

"It's been going on for weeks now. I feel sick pretty much all of the time, and I keep falling asleep after our evening meal. Maybe I'm anaemic or something? I've even gone off tea and alcohol, which for me really isn't normal." I was sitting forwards, eagerly describing my symptoms.

The doctor started smiling, which hardly seemed like the sort of reaction a health professional should be having with a patient who was worried about her health. I felt annoyed rather than reassured.

"And, have you considered that you could be pregnant Katriina?"

"No, it's not possible, I've got a coil . . ." But, even as I spoke, I knew I sounded naive.

Of course, Max was completely cock-a-hoop about 'our pregnancy'.

He jumped up off the sofa and dashed over, almost losing his footing on the varnished floorboards. "Are you kidding me?"

I cried, and he placed his arms around me.

"Aren't you happy, my love? Is it too soon?"

"I'm not sure. I think I'm in shock. Stupid, but I hadn't even considered it. She thinks I'm about fourteen weeks."

As I laid a hand over my abdomen, I pictured a tiny but fully formed baby, swimming around inside me, turning little somersaults every now and then.

After a few days I came to terms with what was happening, and I soon embraced the idea of motherhood wholly and completely, and without holding any doubts or worries about what the future held for us. I was both baffled and amazed at how I hadn't realised I was pregnant. I hadn't even registered my absent periods. Initially, I was concerned that my coil would damage or interfere with the baby's growth, but one detailed scan later confirmed that mysteriously there was no coil. The doctor concluded that although it was unusual, my coil had fallen out at some point during the past four months. Casting my mind back, it came as no great surprise when I realised that losing my coil coincided with the time I had seen the children up at the rocky outcrop.

149

CHAPTER TWENTY-NINE

The Man from Mars

Despite the morning sickness, which as per the textbook lasted three to four months, I felt surprisingly well throughout my pregnancy, and I was able to work right up to my due date. As my colleagues wished me luck on my last day, amidst predictable jokes about cabbages and leaking boobs, I realised that I hadn't given a great deal of thought to how much our carefree lives were about to change.

My ever sunny mother painted such an idyllic picture of motherhood, often telling me what laidback babies my sister and I had been, that when I went into labour and arrived at the hospital in excruciating pain, I firmly believed that the birth was going to be the hardest part. If the baby and I could get through the labour relatively unscathed, then the rest would be plain sailing.

The birth turned out to be anything but textbook, with a labour that lasted two days and culminated with a baby in foetal distress, a trolley loaded assortment of shiny, but medieval looking contraptions and twenty-two stitches in my nether region.

Once we were safely settled onto the maternity ward, I thanked God that the tricky bit was over and that our baby had been given a clean bill of health. I felt exhausted but euphoric with my angelic baby, Louis Maxwell O'Donnell, all 8lb 1oz of him, lying pink and content in my arms.

Louis slept for a full twenty-four hours, after which our world imploded, with both Louis and I crying continually. The midwife said it was just my hormones, but on top of cracked and bleeding nipples, and having no sleep whatsoever, I soon plunged headfirst into the depths of despair.

After our first night at home as a 'family' I rang home, and blubbing pitifully, I pleaded for Mum to come and rescue us. True to form, she got straight in the car and arrived a few hours later complete with a huge tube of nipple cream, one fresh savoy cabbage and a truckload of love and sympathy. Max admitted to feeling as overwhelmed as me and we welcomed Mum with flummoxed faces and chilled champagne.

Mum loved every minute of caring for Louis, even when he kept us up half the night. And, I learned so much about patience and perseverance, especially when it came to breastfeeding. Although I was well-equipped, I couldn't understand why Louis wanted to feed all night, even after feeding non-stop all day. Mum gently encouraged me to stick with it and after one extremely long and painful month, Louis began to settle, and the intervals between feeding grew. In the end, we kept Mum hostage for six weeks, after which we finally allowed her to return home to her own life and husband.

To celebrate Louis' first sixth months, we went for lunch in our favourite pub, The Pig & Whistle. Louis was conveniently sleeping like an angel in his portable car seat. We were chatting about the logistics of my returning to work, and how we were going to share the ferrying of Louis to and from nursery. Before Louis was born I confidently told work I'd be returning full-time, but as D-day approached I couldn't imagine leaving Louis with strangers all day, let alone being able to cope with getting up for work and driving here, there and everywhere across the Highlands.

Max sensed I was struggling with the whole idea too.

"You know you don't have to return to work. I'd love to support you if that's what you want. And you know we can afford for you to give up work for a while."

Louis snuffled in his sleep and Max rocked him gently back and forth with his foot.

As I watched them my throat tightened, and I couldn't speak.

"Don't decide yet. Have a think over the next few days." He rested a hand on my knee and smiled adoringly down at Louis.

I looked at Max and felt a sudden, deep rush of affection for him - always so supportive, thoughtful and selfless. Then I looked down at Louis sleeping peacefully, head lolling slightly to one side and a sweet lopsided smile coming and going with a bit of wind, and I wondered why I was worrying myself stupid about work when I didn't have to.

My eyes welled with tears, and as they spilled over and ran down my cheeks, I reached for Max's hand.

"I don't want to leave Louis, and I don't want to go back to work. At least not yet."

"Then don't, my love. Do what's right for you, what's right for Louis," he said, and stroked my hand.

With my decision made, I broke the news to work and became a stay at home mum. I exclusively breastfed my babies during their first year, made them organic baby food, and joined every mother and baby group within a twenty-mile radius. I even learned how to knit so that I could make them wee Scottish jerseys, albeit more of a fisherman rib, rather than fair isle knit variety. Max found the knitting highly amusing, especially when Louis poked his podgy little fingers through the holes that appeared here and there.

Sex definitely took a back seat when the babies came along, but we made up for its infrequency by grabbing opportunities as they arose, somehow making it all the more illicit and thrilling.

When Louis was just a few months old I went out shopping for new clothes in Ullapool, but wasn't able to try anything on as Louis was unsettled, demanded to be fed and was generally grizzly.

"Go on then, show me what you bought," said Max, lolling back in a dining chair, his size twelves propped up on the table.

"How about some catwalk action?" I said, and ran back into the living room where I'd dumped the bags.

"Yes please!"

I threw my jeans and T-shirt onto the sofa and buttoned up a purple checked shirt and pulled on a pair of burnt orange leggings. As I sauntered back into the kitchen, I demonstrated my most seductive walk.

Max's eyebrows shot up. "Wow. That's a colour combo I don't often see. Thankfully." he muttered.

"Pardon?"

"Nothing, my love. I was just swallowing."

"Anyway, I wasn't planning on wearing these two together - it's what came out of the bags first."

"What are the funny, flappy things . . . over your boobs?" He got up to take a closer look.

"Oh yes, well it's actually a breastfeeding smock. To make it easier to feed Louis."

"Really? Not seen one of those before." He sounded curious. "How does it work exactly?" He undid one of the buttons and lifted the flap.

"Christ almighty!" He jumped back. "Brings a whole new meaning to the concept of peephole bras." He slipped his hand in and squeezed my naked breast.

I laughed. "I didn't realise it would have more than one use. Guess it is a wee bit kinky."

Max undid the button over my other breast and proceeded to check the flap worked on that one too.

"Just verifying it's fit for purpose," he said, and then pushing me up against the worktop, he lowered his mouth over my nipple.

"Mmmm." He moaned. "Who needs racy lingerie when you've got one of these? You should wear it even when you've stopped breastfeeding." He grinned lustily up at me before swapping sides.

"Stop talking Max and kiss me will you?"

And so it was that we snatched moments like these, at least until Louis was old enough to walk and make unannounced appearances. Sometimes sex was funny, and at other times it was downright desperate, but we could only occasionally indulge in the long and leisurely sex sessions we'd enjoyed before babies.

Without my salary I didn't notice that we had any less cash available, and if anything, we seemed to be more flush, with money pouring in from clients left, right and centre. One evening, not long after Lyssa was born, we were discussing taking a summer holiday, and I suggested we buy a tent so that we could go on some cheap family breaks.

"I'm not sure how we'll keep them entertained when it pours down," said Max, with a puckering of the brows. "It's hard enough when we're cooped up indoors with Louis trampolining on the beds and climbing the banisters. Plus, you know how many changes of clothes they get through. How do you think we'll manage all the washing and drying?" he added with a grimace.

Trying to recall the last time I'd seen Max load the washing machine, I suddenly pictured myself squatting at the edge of a stream scrubbing one soiled baby-grow after another.

"We'd be better off visiting your granny and gramps in Bergen," he continued. "Their house is huge, and Louis can learn a bit of Norwegian - nurture his cultural roots. Can you imagine how excited your grandparents would be to see us all?"

This tipped it for me, and I jumped at the idea, not bothering to question where the money would come from to pay for such a trip.

Max was a wonderful dad, by day that is, not so great at night or at the first pale streak of dawn, when both Louis and Lyssa frequently felt the urge to play. During the daytime, whenever he wasn't working, Max would carry them round endlessly when they were teething, play games on the floor with them, change nappies without being asked and love them unconditionally even during their most hideous tantrums. However, he never seemed to hear them cry at night or if they wandered into our bedroom while we were sleeping. It always ended up being my job to sit with them, comfort them when they were teething, change dirty nappies or dispense fever medicine. I would often accuse him of pretending to sleep so he didn't have to get out of bed, but he swore otherwise, and with a whimsical smile would say he was an unusually heavy sleeper. Even if I kicked him when one of the kids started to cry he'd just groan and roll over. We had some massive stand-up rows during the early years of parenthood. I was often completely exhausted, and Max just seemed to take it all in his stride, sleeping soundly at night and even lying in at weekends.

One particular Sunday morning I'd been up with Louis since before five, playing trains on the living room floor, and by nine o'clock Max still hadn't emerged from our bedroom. I went in to see if he was awake and he yawned, stretched leisurely, then tried to grab me as I passed.

"Come back to bed Kat, I want you." There was a stress-free sleepiness to his voice.

"Get off me! Louis' up," I snapped. "Can you get up and play with him so I can at least have a shower?"

"Sure, in a bit. Can you bring me a cup of tea then next time you're making one? I'm parched," he said, smiling lazily then shutting his eyes again.

"I beg your pardon?"

"Can -"

"Yes, I know exactly what you said," I barked, and stormed into the en-suite. I let the cold tap run for a minute and poured a large glass of cold water, fresh from the hillside. Then I marched back into the bedroom, ripped back the duvet and poured the water over his naked body, putting a complete damper on his morning glory.

"There you go. Still parched?" I snarled, and left him gasping and spluttering away to himself.

After a while, I gave up feeling exasperated with him and found life easier doing the night shifts myself, even though it was often night after night. I soon concluded that Max's lack of night-time involvement was one of the reasons I was unable to cope with a return to work, as some days I felt so sleep deprived I wouldn't have felt safe driving anywhere, let alone driving our young children around first thing in the morning. Despite this, I felt myself fortunate that our finances allowed me a choice of not working and I marvelled at some of my new mummy friends who combined careers with looking after their young children.

Within two years, the business was doing so well that Max had taken out a lease on an office, employed two trainee junior architects and even brought in a fully qualified architect, Kurt Trussler, whom he quickly made a partner in the business. Kurt was the same age as Max, and they'd been on the same postgraduate course at Strathclyde. I thought it was strange that Max hadn't introduced him to me while we were at Uni, but he explained that Kurt had travelled into Glasgow every day from his parent's home and so consequently rarely hung out after his lectures. I didn't automatically take to Kurt as I found him egotistical and arrogant. Everything said, he was by all accounts immensely successful at finding new clients, and his designs and the way he worked fit well with the environmental values of the business.

As Kurt was new to the area he would often come to ours for dinner, but almost every time he would bring a different woman, most of whom were completely gaga about him. One girlfriend, Bethany, who worked as a paediatric doctor, was particularly lovely. One Saturday night as we sat eating and talking around the table, I'd found her intelligent and witty, just the sort of person who would make a great friend.

"He's not even that good looking." I complained to Max after they'd retired to the guest room. "He'll have dumped her in a few weeks. Honestly, he's such a terrible Lothario. He gets what he wants, probably plenty of blowjobs and doggy style shags, and then he spits them out. It's bordering on sociopathic behaviour actually." I switched on the bedside light. "Every time he introduces me to his latest girlfriend and I see him fawning all over her as though she's the love of his life, I feel like warning her and wishing her good luck."

"Hey, come on now. He's a great guy, and a good friend. He's super clever, and a brilliant architect. Plus, there's nothing wrong with a good blowjob, you're quite the expert."

"Do you think so? Thanks," I said.

"Anyway, what about Rosie, I couldn't keep track of her conquests at Uni?" Max put his hands on my hips and kissed me on the lips.

"Yeah, but look at her now, a completely reformed character, engaged and totally serious about Will? And as far as I'm aware she hasn't slept with anyone else since she met him."

"Wow! You mean she's been faithful?" he said, and grinned.

"I just think by the time you reach your late twenties you should start taking relationships more seriously, quit using and messing people around." I felt irritated and twisted out of his grasp.

"Yes, but that's you Kat, and not everyone is as mature and sensible as you are. Anyway, you should know by now that men mature later than women, apart from yours truly of course. That's why so many men go for younger women, they simply relate to them better."

"Don't you mean younger woman, singular? Not a different younger woman every other bloody week. The truth is some men never make it to full maturity." I flung my knickers at the wash basket and overshot by several feet.

"Oh shut up and come here will yer?" He grabbed my waist and pulled me to him. "I hope you're not turning into a man hater my lovely. Where would that leave me?" He pulled a ridiculously sad face.

"In deep trouble." I giggled and nipped his neck. Then sidling up against him, I said, "I'll leave it to you to save me from my misanthropy."

CHAPTER THIRTY

Concord Collars

During these early years of parenthood Max rarely mentioned his father, who remained in prison. From what I could glean from him and then Iona, during one of the rare occasions I saw her, parole had been declined a number of times, though I never was able to find out why. During one or two opportune moments I tried talking to Max about the length of his father's sentence. I even suggested we take Louis and Lyssa to visit him, but Max was so adamant that his father didn't deserve to see his grandchildren that I didn't feel I could push him further. I felt that as a family they were becoming more and more estranged, and ultimately I wanted our children to know both sets of grandparents, even if one of them were a convicted thief.

Periodically, we met up with Iona, but Max told me it upset her to talk about his dad, and we should avoid the subject as much as possible. I wasn't entirely convinced, as Iona mentioned Brian a few times herself without any suggestion from me. Eventually, I determined that it was, in fact, Max who found it upsetting to talk about his dad.

Then one day as we were driving home from visiting friends, Max announced that his father was out of prison and his parents were travelling over to visit us the following weekend.

"Are you OK with him coming?" I asked.

"Can't say I'm over the moon, but I don't exactly have a choice. He is Louis and Lyssa's grandfather, and he's a right to see them."

My words exactly, I thought, but I bit my tongue.

"They're only staying two nights as Mam has to get back to work." This was said with an edge that made it clear he didn't approve of her still having to work full-time. "When I spoke to Mam, she said he was out and about looking for work, but because of his history, he wasn't getting interviews. I suggested he'd have to prove himself honest again before anyone would be likely to give him a fresh chance."

It was clear Max wasn't only talking about prospective employers.

Later that evening we cozied up together on the sofa, sipped our wine and listened to music.

"You know Max, I'm so pleased to be meeting him at last. I can't wait to see how alike you both are, and to Louis and Lyssa as well."

His body stiffened, and he looked as hurt as if I'd slapped him in the face.

"I mean to look at. Obviously, I realise you're both completely different character wise," I added swiftly, and draped an arm across his shoulder. I kissed him lightly on the lips, and he obviously forgave me because he kissed me back unreservedly.

Max was on tenterhooks all week, fretting about the piles of clothes and clutter in the guest room, being unusually keen to hoover and tidy the house, and even doing the supermarket shop to ensure we had plenty of nice food in. On the Friday morning when Max left for work, I ran around the house doing a last minute tidy up. In Max's office the waste paper bin was overflowing. I tipped the contents into the bin liner and spilled a couple of scrunched up pieces of paper onto the floor. As I picked them up, I noticed my name written on one and so I unfolded it. Max had written a list of things that didn't look like work. It read:

- Introductions
- Tour of house – Inside & out
- Eco features, wind turbine, solar etc.
- Dinner, free range roast chicken & Yorkshire puddings
- Play music - Rolling Stones, Dusty Springfield, Pink Floyd
- Tired - early night!

Saturday
- Breakfast - porridge, bacon sandwiches
- Play with kids

- Lunch - soup & crusty bread, pork pie, salad
- Drive to show Dad the office
- Butchers
- Dinner - lamb shanks & mash

Sunday
- If weather OK - picnic – including ~~Guinness~~ Champagne
- If bad weather - play trains, cards or game of life!
- Leave 3 pm!

There were several other similar lists, all discarded. Poor Max, I thought, having to list what he was going to do with his dad. He must be feeling horribly anxious about it all. It unnerved me, as he was usually so laid back about having people to stay, or the general untidiness of the house. I began to wonder what his dad must be like, to make him so apprehensive about seeing him again.

Iona and Brian arrived punctually at a quarter past six. I welcomed them in and introduced Brian to Louis and Lyssa, now six and two respectively. Brian got down on his knees to speak to them and chatted away in a deep Irish drawl, and when I turned away he sounded so much like Max, even using one or two Max'isms as I called them. He kissed me on the cheek and asked me a few harmless questions about myself and the kids, and I felt myself begin to warm to him despite my initial unease at meeting him, driven by Max's obvious apprehension.

At six-foot-tall, Brian was a couple of inches shorter than Max, but much stockier, which I figured must be due to his lengthy stay in prison without a great deal of activity. I could see he had once been handsome, though his thinning hair was completely grey and his face was bloated and ruddy, which veiled his features somewhat. The blue shirt he was wearing clearly dated back to pre-prison, slimmer times with its pointed concord collar and buttoned front that gaped a touch across his protruding belly. Hard though his lengthy stay in prison must have been, he certainly hadn't been on any hunger strikes, I thought. He shared Max's generous mouth and broad shoulders, and overall, it was clear to see Max was a fine blend of both of his parents.

Max arrived back from work a short while later, and I met him in the hallway.

"Darling," I kissed him on the cheek. "Your parents are in the living room playing with Louis and Lyssa," I confided quietly. "Your dad is quite charming. Louis and Lyssa have really taken to him. I think we're going to have a wonderful time, honestly."

"I need a whisky Kat. I feel sick." His brow furrowed as he glanced anxiously up the stairs.

"It's been so long since you saw him, you know, properly, and the first time he's been here or seen the children. It's natural to feel nervous." I took his hand.

"Hello, son. Been a while, eh?" Brian stood half way up the stairs with Lyssa on his hip.

"Daddy," squealed Lyssa.

Max gave a wave to Lyssa. "Dad. Good to see you." He walked slowly up the stairs and on drawing level, they continued together up the final few steps.

I ran up behind them.

Up in the living room, I said, "I'll fetch us some drinks."

I watched as Max and his dad exchanged looks of acquaintances rather than of father and son.

"A wee dram perhaps, Brian, Iona? You won't have had chance for much of the good stuff when you were in pr . . . I mean, for a while." I bent over, cringed at my faux pas, and removed a Lego man from Lyssa's mouth.

"No, no, we don't drink spirits do we?" He grimaced as though I'd offered him something illegal. Brian turned to look at Iona, who nodded agreement. "A beer or a Guinness if you have any?"

I turned to Iona.

"Yes, the same for me. Thank you Katriina."

"OK, of course. Max?"

"Sure, that'd be grand." Max sounded bright enough, but still looked decidedly uptight.

I returned a couple of minutes later to find Iona alone in the living room with Louis and Lyssa. They were playing ring-o-ring-o-roses, and both children giggled hysterically each time they fell down.

"Max is giving Brian the house tour. He's been itching to see it and has always asked me so much about it. But really you can't do it justice, describing it." Iona took Lyssa's hand. "I suppose I should have taken more photos, but I always end up taking so many of the children."

"Again, again Granny," shrieked Lyssa.

As I watched them play, I smiled, and felt happy with the way things were going; the children bonding with their grandparents, and Max finally renewing his relationship with his father.

When I stepped out onto the landing with the drinks I overheard Max and Brian talking in the office. Something made me hesitate.

"I'm proud of you son. This is what I planned for you. Your own business... decent money, a family, and you even managed to give me a grandson first."

"Thanks, Dad. I'm proud of Katriina and the kids too." Max sounded more upbeat.

"Now aren't you glad I pushed you to do well at school? If I hadn't, who knows what you'd be doing now. Probably working in Burgers 4U," he said. "And I can't imagine you would have caught a cracking lassie like Katriina, eh?" He let out a sleazy chortle.

My blood was beginning to boil; digs, cleverly disguised as compliments. I continued eavesdropping.

"But Dad, you haven't been in my life for so long, and it's been tough for Mam. Can't you see she's exhausted? And she's stuck by you, despite everything."

"I know son. And I'm going to make it up to her, earn some decent money so she can give up work. I promise you." His voice was full of false confidence and bluster.

I'd heard enough, and I returned to the living room, drinks still in hand.

It wasn't until I had bathed and settled the kids into their beds, on my own, that I saw Max again. I searched his face for clues as to how he was feeling. He didn't look like the honoured son, proud of his achievements, glad to have his father back. He sat slumped on the sofa and as he talked to his parents, he looked edgy and tired. And I could suddenly see what had made Max so driven these past few years, driven to succeed in first building our house and then to put in the endless hours needed to make the business a success. I guessed much of it was done to gain approval from his dad. Though I knew

Max was happy with me, with the children, I knew it wasn't making him happy to have his father slap him on the back, for it was clear to see any respect he once felt for him had well and truly departed.

As we ate dinner, I rested my hand on Max's thigh in between mouthfuls. I touched his arm and tried to bolster his mood and reassure him with my presence. Straightaway, I noticed that the way Brian spoke to Iona veered between patronising one minute to flattering the next as though to make amends for an earlier remark. Beside Brian, Iona was much quieter than the bright and self-assured woman I'd grown to know, demure almost, and she never bit back at anything he said that was a little dig or an attempt to put her down. I tried hard not show my irritation or interfere, but I couldn't help but add a careful observation here and there in favour of either Max or Iona.

At bedtime, Max curled up and faced away from me. He yawned as I got into bed.

"Are you tired?" I whispered. He didn't answer so I snuggled up and pressed myself against his back, tucking my knees in behind his. I slid my hand over his hip and shifted his inner thighs.

"Mmmm," he mumbled softly.

"You OK?"

"Sure. You?"

"Yeah," I paused. "I can see why you were a bit worried about seeing your dad again. He's kinda complex."

"He hasn't got a clue what it's been like for us, for Mam, all these years. At least I've moved on, but poor Mam, I think she might be happier if he'd never come home."

"Oh Max, you can't mean that. I'm sure she must still love him."

"I think she did, but I also think she's got used to him not being around. And now he's back he's not even nice to her. Did you hear his spiteful comment about buying clothes too young for her?"

"It was unkind and humiliating, wasn't it?" I kissed the back of Max's neck. "And in front of us. How did he get onto the subject?"

"It was 'cus Mam said she liked your shorts and asked where you shopped."

"Oh yeah."

"I liked your subtle retort. 'The thing is, when you're nice and slim it's such a pleasure to buy new clothes that you know will suit you.' Nicely off the cuff, my love."

"It's true anyway," I said. "Your mum is beautiful."

"I wish Mam would put him in his place. But she won't say a word against him. When I was showing him round, he said he was pleased he'd pushed me at school. He tried to take the credit for what I've achieved, for what we've achieved here." Max huffed. "He's conveniently forgotten he wasn't around through high-school, A-levels, Uni. To me, he feels more like a stranger."

As Max talked, I planted soft kisses on the bare slope of his shoulder.

"Dad was so competitive when I was young. Pushy, and made me feel bad if I didn't come top in tests or win races on sports day. Anyway, once Dad was in prison, it was down to Mam to help me with school work. He didn't have any input then, how could he?"

He turned to face me, reached over and stroked my back and ran his hand over my bottom.

"And another thing... he promised to write and wanted me to write back, tell him what I'd been doing at school. But after a couple of months, he gave up replying." Absentmindedly, Max fondled my breasts. "I carried on for a bit, but I gave up too. Mam has always written, but he rarely wrote back, said he preferred to talk face to face."

"Mmm." I struggled to concentrate. "It must have been tough...like he'd deserted you."

"Exactly. Mam defended him. She said it was hard in prison, that it affected him mentally and made him depressed." Max snorted in disbelief.

"Mmm, yes well it probably was vile in there - rapists, paedophiles, drug dealers, wife beaters for company. Did you visit much?"

"Mam made me go most months, but I hated it. I was angry. He put himself there. He didn't need to steal. It's not like we were poor."

"True, but he's more than paid the price for it, surely? Maybe he needs to readjust to life outside."

"Maybe."

"It'll help when he's working. I imagine he feels guilty about your mum having to support him. It can dent a man's ego if he's not providing. Imagine how you'd feel?"

"Well, I wouldn't put you down publicly, humiliate you, make you feel bad just because I did."

"No, you wouldn't," I said, and kissed him. "You and he are different men Max. Maybe him being out of your life for all these years has made you a stronger, better person. I dunno. It's hard isn't it?"

"You're not kidding." He stroked my inner thigh. "Anyway, I'm tired of talking about him. I know what will make me feel better."

"Oh? What's that?" I ran my hand through his hair and snuggled up.

We kissed and caressed one another, and just as things were heating up, there came a long, high-pitched scream.

"Lyssa. That's Lyssa." I threw back the duvet and flew out of bed. Her cries sounded far more urgent than her usual half-hearted shouting, so I ran down the corridor and pulled my robe about me. As I reached her door, Brian walked out of her room. I brushed past him and switched on the lamp above the bed. Lyssa was sitting up and crying hysterically. I scooped her up.

"It's OK baby. Mummy's here."

I heard a movement behind me, turned and bumped into Brian.

Lyssa cried harder.

"I'm sorry Katriina, I went to the toilet and came in. Only to watch her sleeping. I didn't want to wake her." He smiled and tickled Lyssa under the arm.

I felt Lyssa shrink from his touch and I stepped back. "It's fine, she'll settle in a minute. She doesn't know you well enough. Shh. It's OK petal." I looked straight at Brian. "You must have startled her. Go back to bed, she'll be fine."

After he had apologised again, he returned to his room.

What a complete prat, I thought, coming in and scaring her. Poor Lyssa was inconsolable. She sobbed and clutched onto me, so I took her upstairs and warmed some milk.

When we returned to her room, I lay in her bed, with Lyssa hooked in my arms like a new-born. Her little hands gripped her Minnie Mouse beaker, and she gazed up at me with adoring, sleep filled eyes. I stroked her glossy brown curls, and she soon closed her eyes and drifted off to sleep.

Instead of returning to my bed, I looked in on Louis who slept peacefully, then I went back to Lyssa's room and snuggled down next to her. I knew she had been badly shaken by Brian's night-time appearance, and I wanted her to feel fully reassured.

Just after seven, I awoke to Lyssa singing and stroking my face.

"Wo wo wo your boat, gently down the stweam.

Mewily mewily mewily mewily life is but a dweam."

"Morning sweetness," I said, and stretched. "Sleep well?"

"Yes, Mummy. I like sharing my bed."

"I do too petal. Now, how about we read a story?"

A short while later, we sat around the breakfast table.

"What was up with Lyssa last night? Bad dream was it?" asked Max.

"Something like that." I glanced at Lyssa sitting on her booster seat, as she happily spread far too much butter on her toast. "I decided to stay with her. She was rather unsettled." I caught Brian's eye.

Unfazed and clearly deciding that no explanation on his part was necessary, Brian brazenly winked and continued to shovel down his breakfast.

Inside I seethed, but I reigned it in and resolved to diplomatically ask that he didn't go into the children's bedrooms during the night. I also felt it would be prudent not to mention it to Max, to avoid creating any further tension between the two of them.

As the weather was dry, we filled a picnic basket to take up the hillside, though I didn't expect us to get all that far. Lyssa walked well, but generally when we attempted to go for family walks, she would become temperamental, especially when a hill was involved, which was impossible to avoid around here. I knew Max or I would end up carrying her some, if not all of the way.

Brian took Louis' hand, and they walked up the stony path as the rest of us followed behind. Max and I had walked up that stretch with the children dozens of times and each journey had been different, as they always discovered new things to look at, touch and experience along the way. The long summer grass tilted slightly, laden with dew, and the heather and undergrowth either side of the path held beautifully intricate webs, covered with fine dewdrops. Max stopped beneath a birch tree and broke off a couple of twigs. He stripped them back, shaped them like catapults and held them out in front of him.

"What are those for?" I asked. "Are you going to teach them how to catapult?"

"Not exactly. Louis, Lyss, come here. I've got something for you."

"It's a stick Daddy." Lyssa took one and held it up to examine it.

"D'ya see this little web, all covered with teeny, tiny water droplets?" He guided Lyssa's hand and brought the Y-shaped stick up under the web to gather it gently across the gap. "Hold it up, and you'll see all the delicate threads the spider has spun."

"Ooh Daddy, it's so pwetty." She gazed and tilted it at different angles. "But where's the spider gone?"

"He's crawled off to weave some more webs. You need to catch another dewy web, and then some others and you'll end up with hundreds of tiny webs all laced together, like a miniature lace blanket."

Louis had already moved off amongst the heather and gathered little webs as he went. "Daddy look. I've found a massive one," he called out.

Max marched over to take a look. "Now that is huge. Must have been a big spider to weave that one. We have to keep moving up the hill though Lou. I think the best webs will be a bit further up."

I took Max's hand. "Why haven't you shown me this trick before? It's beautiful, and they're loving it."

"Because I've only just remembered doing it. I sometimes did it with Mam and Dad. You know, it's bringing back memories." He smiled and squeezed my hand.

I don't think the diversion helped us to travel any greater distance that morning, but no one complained about tired legs.

When we stopped for lunch I realised I'd left the drinks on the kitchen table, and so I volunteered to fetch them. I grabbed the jute shopping bag with glasses, a bottle of champagne, pear cider and orange juice cartons, then slogged back up the hillside. It was as I rounded the edge of the rocks that I heard the children's shrieks and laughter echoing all around me, and even before they came into view the sound triggered the reoccurrence of a memory held dormant for several years. As I drew near, I saw Louis and Lyssa, with Iona and Brian nearby. I watched my two beautiful children balance stones one on top of the other, then squeal with excitement as they fell into a heap.

I looked around and saw Max sitting on the crest of the highest rock, Nikon in hand, as he took photographs of the happy scene. He smiled and waved, then pointed the camera my way. It felt surreal, and I remained there and watched them from a short distance away as tears formed in my eyes.

It was only then that I knew, without a flicker of doubt, how several years previously and before either of their births, I had encountered my own children through some kind of mystic doorway to the future.

CHAPTER THIRTY-ONE

Au Naturel

In the world of contemporary architecture and house building, Max's name and business had established a well-respected reputation and had recently featured in several prominent newspapers and magazines. Only last month he'd won a prestigious prize for his innovative eco-design of a modern art museum building in Aberdeen. The journalist covering the story arranged to interview him at home.

"Hi, I'm Jane Peplow." A pretty, elfin-like woman with long poker straight chestnut hair, introduced herself, in her highly affected Edinburgh accent. She extended a dainty, well-manicured hand. "I've come to interview Max O'Donnell." She peered inquisitively behind me.

"Hello, yes Max said you were coming." I shook her hand. "I'm Katriina, come through." I held the door. "Can I get you a tea, coffee?"

"That would be super. Coffee, black, no sugar." As she spoke, she didn't catch my eye and instead gazed up, taking in the large atria space.

"Max," I shouted upstairs. "Jane from Green Build is here."

Max appeared on the landing and jogged downstairs.

He took her hand in both of his and said, "Great to meet you Jane. We'll talk in the living room, beautiful views. Can I get you a coffee?"

"Thanks, Kathleen is getting me one." She beamed up at him. "This is an amazing house, Max. Did you design this?"

"It was my first project, wasn't it Kat? We lived in a caravan while we built it."

As they made their way upstairs, I heard her gushing compliments, and when I walked into the living room a few minutes later, they were sitting side by side. I immediately noticed their legs touched. As I placed the tray on the coffee table, I watched Jane nod keenly at his every word, and smile inanely.

"Hey, Katriina, Jane's keen to include some stuff on Wolfstone House in her feature. You OK with that?" Max handed Jane her coffee.

"I guess so, if you want to." I settled myself in the rocking chair by the window, opened my book and sipped my tea. As I half-listened to their conversation, I began to feel slightly ill at ease.

When they got up, I felt compelled to speak.

"Excuse me, Jane. If you do use Wolfstone in your feature, please can you not state exactly where we live?"

"Oh, absolutely. No problem at all," she replied, cheerfully.

As Max led her away for a house tour he glanced back briefly, smiled and winked. I didn't smile back. Jane was already snapping away with her camera as she went and I realised many of them would be unusable, as neither Max nor I had done any tidying up in preparation for her visit and the house was full of the usual tedious detritus left over from our busy lives.

After a while I heard them head outside, so I pulled on my jacket and joined them at the front. Louis and Lyssa were walking back up the drive, returning from their riding lesson at nearby Woodside Stables.

"Hi, guys. Where did you ride to?" I said.

"We rode through Cramback Woods, and along the beck at Fairy Glen." Lyssa came up and took my hand. "I rode Grecian. He's so fast Mum, I could hardly stop him when we got to the beck. I thought he was going to leap right over." She looked flushed and happy.

"OK. But I'm not sure I want to know that. Personally, I think Bramble is a more suitable ride on a hack. Bombproof on the roads too."

"He's way too slow. Louis rode him anyway, didn't you?" she said, and grinned at Louis.

"I got waylaid by Megan, and then I didn't get a choice," he grumbled.

"Megan fancies you, Lou. Did you know?" Lyssa said, with a giggle.

"Shut up," Louis snapped. "My legs are like jelly. Bramble doesn't respond to a squeeze, needs more of a hefty boot in the ribs. I spent the whole ride shouting at the others to wait for me."

"I tried Lou, but Grecian only likes being in front."

"Come and say hello to Jane," Max said, and beckoned them over. "She's going to be writing about our house. Exciting eh?"

Louis and Lyssa went over, none too eagerly.

I wandered off and pulled up a few weeds that were sprouting up through the gravel.

Max called over, "Guess what Kat?"

I joined them beneath the wind turbine.

"Jane's also working with BBC Scotland who are about to start filming a documentary about zero carbon homes. She thinks ours would be perfect for it. What do you think? It would be fantastic publicity for the business."

"I guess. What would it involve?"

"Only a half a day's filming. I'd be interviewing Max. You don't need to be involved if -"

"But I'd like Kat and the kids to be involved," Max said, putting his arm around my waist. "This is our forever family home, and my family is what this is all for."

"Of course. Super. And your kids are gorgeous, perfect for television," she said, and scribbled something in her notebook.

Her sycophantic crawling was turning my stomach, and I turned away, resisting an urge to stick a finger down my throat.

"What are you building over there, is it a studio?" She pointed to a small square of newly laid foundations to the front of the gravelled area.

"Actually, that's going to be our sauna. Should be up and running in a couple of months," explained Max.

"Ooh! Really?" she said, and giggled girlishly. "I must think of an excuse to come back when it's finished."

"It'll be fabulous for those cold winter evenings," Max continued.

"And will you be sitting au naturel?" Jane flipped her hair off her shoulder and tilted her head to one side.

"Umm, I certainly hope so." Came Max's good-humoured reply.

I was gobsmacked at her barefaced flirting, and with me standing just feet away.

Swinging back around to face them, I said, "Yes, and I can assure you, Jane, we won't only be sitting there au naturel, will we Max?"

Max shot me a look and burst out laughing.

"In that case, I'm going to place that order for the sauna stove right now."

Jane pursed her lips, and changed the subject. "Now Max, how about a photo of you and the kids in front of the house?"

Louis started to make a quick getaway.

"Ahh, come on Lou. It'll be cool, honest." Max jogged over and put a hand on Louis' shoulder.

Jane spent the next few minutes rearranging us into various positions and taking shots from different angles with the house in the background.

"If you could stand from smallest to tallest, and look up at the wind turbine. Ya, great, don't smile, just gaze up in wonder. Hold it." Jane lay on the gravel aiming to achieve a sufficiently arty angle.

I tried not to laugh, which after seeing her flat on her back, was impossible.

Afterwards, when she showed them to us, I could see we looked like the model family. Attractive and fair Max, complete with designer stubble, Louis and Lyssa both undeniably beautiful children and even I was managing a genuine smile. The house looked stunning too. The roof was thick with grasses and speckled with colourful wildflowers, and the shrubs and trees we'd planted strategically around the house were fully established and blooming with midsummer foliage.

As Jane hugged and kissed Max goodbye, I heard her say in her shrill, singsong voice.

"I'm so happy to have met you and your family, Max. The magazine editor is going to be over the moon with my feature. I honestly can't thank you enough. I'll be in touch."

We waved her off with the promise of seeing her again for the filming for the television programme.

Once her car disappeared down the drive, Max said, "If it didn't look as if Kurt was finally serious about someone, I'd be thinking about introducing him to Jane. They'd be perfect for one another. And she told me she's single. "What do you reckon?" he said, eyes alight with amusement.

"Absolutely bloody perfect," I replied, and leaned into him. "Hold that thought though. I'm sure things will become considerably less serious with Fleur before long."

CHAPTER THIRTY-TWO

Little Miss Polly Perfect

Beneath the spotlight, the fine lines on Max's face seemed more pronounced and the shadows beneath his eyes darker. "Your car was abandoned in a layby just outside Arrochar. At the same time, a car was reported stolen from the village," said Max. "It was low on fuel so either he has no money, or he knows better than to risk being recognised at a petrol station. The whole of Britain must have seen that picture." Max took two cups from the cupboard. "I need caffeine."

"Oh, so you do believe I remembered what he looked like." I couldn't disguise my sarcasm. I digested this new piece of crucial news. The name of a village. That meant the police were getting closer.

Max slammed his fists against the overhead cupboard and the sound of breaking china filled the kitchen. "Jesus Fucking Christ!"

About time, I thought, a show of emotion. A reaction to show he felt something. I left him there as he cursed and picked the broken china out of the sink and I rang the police. Constable Pearce told me the stolen car was a blue Nissan. I wrote down the registration on a scrap of paper and slipped it into my pocket.

"Has he still got her though?" I said to Max afterwards. "Oh Christ. I forgot to ask if it was a hatchback or saloon. That could be significant, couldn't it?" I turned it over in my mind. "Why though, what does he want? Oh God, what's he done to her?"

"Come here, Kat, please. We can't think like that."

I noticed Max trembled as he wrapped his arms around me.

"We've got to focus on finding her," he said. "We will too, the police are on his trail." He held me tightly and stroked the back of my head over and over.

"Why Loch Lomond?" I asked. "Does he live there?"

"We will find out." Max pulled away, screwed the lid back on the milk carton and put it back in the fridge.

"It's not like we made any enemies at Uni is it?" I continued. "And that man dying on Benn Arum. We did what we could, didn't we?"

Max tore off a sheet of kitchen towel and blew his nose.

"Max?"

"Of course we didn't do anything wrong," Max replied. "Where your car was found has nothing to do with us, and he might've driven on somewhere else." Max turned to the door. "I'm sure I heard a car." He marched out of the kitchen and shouted back. "Just your parents. I'll tell them what's happened."

"OK, my loves, dinner. And don't try telling me you're not hungry," said Anna.

"Thanks, Mum. Soup would be fine though."

"I know, but I need to do something. Anyway, my fish pie has always been your favourite." She placed the crispy topped pie onto the worktop. She looked at me as she twirled the pendant on her necklace. "You look white Katriina. You don't look right at all." Her face suddenly crumpled, and she turned away. "We're all trying to be strong, but how can we?"

I got up and held her. "What if we don't get her back, Mum?"

I burst into tears, and Dad and Louis cried with us. It felt cathartic, but at the same time I felt I had accepted the inevitability of Lyssa never coming home.

On the ten o'clock news they showed the photo-fit again and the blue Nissan. Soon afterwards, Louis and my parents went to bed leaving Max and I alone in the living room.

"Want one?" Max said, and got up to pour himself another whisky.

"No and you shouldn't either. We could get a call and have to leave." I watched as he poured his drink, how his hands shook, and it sloshed onto the floor.

"Christ Max, you've poured yourself at least five shots. You'll be pissed and ill."

"I need it, even if you don't," he snapped back.

"I do need it, but what's more important?" I said. "I couldn't stomach it anyway."

I thought for a second about telling him I was sure I was pregnant. But it seemed so absurd to even be pregnant, let alone think it a good time to announce it, like a piece of good news to plug the hellhole we were in. I quickly shelved the thought.

Max downed his drink, got up and poured another. He lifted his glass and slurred, "Sainte!" before he dropped onto the sofa, bottle and glass in hand. He swirled the whisky around his glass.

"Stop it, Max. You're fucking irresponsible." I snatched the bottle and glass from him and carried them into the kitchen.

When I returned, I found Max in tears, and his shoulders shuddered with each rise and fall of breath.

I sat down and put my arm around him.

"It's OK to cry."

"You don't understand, Kat." He smacked his forehead with his fist.

My mind reeled. "What Max? What don't I understand?"

"Our baby. Beautiful Lyssa. It's my fault," he blurted, and turned away.

"It isn't. It can't be."

He drummed his fingers on his temples.

"Why would you say that, Max?"

He muttered through his tears, "I'm sorry Lyssa, forgive me."

Stunned, I jumped up. "What the fuck do you mean, forgive me?"

He glanced up at me and I saw in his eyes a dark weight of shame.

"It's my fault. And Lyssa might die."

I fought to keep my voice level. "You'd better explain Max - right now."

He shifted awkwardly and with eyes fixed on the blackness outside said, "I don't know how to start. You'll despise me, and Lyssa still might die."

I trembled, unable to speak.

"But I have to tell you. It might help - it might not." His words slurred and I shuddered at what he was about to say.

"Tell me Max."

174

He searched for something on his phone, and passed it to me. "This will explain."

The pain etched upon his face terrified me and my hands shook as I took the phone from him. My legs folded. It was Lyssa, ashen face, blindfolded, her arms held behind her.

I read the message beneath.

'Want her back alive. you no wat to do. Give me whats mine or she is no more.'

Bile rose in my throat, and I coughed and retched.

I turned to Max. "How? When did you get this? What belongs to him?"

"I never thought this would happen. It was stupid, so feckin stupid." Max clutched his head as he spoke. "I was young, naïve, and the worst thing is, all this time, his face has never left me. He's always in my head, my dreams… my nightmares. I've tried to justify it, but I can't." He wiped his nose. "I almost told you so many times, I swear. But I was scared you'd leave me. I couldn't risk that."

"Please, Max."

"It's the worst thing… our baby girl."

"What did you do? Who is he?"

"I killed him, Kat. I killed his dad."

My head spun and rolled in somersaults, like a vast windstorm that had sucked everything up in its path and churned everything round and round in ever widening circles. I wanted to scream and hit him, force Max to speak his name. Anger clung to me and suddenly the truth dawned. And I knew who he had killed.

"It was Benn Arum, wasn't it? It was Roy?"

His tears streamed and he nodded.

For a moment I shut eyes and wished that the last two days had been one vile joke.

"You have to tell me everything," I said. "You can't hide any longer." I lifted his chin. "Look at me Max. You know that, don't you?"

His eyes flickered.

"You need coffee," I said. "Let's talk in the kitchen."

We sat across from one another and I watched Max. His greasy hair plastered to his forehead, the shadows on his face had grown darker and the hollows of his eyes had become deeper. Every so often a drip fell from his nose. This wasn't my handsome, funny and loving husband before me, but a broken man who had risked everything he held dear.

"Do you remember when I spotted him as we started down Benn Arum, that storm taking us all by surprise?" Max lifted his cup, drank a mouthful and swallowed. "The wind, the rain, the noise. It was a miracle I even looked across in his direction. So many times I've wished I never had. But I did. We tried to help him, didn't we? But neither of us knew what to do, other than try to stop the bleeding and talk to him."

I nodded, and it dredged the memory from the hidden depths of my mind.

"Then you left us so you could find help. You knew how to navigate mountain tracks better than me, didn't you?" He paused, and waited for some signal of agreement from me.

"Go on, Max."

"After you'd gone I talked to him to keep him alive. The rain wasn't letting up; the wind was pulling at the tent cover. It seemed like forever since you set off, but might have only been a few minutes. I climbed over the rocks nearby to look for something that might offer a clue as to who he was, something that belonged to him. And then I did find something." He hesitated, and his eyes shifted sideways, unsure whether to continue.

"What did you find, Max?"

"A bag, tucked behind a rock. Not a rucksack, but a small holdall. I brought it to him, tried to wake him, said I'd found his bag. I knew it could hold a clue as to who he was so I opened it. There was a black plastic bag, full, and a small trowel. The plastic was thick, stapled and I couldn't tear it open. I ripped it with my teeth." He paused, and lowered his voice. "It was full of notes - big ones. But the next part is muddled. He grabbed my leg, and his eyes were open and he was trying to sit up. He was scratching at my legs, my arm and, I don't know, I didn't like him touching me. So I pushed him off. Shoved him I suppose." Max closed his eyes and relived it. "I shouldn't have done that. He was too weak. If I'd only pulled away. When he fell, his head hit the rock. And he started fitting, shaking, thrashing his head against the rocks." Max paused, and massaged his temples in small, feverish circles. "It went on and on, then just as suddenly he stopped. He wasn't moving, or breathing."

"Oh God, Max. You told me about the fit." But he'd been selective with the reason for its sudden onset. "You were upset in the helicopter." I tried to figure out the chain of events up to when Max pushed Roy away and thought that this, on top of his already desperately fragile condition, could well have contributed to his death.

"The money, Max - what did you do with the money?" I already knew the answer, but I needed to hear him say it.

"I didn't know what to do. I was in shock, him dying." Max looked me in the eye and with a small shrug said, "So, I kept it." He watched for my reaction.

I stared back, my expression blank.

"I hid it at the bottom of my rucksack. All these years, I've tried to justify taking it. Telling myself that he was dead so no longer needed it."

I tried to absorb his words and the enormity of his lies that penetrated deeper than any blade could reach. It seemed impossible to process. I could only wonder how he'd managed to keep it to himself that day, that night . . . for twenty years. Max wiped the hair off his forehead. He looked ahead and waited for me to react - to say something.

"But you stole that money." My voice sounded strangely matter of fact. "I'm not sure you intentionally killed Roy, but I can see why the guilt has stayed with you. If only you'd told me. Oh Max, why didn't you tell me?"

"I wanted to."

I walked over to the window and stared at the impenetrable dark wall, then I turned back to him. "I don't understand you. All these years we've been together. Twenty years. Jesus Max. All of this, our children, our home, the business. It's all built on a lie." I wept. "There was no inheritance was there?"

"We were just getting to know each other. And I wanted you. More than I'd ever wanted anything. I remember so clearly you held me in the helicopter. You were lovely, and all I could think was how much I wanted that - wanted you. I felt guilty at the campsite, but you came to find me - and you kissed me. Everything was falling into place. You liked me, let me share your tent. And that incredible first night together. You felt it too, I know you did. That's why you're here with me and with our amazing children." He sighed heavily. "At the hospital that officer didn't mention any missing money. His wife didn't report it missing, or we'd have heard, wouldn't we? The police never contacted us again. No one even knew about the money."

I couldn't listen any longer. He wanted to convince me that what he'd done had been justified in some way; that his behaviour was rational. In some bizarre, warped way, he still believed his actions were defensible, but now his guilt had resurfaced because of this man, this psychopath, whoever he was and what he was capable of.

Then another thought occurred to me. Was this the first message? Were there others?

"Shut up about the money, Max. We need to figure out how to talk to him… to find Lyssa."

"I know, but it won't be easy."

I searched for the words. "Max, is this the only message? Have you replied?"

His eyes flickered, and I saw guilt carved across his every feature. "This is hard to say, and I know when I do you'll never forgive me." He breathed deeply. "I've been getting messages for nearly two months."

I felt the sweat break out on my neck and chest. "What?" But I didn't wait for a reply. "You're out of your tiny fucking mind. Why didn't you tell me a maniac was on the loose and threatening you?" I cried, enraged, and wanted to strike him.

"At first, I thought they were a joke from someone who hated me. They were cryptic. I had no idea who he was. I thought it was someone who fancied you or you'd had an affair with or . . . still were."

"For Christ's sake. You really thought that? When have I ever given you a reason to think that way?"

"You haven't. I know I was crazy. You can't see it Kat, but you have a hold over men. You only need to look at them, and they're hooked. I see how they look at you - their eyes. I thought maybe you were fed up with me."

"Jesus, Max. OK that's for later, not now for Christ's sake."

"If you read the messages you'd understand."

I sniffed. "I doubt it, Max, but please do go on. When exactly did you realise who this lunatic was and what he really wanted?"

"A couple of weeks ago. The emails became threatening, and he told me in a roundabout way that I'd killed his dad and stolen his money. At first it didn't occur to me who he was, I swear to God. I don't know why. I thought it was someone I'd done business with. I remember you telling me about his wife and son after we left the hospital, but perhaps it was because I was in shock or had never spoken to them myself. One night I woke up thinking about the messages and the penny dropped. I should have known earlier, and I should have talked to you... to the police."

"But you didn't, because you stole the money and you knew you'd be found out. Instead, you chose to put your family at risk."

"It wasn't like that."

"Blood money, that's what it is. Our daughter's blood." I'd lost all semblance of control. I sobbed and imagined Lyssa lying face down in a ditch.

"Don't Kat. She's going to be all right. She has to be."

"She could be dead, and if she is, you're to blame. Do you understand you bloody bastard?" I spat the words in his face. "And if by some miracle he hasn't hurt her yet, abused her, raped her, she'll have to live with it for the rest of her life - the trauma."

Max paced back and forth the length of the kitchen, and his hands scratched back and forth through his hair. "Before I knew who he was, he asked me to meet with him - twice. And I was there, but he never showed up. I said I'd sort it out with him. I did everything I could to resolve it but he must have got angrier and kidnapped Lyssa for ransom." Max stopped pacing. "What a mess, Kat." He thumped the table and kicked a chair across the floor.

"How did he know who you were - that we were with his dad when he died?" I asked.

"He said he saw us, our house, on that homes programme. Said he knew you straight away, remembered you from the hospital. Said he saw our home, our perfect family, our perfect life he called it. Called me a fucking smug bastard."

"I knew we shouldn't have done that programme," I said. "It seemed all wrong at the time. And that hideous woman who came here. What a bootlicking sycophant." I picked up the chair and placed it back under the table.

"Aren't you clever?" Max threw back in a sardonic sing-song voice. "But how could I have known it would lead to this? It made business sense at the time."

"No, you only wanted the publicity for the business, nothing whatsoever to do with fame and seeing yourself on TV."

"You're right, you're always bloody right aren't you?" Max shouted. "Little Miss Polly Perfect does it again. If only I were as perfect as you."

"Stop it!" I screamed. "This isn't about who's right, who's wrong. It's our baby. It's only about Lyssa."

He was no longer listening. Muttering and lost in his own troubled thoughts.

"Max, can't you see that?" I raised my voice to drag him into the moment.

He swung around to face me.

"He says we killed him to get the money. And it's eaten away at him, stopped him from succeeding in life. For years he's tried to find out who we were. He wants to repay us for what we've done. He wants me dead."

"Don't you dare use 'us'. It's you who has to take responsibility."

"You've been happy living here, spending the money." Max looked me in the eye for a moment before he turned and walked to the sink.

"Do you think I'd have ever had anything to do with you if I'd known?" I said. "You're living in a fantasy world."

Max stood with his forehead pressed against the overhead kitchen cupboard.

"If his mum didn't mention the money at the time Roy died, how come his son knows about it?" I said.

Max swung around to face me. "I dunno. Perhaps it was stolen, or he was a drug dealer. I think he was going to bury or hide the money. A pretty stupid thing to do though."

"Not as stupid as stealing it," I said.

Then I pictured the boy, the desperately sad face of the child who had learned of the death of his father. And that young innocent face I now saw in the man's reflection in the wing mirror. Strange, but even after all these years, I realised his face was familiar - the sharp arch of his eyebrows, the outline of his chin.

I pushed back my chair. "What's his name? I'm ringing Inspector Keir."

"I don't know," he said. "There's no clue in the email address. But do you remember Roy's surname was Simpson? Not the most unusual surname in Scotland."

"I only remember he was Roy," I said.

"I tried looking it up, but there are so many Simpsons around Loch Lomond, in Scotland, in Glasgow, that I didn't know where to start," he said. "I wasn't sure what I'd do if I did know where he lived. I couldn't just knock on his door and hand the money back could I?"

"But you could have offered some money or exposed him to the police. But you didn't want to. You were afraid of the repercussions for yourself, for the life you've made. Forget that - stolen."

He wept. "I know. It's pathetic."

The truth had sunk in about our daughter's abduction and he sounded pitiful. Anger prevented me from feeling sorry for him. No, if Max was in pain because of his wrongdoings, let him feel it, every splinter, every razor sharp edge. I wouldn't protect him. He would have to face up to the aftermath.

I said, "I'm phoning her now."

Max slumped onto the chair. His head hung in shame.

The phone rang twice before it was answered.

"Inspector Keir please, it's Katriina."

The line became silent for a moment, then her voice sounded in my ear, expectant.

"Katriina?"

"We know who he is. We know who's got Lyssa."

CHAPTER THIRTY-THREE

I rushed my words; the emails, the photo of Lyssa bound and gagged, the death of the abductor's father, Roy Simpson, twenty years ago, and Max's involvement, the stolen money.

"Roy's death will be in police records and from that we'll know who his son is. I'm sending a car for Max. Tell him to be ready to leave with his phone. Just a moment."

I heard a muffled exchange before she came back on the line. "I'll ring as soon as I have his full name. Our officers have been searching Arrochar and the surrounding area, showing residents the photo-fit to see if they know or have seen anything. But I told Max earlier, he'll have told you."

"No Inspector, he hadn't told me."

In the time it took for the police to arrive, Max showed me the emails exchanged between them, but I was still at a loss as to how he'd avoided confessing the truth. How could he have kept something like this to himself? I'd have shared straight away. But then I also knew I wouldn't have kept the money in the first place.

I read a message received a week ago and my head throbbed with rage. "Why do u deny what you stole? Confess and repay or I promis u I will hurt your family, your sexy wife, your young inosent daughter and prized son."

Another message said, "I know where u live. I will visit. It might be when you're out, when your wife is alone with your kids. I will come."

The more messages I read, the more terrified I felt. I realised how angry and bitter he was, how he intended getting his money back, by whatever means he could. He relished the control and intimidation, the threats, the possibility that he could wreak irrevocable havoc on our family in order to repay Max in full for his wrongdoing.

I realised too that the deep love and intimacy Max and I had always shared, had in a single moment been rendered false and our relationship was nothing more than a synthetic imitation of something real.

I had neither the time nor desire to fix a marriage on the brink of collapse, and the way I felt at the moment, I never would.

When two officers arrived at the door, I stood aside and let Max leave. He knew better than to offer me reassurance. I knew with absolute certainty that there would be no going back for us from this, whether Lyssa was found alive or not.

CHAPTER THIRTY-FOUR

The Sins of the Father

The onset of sleep freed Lyssa from her nightmare. In her dream she was home – her loving mother watching over her and talking together about her friends and school. Sometime later, when she awoke she sensed a dazzling light, and for a moment thought it was the sunrise stealing through the blinds of her bedroom window. But then she saw him, the way he slowly beamed the torch around the room, and her fear returned, and jabbed at her throat like a shard of glass. She sat up, swung her legs over the side of the bed and tried to blank out reality.

In her confusion, Lyssa wondered if the chair had been in the room before, or had he only just brought it in? It was strange how it looked like one they had at home, old and with long, curved armrests, the one her mum liked to sit on. Her mum said it was a chair with memories. Lyssa remembered her Dad offered to varnish or paint it. He said it would make it look even better, but her mum had refused.

Her mum was often like that, always knew what she liked, even if it was something no one else would want.

"Do you want a drink?" His black eyes narrowed, and his forehead creased together like corrugated iron.

Lyssa didn't want to speak, but she was desperately thirsty and could hardly move her tongue. Her mum had always nagged her to keep hydrated, and she knew that if she got ill it would be difficult to run away.

"Yes," she replied.

He pulled a can from his coat pocket and held it in front of her. He sniggered. "Where are your hands?" Then he tugged roughly at the baling string. Lyssa looked at the angry welts that circled her wrists, and rubbed them to regain some feeling. She felt his heavy hands pressed against her back, and she held her breath until slowly he moved them away again. When she pulled the can's ring, the drink spurted and splashed onto her legs.

"Ha-ha-ha." He laughed loudly as though he'd invented the prank.

The drink fizzed and seeped through her skirt and in-between her legs. Lyssa shuddered. As she drank and swilled the cold fluid around, her mouth tingled. She swallowed, and continued taking long gulps until a burp rose up her throat. She let it out, long and loud. Normally, she would apologise or laugh, depending on who she was with, but she did neither of these things.

He nodded his approval and snorted. "Dirty bitch." He unravelled the string, pulled her arms back again and bound her wrists tighter than ever. "Do you know why you're here . . . Lyssa?"

She shook her head and lowered her gaze to the filthy mattress, with its pockets of thick black dust over the buttons. She thought the stripes had been green once upon a time.

"It's your Dad's fault. But I'll thank your mum for making it easy to snatch you. What was she doing?" He paused, and his brows rose, expectant. "Made my job easy." He sneered, his anger and frustration suddenly on the tip of a knife. "It's 'cus your dad... and I hate thinking about it."

Lyssa stole a glance.

He shook his head, and his eyes darted about. "He killed my dad, and stole his hard-earned cash. That's why you live in a massive fuck-off house. I saw it on TV. And your dad, what a fuckin smug bastard he is, telling the presenter how he built it. As if he'd rolled up his sleeves, got his spade out, instead of swanning around and barking out orders to his lackeys. Must've been tough for him working with his half a mil' budget, huh?"

Lyssa trembled and her stomach juddered in pain. She groaned and turned away.

"Your dad spent my dad's cash. Money that my Dad wanted to spend on us. He was going to buy us a house so we could move out of the filthy, stinking flat." His every word was spiked with bitterness and anger. "Your mum could have helped kill him too. But this is where my memory gets mixed up. I remember that copper saying it was your dad that stayed with my Dad. And I've thought about it. I don't reckon your mum's the sort to kill. But your dad is, without a doubt." His mouth had set in a knotted snarl. His fists clenched, knuckles white, and they readied to react to the slightest provocation.

Lyssa knew it was lies, every rotten word. Her parents were wonderful people. Always kind and loving. And she knew her dad could never hurt anyone. He never smacked her, or even shouted and Eve said her parents were always smacking her. No, he was wrong about her dad. But she wouldn't tell him that.

CHAPTER THIRTY-FIVE

A Stab in the Dark

As I watched Max leave, I felt detached from him in mind as well as body. My husband, whom I thought I would love until the day death separated us was not the man I'd believed him to be for all of these years. How could he have misled me all of this time? How could I have allowed myself to be so fooled by him? I knew our relationship had always been intensely physical and perhaps that had masked my judgement; had stopped me from seeing his faults or at least from properly acknowledging them.

For the moment, I remained alone in the silence of the night, to figure out what to do next. Should I sit it out, let the police do their work, which up to now I couldn't exactly fault, other than they hadn't actually managed to locate Lyssa? Or should I search for her myself. In my visions I had heard Lyssa, she'd spoken to me, and it made me wonder if I might be capable of finding her through less orthodox means.

I was desperate to hear back from Inspector Keir about the abductor's full name and possible whereabouts. My thoughts and any measures I could take ran riot in my head, and my mind grew ever more confused. I felt exhausted and struggled to link any of the strands together.

Overwhelmed, I lay on the sofa, switched on the TV and turned to the news channel. I wouldn't do anything until I'd heard from Inspector Keir. Lyssa's abduction filled the headline and they showed a radius that covered their most likely location. I wondered how they had come up with that radius. Surely he could have driven miles away by now unless there had been further sightings.

The report switched to Inspector Keir, her face drawn and pale, but her tone resilient and confident. "We're following significant leads and want to urge anyone who believes they have any information to come forwards. The family are desperate and we must act quickly to apprehend this man."

I thought, yes find him, but more importantly, find Lyssa. Why hadn't Inspector Keir emphasised that? I muted the sound. If I had the energy, I'd jump in the car and drive straight to Loch Lomond. Instead, I closed my eyes, and exhaustion shrouded my fears and tangled thoughts.

In the hazy half-light of the narrow woodland track, I couldn't tell if it was dawn or twilight. I had no concept of time and no memory of why I was there. Whatever the reason, I continued along the path, compelled, though I had no idea where it would take me. I became aware of an odd, weightless feeling, as though I was floating. I picked up pace, took long strides, and made easy work of the sharp incline. I rounded a bend in the path where the way ahead appeared clearer, and I figured the sun had risen. But, my progress suddenly faltered, and my feet sank into the mud at each step. I saw hoof prints in front of me, fresh in the wet earth. They were large, cloven and unusually spaced, one print followed by another a yard in front. What creature did they belong to? My unease mounted and I followed the unfamiliar prints. Time compressed, or stretched, and the prints led to an old stone carriage arch in front of a rundown farmhouse. I paused beneath the archway and saw the prints continued to a door, left slightly ajar. A bright shaft of light spilled onto the grass, as though it invited me to enter. I shifted position to remain hidden.

My gaze was drawn to a small upstairs window, softly lit from within. Malevolent shadows darted about and shifted across the walls and ceiling. Shrill, terrified screams spliced the silence. I knew someone needed help and I moved, but my feet were held fast. The unrelenting screams filled my ears. Then one small hand pressed against the window and when a young, terrified face appeared, a bolt of fear ripped through my heart.

'LYYYSSSAAA... LYYYSSSAAA."

My eyes flashed open and I saw the flickering light from the soundless television.

Instantly, I knew it had been no ordinary nightmare, but something that had happened, or a forewarning of what was to come. I prayed for the latter.

I ran it through in my mind and searched for clues that could help me to identify the location of the woodland, the farmhouse. Doubt edged its way in. What if it was merely a dream and my mind played cruel tricks on me? No. I suppressed the uncertainties; there was more substance to it. It felt entirely different to my usual dreams; it had been more lifelike and tangible.

If the police believed that Lyssa was near Loch Lomond, then it seemed logical that the woodland and farm from my dream were there too. I had walked in that area several times, hiked through too many woods and forests to place them individually, but all occasions had been during my childhood or time at University. The connection, of course, was Roy Simpson and Benn Arum, but in my mind I couldn't recall that I'd walked the same path or seen the same woods and farmhouse as they appeared in my nightmare. Yet that fateful hike had been twenty years ago. I could vaguely picture the inside of the pub but not the name of it. I could visualise the hostel, but I couldn't remember the name of the village? That was a good place to start. I thought back to the first night Max and I slept together, but the name of the campsite eluded me? Had it been the same village where the police had found my car? Damn, it was too long ago.

Over the years, whenever I walked a route I had ensured I carried the relevant Ordnance Survey map. I went to the bookshelf, climbed the ladder and located two maps for the area. I recalled our weekend at Benn Arum, that first momentous weekend with Max. I would never forget that hike, that death, that night together. Both maps included Benn Arum and I unfolded one and lay it out on the floorboards. I leaned in and traced my finger over Benn Arum and the surrounding villages and houses that clustered around them. There were more than I remembered. That area always seemed so wild and expansive. Youth Hostels narrowed down the name of the village, and more importantly, the start of our walk that day. There were three in the area. I switched on the iPad, and found Google maps. I soon located the three Youth Hostels. I tapped one of the YHA symbols, which linked me to its web page. The Hostel, a red brick building with a large timber annexe, didn't look remotely familiar. I returned to Google maps and tapped another Hostel symbol and again it linked me to its webpage. I zoomed in. I stared at the familiar large and attractive double-fronted stone house with a grey, slate tiled roof, more reminiscent of a four-star country hotel than basic accommodation in shared dormitories. In the photo, I saw a beautiful display of purple wisteria in full bloom. Tippelin, the village where we had begun our fateful hike.

I was certain now and surely by no twist of fate, only a short distance from Arrochar, where they'd found my abandoned car. I studied the map and noticed a few footpaths and bridleways that headed up Benn Arum. There were extensive areas of woodland and two farms a mile or so apart - Edge Farm and Deeren Farm which echoed my dream. Deeren Farm looked nearer to the village and on a more direct route towards the summit. Perhaps Roy Simpson had lived there and the farm belonged to the family. The more I stared at it, the more convinced I became. Something clicked into place and I knew what I had to do.

On the sideboard, the fluorescent numbers on the DAB radio said four forty-six am, and Max still hadn't returned. Not that I was keen to see him; quite the opposite. With no intention of waiting for his return I went silently to the bedroom, lifted my rucksack off the hook on the back of the door, and shoved a fleece and T-shirt into it. I put on my coat and boots, then returned to the kitchen and collected food supplies, water, an inhaler and emergency asthma steroid tablets. Finally, I wrote a note which explained my intention to find Lyssa and not to try to stop me. I leaned it conspicuously against the tall pepper grinder in the middle of the table. Ready to leave, I paused in the doorway, spun around and went to the knife rack and picked out a small sharp blade. I'd never used a knife for self-protection and I hoped to God nothing would make me resort to using it. I shivered at the thought, but knew that if Lyssa's life depended on it, I wouldn't hesitate for a second. I grabbed Dad's keys from the sideboard, let myself out and shut the door softly behind me.

CHAPTER THIRTY-SIX

Treading Softly

"I might not hurt you if you do all I tell you to do." He watched Lyssa closely. "And if your dad loves you enough to do what I tell him to. Understand?"

Lyssa nodded. What did he want her to do? She couldn't tidy her room, clean out the rabbit or brush her teeth. She took slow breaths and tried to think happy thoughts.

"My feet are tired and I want you to massage them." He stood close and Lyssa felt his breath on her face. "I'll untie your hands. You'd like that, wouldn't you?"

She looked at the floorboards, and wished she was at school with Eve and Jules, talking about the ponies at the riding school or the play they were doing that term.

He pressed a filthy finger beneath her chin and lifted her head. "I said, if you do everything I want, then I won't hurt you. Understand?"

She looked away but he pinched her chin and forced her to hold his gaze.

"I need to eat," she said.

It was true. She didn't have the strength to touch anything, least of all his feet. The thought alone made her tummy twist into painful knots.

"For fuck sake," he said, and kicked the bed.

"Sorry." Lyssa recoiled and knocked her head against the wall. She clutched her head and cried.

He stormed from the room and banged the door behind him.

Two minutes later he returned and dangled a bag of Maltesers in front of her. He tore open the bag, lifted it to his face and inhaled deeply.

"Open up" he instructed.

The choking smell of sweat and rancid breath drifted up her nostrils and lingered on her tongue, like the vapours from a rotting animal carcass. She noticed black filth trapped beneath his fingernails. But, she gazed at the chocolate and it made her mouth ache and salivate. She felt torn between a surge of revulsion and a need to eat. He placed one in her mouth, and his finger lingered on her bottom lip. Lyssa held back an urge to bite him, and drew away and closed her mouth over the chocolate. With each chocolate she felt guilty and knew she should have refused, but also knew she could not. Her parents' words of warning about never accepting sweets from strangers rang in her ears. She hoped they would understand.

He grabbed a handful of chocolates and stuffed them into his mouth. As he chewed, the noise of his slapping lips filled the room. Saliva and chocolate dribbled from the corners of his mouth.

He folded over the top of the bag and stuffed them in his jacket pocket. "You'll have to earn the others and we'll start with that foot massage." He removed her hand ties.

"And don't try anything on, or I'll wallop you with my belt." He rubbed his hands together in anticipation. "A good thrashing never did me any harm. Dad hit me and it taught me discipline. Your mum or dad smack you and your brother then - or each other?"

"No," she said. "They don't believe in corporal punishment. They think if they smack us, we might smack someone else."

"Well, well, well." He laughed and revealed the gaps in his teeth. "I only smack someone if they deserve it... Lyssa. And I've done worse than smacking."

He sat beside her, removed his trainers and socks and rolled up his jeans. He lifted his feet onto the bed and took Lyssa's hands in his. Lyssa wanted only to pull her hands away and rub them on the mattress to remove his touch, but her strength dissolved. His hairy feet disgusted her. They weren't like her dad's or Louis' and even more strange were the scaly toenails that curled over the tips of his toes like hermit shells.

"Our feet link to different parts of our body. So if you massage my feet it's like you're massaging me all over." He smiled a crooked smile. "I saw it on TV. There are massage parlours where you can get it done but it's pricey. We'll try. You've gotta move your hands."

Lyssa's hands trembled. He grasped her wrists and dragged her hands back and forth over his feet and up his legs. He had a crazed look in his eyes and rolled his head back and forth, his breath heavy. A burning fear bubbled within Lyssa and threatened to overwhelm her. But a sense of disgust and anger took over and she curled her fingers and scraped her nails across his skin as hard as she could. He lifted his head sharply, jumped off the bed and stormed from the room. Lyssa heard another door slam nearby.

She glanced at the open door. Desperate, she tugged and pinched at the knots to loosen the string around her ankles. She heard a door open and footsteps again. She froze. He appeared in the doorway, shut the door and thundered down the stairs. This was her chance; there was nothing to stop her, as long as the door was unlocked.

A floorboard groaned as she tiptoed to the door. She turned the handle and the latch clicked open. She slipped her head through, and saw a long corridor with a low ceiling. A door led off it and daylight spilled through onto the threadbare carpet and faded floral wallpaper. She saw the stairs to her left.

Her heart pounded. She must be brave and do all she could to get away. The thought of what he would do to her gave her the courage. Her fingers rested on the handrail and she stepped quietly down the stairs to the darkened hallway below; the front door a few feet away. A clatter of furniture nearby made her race to the door. She turned the handle.

"What the hell are you doing?" He grabbed her hair and dragged her back across the hall.

She stumbled and fell to her knees but he seized her arm and yanked her back up, hard.

Lyssa screamed. "Stop! Please…"

He jerked her head. "Shut that mouth."

At the bedroom doorway he shoved her into the room and locked the door behind her. She fell onto the hard, wooden floor and lay still and stunned. Blood dripped from her nose and there was a sickly, metallic taste on her tongue. Carefully, she stood up and stumbled to the bed. Then she cried - for her bleeding nose, for missing her parents, but mostly from fear of what might happen.

Whatever the reason he had taken her, she had to get away before he hurt her, or worse. She wept into the sleeve of her cardigan and thought about home. And she pictured her bedroom with her pony posters and photographs on the wall, her favourite teddy and her warm, soft bed with its brightly coloured duvet and pillow. She imagined lying on her bed at home, her head sinking into the pillow and her mother calling to her.

"Lyssa, it's Mummy. Can you hear me?"

"I hear you Mummy," she whispered.

CHAPTER THIRTY-SEVEN

Money Problems

Max sat on one side of the interview table, and opposite sat Inspector Keir and Detective Brooks. Their eyes burned into him and he felt the leaden weight of their attention.

"You know why you're here don't you Max?" Inspector Keir spoke without her usual warmth.

Max nodded.

"Speak up Max, we're recording the interview," Detective Brooks cut in, his tone dry.

"Yes, I know why. But this won't help Lyssa. You should be out there searching for this maniac," Max said. "I'm not the one holding her. I've tried everything to contact him - to meet him. But he's ignoring all my messages."

"Trust me, we have plenty of officers out there doing their utmost to find your daughter. But we need to establish precisely what it is that you know." Detective Brooks rested his elbows on the table and made a steeple with his fingertips. "You want us to find her, don't you Max?"

"Of course I do."

Detective Brooks eyes didn't waver. "It's been two days now, and I don't need to remind you that acting swiftly is key. The longer Lyssa is with him, the higher the likelihood of her coming to some sort of harm. Am I making myself clear?"

"I would hardly call two days acting swiftly. Could we just get on with it?" said Max.

"Our point exactly. Two days ago you should have informed us of everything that you knew," replied Inspector Keir. "However, moving on. Is this your phone?" She placed Max's phone on the table.

"You know it is." Max reached to pick it up, but Inspector Keir retrieved it.

"And how did you and he exchange messages?"

"Email. My work email."

"He's never phoned, texted, messaged on Facebook?" she asked.

"He hasn't got my number."

"But he found your email address, and there are ways."

"Have you deleted any of the messages?" asked Detective Brooks.

"I don't think so."

"So are you saying you might have deleted some?"

"Unless it was by mistake then I haven't."

"Would you show me where the messages are?" said Detective Brooks, and he slid the phone across to Max.

"He first emailed at the beginning of April, and he kept messaging, one every couple of days. I always replied," Max said, returning the phone.

Detective Brooks and Inspector Keir read the messages for several minutes. Every so often they exchanged incredulous looks.

Inspector Keir tore a sheet of paper from her pad, and placed it with a pen in front of Max. "I want your login details for Facebook."

"Why? He's hardly going to be a friend," said Max, and snatched up the pen.

"I'm going to hand your phone to my comms officer," she continued. "We'll see what intelligence we can gather."

As Inspector Keir left the interview room, Detective Brooks watched Max. The two men remained silent until she returned.

"I have information on Roy who died . . . while in your presence," said Inspector Keir. "We're running a full check on him and his son. And, I'm sorry to tell you, Max, that his one son, Corey, is already on police radar." She paused. "Although he isn't a convicted paedophile, he was arrested last September for pestering children in his hometown Cumbernauld, Glasgow. He shared alcohol and drugs with the youngsters. And we know of one fourteen-year-old girl he invited to his flat. Fortunately for the child, her mother found out about the arranged meeting and reported him."

Unable to contain his anger, Max stood abruptly and slammed his palm onto the table. "I'll kill him..."

"You must understand the consequences of your actions Max, your delay in coming forward with this crucial information, and the impact it's now having on your daughter - on your family."

"I need..." Max's voice cracked, 'I need water." He turned away.

Inspector Keir sighed. "I'll go."

"Max, please sit down?" said Detective Brooks. "Are you sure you've never spoken with this Corey? We are running a check on your calls, office and landlines too."

"No I haven't," Max replied through gritted teeth and sat back down.

Inspector Keir returned and set a plastic cup on the table.

Max drank it back and slowly crushed the cup in his hand.

"Another thing I'm surprised about is that you hadn't considered the potential for this sort of development." Detective Brooks tapped his pen lightly on the edge of the table. "I'm at a loss as to why you didn't mention such vital details sooner. I can't imagine Katriina withholding any information that could lead us to Lyssa. I'm sure she's wondering why you'd deliberately mislead us."

"Yes, I know," said Max. "Katriina won't forgive me, and who can blame her."

"I understand why Corey is out to get you and your family, but you're not off the hook. You stole a huge sum of money, and for all we know you finished Roy off, to ensure you could keep it." He paused. "Am I right?"

"I only wanted to help him," said Max.

"I'm also wondering if you already knew Roy. Knew about the stash of money and that he would be up Benn Arum when you were. The reason I'm wondering is because we've run a detailed check on you and your family, and more specifically, your father. As you are aware, your father is no stranger to money problems, and I'm hazarding a guess that these issues have had repercussions for you and your outlook on money."

"It doesn't follow that I'm a criminal does it, just because my dad was?"

"But you are, Max? I'm not getting through to you am I? You're still in denial. I hate to break this to you, but you did steal the money, money that wasn't yours to take. Stealing makes you a criminal. You have no idea where it came from – dealing drugs, someone's hard earned life savings. He sat back in his chair and folded his arms.

Max cleared his throat and spoke steadily. "When I found the bag, I brought it to Roy, tried to talk about it. He woke up and grabbed me. I pushed him off, and I think he fell backwards. His head was already badly injured when we found him though. Ask Katriina."

"I believe Max, that when you found the money you were only thinking how lucky you were and how much you wanted to keep it. I also believe you knew that if Roy recovered, you'd have no chance of keeping it. I think the minute you found it you began to imagine what you could, would do with it," he said, and held Max's gaze.

"It wasn't like that."

"But it was Max. Otherwise you would have handed over the money straight away. Wouldn't you?" The authoritative tone of his voice left no room for argument.

"I didn't think that at the time, but . . ." Max held his gaze, and twisted his wedding ring.

"It's a straightforward case of a man in denial Max, and I've seen it time and time again in people just like you. Often highly educated professionals, hopelessly self-seeking in the pursuit of their own selfish ambitions, profoundly arrogant and just as deeply flawed," Detective Brooks said calmly, and then dropped his hand onto the table, like a judge striking his gavel on the courtroom desk. He'd delivered his verdict.

"OK, this is a matter for the courts." Inspector Keir shut her folder and pushed back her chair. "You can rest assured there will be a full investigation into Roy's death as well as the money, where it came from and what you've done with it since. For now, we need to focus on Lyssa. You will remain with us. We will use your phone, with your help when needed and we'll start by trying to bring about an email conversation with Corey. See if we can find out where he's hiding, and hopefully Lyssa, too."

"I can't stay here," Max said, and got up to leave. "I need to be with Katriina and Louis. They need my help. At least let me call her?"

"I think you've already done more than enough to help, don't you, Max?" Detective Brooks replied evenly.

"But I have to make things right."

"You can still try. You're our strongest link to Corey, to Lyssa. Are you prepared to do what it takes to find him…Lyssa?"

"I'll do anything. But I can't do anything shut in here. You haven't arrested me."

"Not yet we haven't," said Inspector Keir, before she turned to leave.

Lost for words, Max fell silent.

"Good boy," said Detective Brooks. "We'll come back when we need you."

CHAPTER THIRTY-EIGHT

Tippelin

Dawn broke as I set off driving and subtle streaks of violet and pink undulated and lit up the sky above Loch Dubh and Applecross, and gave them a surreal, dreamlike appearance. Within minutes, the sunrise created an even more dramatic sky, slashed through with vivid shades of red, which burnished the crests and valleys of the hillsides. Although it dazzled, I knew it didn't bode well for decent weather. I pleaded for the elements to be kind, for I knew how storms, mist and rain could make walking in the hills so much tougher.

Wide awake now in the unambiguous daylight, I convinced myself that what I'd experienced hadn't only been a nightmare, but something tangible, something that would lead me to Lyssa. I would have liked to ask for help from the police, but I knew they wouldn't take a dream seriously. Even to me it sounded ludicrous and hardly a convincing piece of evidence. But something else drove me too. I felt so hurt and betrayed by Max that in my quest there was a part of me that wanted to be far away from him. I was angry and I didn't care if they'd arrested him and locked him up. As far as I was concerned he deserved it.

Thankfully, my hormones remained low, and despite the occasional wave of nausea, I didn't think I'd succumb to sickness. One hour in and the previous snapshot of the resplendent sunrise had given way to a typical misty and murky Highland morning. I switched the radio to the local channel and when the news came on it focussed on Lyssa and the latest developments. At least she was still headline news and hadn't been pushed aside by other stories.

The newscaster said, "Police are urging the public close to Arrochar and Loch Lomond especially, but also throughout the UK, to remain vigilant and to ring the helpline if they see or hear anything suspicious. The investigation is now following significant leads in the area."

As the news ended, Dad's phone rang. I grappled around in my rucksack, but by the time I'd located it, it had stopped. A ping indicated a voicemail. Just moments later, it rang again. I glanced down and saw it was our landline. Mum had found my note, and there wasn't anything else I could tell them right now. Besides, if I stopped to make calls, it would slow me down and I knew they'd only try to discourage me from taking unnecessary risks. Another voicemail arrived. The phone's charge had run low and I powered it off.

The quiet time allowed me some respite to think things through. Deceased Roy Simpson and his deranged son, Max's terrible deceit, everything that happened previously and was happening now. It slowly sank in, and despite feeling sick with fear for what Lyssa was going through, I felt more in control than I had since it had all began.

I continued onwards through Inchnadamph, Ullapool, and Drumnadrochit but I felt dangerously heavy-eyed, and stopped at a roadside garage. As I paid for a coffee, I noticed a young assistant staring at me. Her eyes were thick with lurid make-up.

"I hope you don't mind me asking," she said. "Are you Lyssa's mum, the girl on the news?"

"Ummm, yes," I said, disarmed by her insensitivity.

"What's the latest news?" And without waiting for a reply. "It breaks my heart to think of what he could have done to her. I'm sorry for you... for Lyssa." And she held up her phone to take my photo.

I backed away. "I can't talk."

"I hope she's OK and you find her," she called.

I head for the exit.

I started the car, pressed my foot hard on the accelerator and turned onto the main road. The screech of tyres filled the car. Fierce tears blinded my eyes and I pulled into the kerbside. I had to be right. I couldn't doubt myself or what I was doing. I remembered the calls I'd had and knew I should check my messages. I couldn't afford to miss a piece of vital news. There were several missed calls and three voice messages.

The first message was from Dad. His voice sounded strained. "Katriina, I hope you know what you're doing. We'll call if we hear anything. We love you."

I wiped my eyes and blew my nose.

The second was from Max.

"Kat, I can't come home right now. Inspector Keir thinks I can help get in touch with Roy's son. His name is Corey. Call me when you get this. Please, Kat, it's important."

The third message was from Inspector Keir.

"Katriina, I know what you're trying to do, but you should leave this to the police. We know who he is and you cannot tackle him alone. He isn't at his home address, and we've checked all other likely locations. This man is extremely dangerous."

I snorted at her final comment.

Such words from a senior police officer was stating the bloody obvious. A child abductor was hardly going to be the sort to invite me in for a spot of afternoon tea, I thought. But I felt more confident about taking things into my own hands and I drove on with added resolve.

I turned to Radio 4 for the national news, but instead a drama about domestic violence had started. I listened for a minute or two before I switched off. The caffeine kicked in and worked its mini-miracle, and I felt re-energized as I continued along the rolling roads through Fort Augustus, Fort William, and Glencoe. Unlike previous occasions, I didn't pull over to admire the magnificent landscapes or take photographs.

With a sense of hope I finally drove through Tippelin and pulled onto the grassy verge in front of the youth hostel. The wall of wisteria greeted me, green but not yet in full bloom. My overnight stay with the walking group twenty years ago came flooding back, with its terrible and wonderful events. Looking at the building now, I even recalled that the upstairs sash window on the right was the same room I shared with the other girls. I could never have anticipated revisiting the same place under such dissimilar circumstances.

The garden, with its lush, striped lawn, sloped smoothly down to the road on both sides of the short gravelled drive, with a low stone wall that separated it from the verge. Dying daffodils sat amidst brightly tipped tulips in the narrow borders that ran the perimeter of the lawns. Mature trees with burgeoning foliage of olive, khaki and bottle greens stood proudly either side of the hostel, and for a moment I returned to that momentous weekend.

A peculiar tranquillity descended. I'd expected sirens or police officers in the village. I thought I'd see them knock on doors, talk to residents, but there was nothing like the hands on, investigative scenes you see on the news.

I stepped out of the car and felt a strong sense of precision. This was the place to start.

I still hoped to locate the same track we had hiked up all those years ago. I unfolded my map. The area had so many tracks, footpaths and bridle paths. A woman with long grey hair cycled down the road towards me and a small black dog sat in the wicker basket that hung on the handlebars. As she neared, she freewheeled, slowed down and smiled in greeting. For a second she looked as if she was going to stop, and I noticed how the dog's gaze mirrored the woman's exactly, before their eyes returned to the road ahead once they had passed me by.

Benn Arum reared up before me like a dangerous wild and dark stallion, its presence formidable and made more so by dense clouds that mushroomed and masked its summit. I estimated it to be a couple of kilometres of gentle slopes before I reached the steeper inclines that led to its rocky summit. Areas of forest and smaller woods swathed the foothills, and although I couldn't see any farms, the OS map showed that Deeren Farm lay amidst woodland.

I focused in on my pencilled area. A footpath approximately a kilometre further up the lane, which appeared to take a rounded but relatively direct route to Deeren Farm, the farm nearest to the village. The map also showed a long farm track that led up to the farmhouse. Studying it, I realised the track might be a quicker and easier way to reach the farm, but if I took that route, it would be difficult to approach it discreetly or to hide if he came towards me unexpectedly. I couldn't afford to risk making any careless mistakes that might cause him to become impulsive or violent. I didn't want to jeopardise Lyssa's safety. I got back in the car and set off in search of a quiet spot to park.

CHAPTER THIRTY-NINE

The Beast Within

Lyssa tried to work out how long she'd been locked in the room. Was it two, or three days?

The cruel deprivation she faced, the lack of light, exhaustion, hunger and thirst all conspired to heighten her confusion. It seemed like forever since the morning; each hour felt like an eternity, as every agonising minute limped painfully on to the next.

With both hands and feet free, she picked up the chair. It felt heavy in her grasp, but she could raise it above her head. She thought about waiting by the door, listening out for him coming up the stairs and then bringing the chair down hard on his head. It would knock him out and she could run away. She set the chair beneath the window, stepped up and looked outside properly for the first time. She pulled the window latch, but found it stuck solid with age old paint. She thought that if she smashed the panes of glass and small wooden frames, she could climb down a drainpipe, or even jump.

She noticed a large outbuilding a short distance away with a broken corrugated roof. The machinery within looked old, rusty and disused. The spring grass grew long, and branches and dead leaves lay strewn about. If it was the garden it was wild and overgrown, unloved, and looked as though it had been that way for a long time. The lush grass gave way to prickly gorse bushes, tall bracken and undergrowth, then a high stone wall with a carriage arch. Beyond the wall stood a fortification of trees, and further still stretched remote, shadowy moorland and a monster of a mountain. Where was the road? Lyssa fought back her disappointment, but she figured that the trees would make a good hiding place when she escaped. She stood still and listened. It seemed quiet - too quiet.

As though he'd heard her thoughts, a key turned in the lock, and the door swung open. He looked at the empty bed then saw her on the chair.

"Get off there."

Lyssa stepped off and backed into the corner.

"Why hasn't your dad paid up?" he demanded. "Doesn't he want you back? Is it 'cus you're a pain in the backside?" He grabbed the chair and launched it across the room.

She glanced at the open doorway and edged nearer. He caught her eye, slammed it shut and pulled her over to the bed. "I might've given you more chocolate, but you've been disobedient and I've eaten them all," he said. "Got some water. Don't want you dying on me yet." He unscrewed the lid of a plastic bottle and gave it to her.

Without hesitation, Lyssa drank, but it tasted strange. "What is it?"

"Squash. There wasn't much and that's why it tastes funny."

She drank again.

"That's enough," he said, and snatched the bottle.

He picked up the chair and sat down, spread his knees wide and looked at Lyssa with threatening eyes. Every now and then, he tilted his head from side to side and rubbed his hands over the top of his thighs.

An unfamiliar sensation began to creep through Lyssa. Her vision blurred and she felt as though she was floating. His eyes bored into her as she lay down, curled up and tucked her hands beneath her chin.

"A good feeling, isn't it?" he said.

"What is it?" she asked, as the room turned slowly.

"Vodka."

Water, juice, now vodka, she thought. She'd seen it in the drinks cabinet at home. Only recently, Louis had gone through the different bottles with her and pointed out the alcohol percentage content of each. There were bottles of lager, Guinness, wine, vodka, whisky. She remembered them all and recalled Louis telling her he could have a glass of lager or Guinness now and again, but nothing stronger as it would make him sick. Her mum and dad let Louis have a small glass of something with his meal on special occasions, and without lecturing him, they'd have a conversation about sensible drinking habits. Her parents didn't always have sensible drinking habits though. She recalled last Christmas Eve, when her parents had too much to drink and were laughing hysterically and being silly, like kids. They were playing charades and her Dad was doing a mime for a James Bond film and had fallen over the back of the sofa making her Mum cry with laughter. It was quite funny at the time, but then Lyssa decided she much preferred them when they were behaving like proper grown-ups.

Lyssa grew sleepier, and as the seconds passed her eyes became scratchy and heavy. She surrendered to the sensations that swirled around her and fell quickly into oblivion, unable to feel her physical surroundings. She could neither see nor hear the beast in the room. At first she dreamt of home, her mummy, daddy, and Louis. Then her loving family vanished, and she felt troubled and disturbed by recent memories.

She looked through the window and saw a log fire that burned in the clearing below, and the bright flames climbed and licked at the night's shadowy blackness. She heard the snap and crack of twigs and the undergrowth moved and rustled. A monstrous, muscular creature moved into the clearing. The half-man, half-beast's fiery eyes scoured the trees and buildings for something. Lyssa withdrew to avoid the beast's gaze. It circled the fire, slowly at first. Then it moved faster – it twisted and turned and lurched from side to side, its arms and face raised aloft. Then, just as suddenly, it ceased its frenzied movements, and knelt down before the fire. It placed its colossal hands on the ground and arched its back up and down in powerful motions. Lyssa tried to turn away, to step back, but her feet were held fast. The beast snorted and grunted. Its voice grew loud and guttural and the vibrations reverberated through the floorboards upon which she stood and made them shudder violently. She grabbed hold of the windowsill to prevent herself from surrendering to the noise. The beast let out a final deafening scream, and its head rotated grotesquely. Its eyes burned as it stared up at the window, straight at Lyssa. She screamed.

Lyssa's eyes flickered and opened, and the room came into focus; the bare floorboards, the small window, and the labyrinth of cracks on the walls, and ceiling. He sat at the foot of the bed with his back against the wall and his heavy lidded eyes upon her.

"Jean looked like you. Big round eyes. She was a proper pain in the arse sometimes, screamed the place down at night, woke me up. Night terrors, Mum called them. But, mostly she was good to have around. I remember Mum taking us to the park most days. There was a tree perfect for climbing, and on tip-toes, I could reach the lowest branch. I'd climb up high and look out. I could see people, but they couldn't see me." He paused and caught Lyssa's eye. "When Jean started school she got the flu. The doctor said it was a cold, that she didn't need antibiotics. A right tosser he turned out to be." He cleared his throat and launched a ball of spit onto the floor. "Jean kept coughing, over and over. One night I woke up and Mum and Dad were screaming. Dad was on the floor, holding Jean. She was lying there all limp and white. Jean liked it when I tickled her, so I tried, but Dad screamed and shoved me off." He fell silent and chewed his thumb.

Lyssa watched the blood bubble up and dribble down his thumb.

"Mum was never the same after Jean died. She stayed in her room and Dad couldn't do anything right. Mum couldn't go to work. Things turned bad without Jean. That's why Dad wanted to sort it for us. Thought the money would help Mum get back to being normal."

Lyssa turned on her side and stared at the wall.

"Then one day, Dad came back from work and was really happy. He was laughing, singing and dancing along to stuff on the telly. When Mum went for her bath, Dad told me he'd got hold of some cash, that it was all legit' and there was thousands - tens of thousands. I had to promise not to tell, not even Mum. Dad said he was gonna surprise her, buy a car, a house, take us to Disneyland. Mum had always dreamed of going. I asked him if he'd won on the horses, but he said all I needed to know was that it was his money." He spotted the dripping blood and sucked it away. "But days later my Dad was dead. Murdered."

He prodded Lyssa in the back, but she pretended to be asleep.

She yearned for her family. She thought about her friends – they would be wondering why she wasn't at school. She never took a day off, unless the snow became so bad their lane was impassable. Was it Saturday? Lyssa loved weekends because Dad was home and they sometimes hired a motorboat at Loch Glencoul or went on a pony trek over Applecross Moor. She wondered again if he was going to do something terrible and she would never see her Mum, Dad or Louis again.

She sucked her fingers and cried quietly.

CHAPTER FORTY

Louis

"What do you mean she's gone to find Lyssa? How does she know where she is?" Max asked Anna over the phone.

"I don't know. I was up at six and found the note," replied Anna.

"Why didn't you ring me?"

"We didn't know where you were. Gordon rang the station. Didn't the Inspector tell you?"

"No, or I'd have known wouldn't I?" replied Max.

"How did you get to the station?" asked Anna. "Your car's here."

"I . . . the police offered to drive me as I'd had a drink and couldn't risk it."

"Oh, I see." Anna heard the hesitancy in his voice.

"Can you try ringing Kat? Has she still got Gordon's mobile?"

"I'm assuming she's taken it and yes we'll try her again."

"If you speak, please ask her to ring me? It's important. Please, Anna."

"Of course. And you'll be doing the same?"

"When I can. I'm scared, this man is extremely dangerous. I can't begin to explain."

"For crying out loud Max, I know he is. He's abducted Lyssa," Anna said, and finally lost her patience.

Anna knew Max was hiding something. She also knew Katriina wouldn't disappear in the middle of the night to search for Lyssa without telling him, unless she had good reason to. They'd rung Katriina, but there was no connection. She was probably out of range. Anna wished Katriina would call if only to reassure them that she was OK. Lyssa missing was beyond terrifying without Katriina turning vigilante.

"Gran, where's Mum and Dad?" Louis' face looked drawn as he walked into the kitchen.

"Come here my darling, let me explain." Anna held out her hand.

"You were on the phone. Was it Dad?"

"Please, Louis."

He took her hand. "Tell me, Gran."

She passed him the note, and his hands trembled as he read.

"What's she doing? Where's Dad?"

"He's at the station. He went last night because he wanted to find out what was happening. Your mum left after him."

"I don't get it. Why would Mum go without Dad, or without waking us?"

"I know it's worrying, Louis, but I think she wants to be doing more. I trust her, she's sensible. She obviously thinks she knows something that can help. And I know she'll be in touch soon."

"Has she got Grandad's phone?"

"Yes. Grandad tried ringing, but you know what reception's like."

Louis began to cry and Anna held him and fought against her own spiralling emotions.

"It's OK my love. This is a terrible time for all of us, but we have to try to stay calm. We'll have breakfast then we'll ring your mum again."

Anna took Louis' hand and led him to the table. She busied herself retrieving bowls and cereal boxes from the cupboards.

"Got through to Kat?" asked Gordon, as he walked into the kitchen.

"Not yet. I know she'll call when she can." Anna gave Gordon a meaningful glare before she glanced back at Louis.

Louis sat at the table and flicked through his phone.

Anna touched Gordon's shoulder. "Will you log into your iPad for me? I want to check something."

"Aye, but you know the password."

"It wasn't working," she said, and nodded to the door.

"I don't want the iPad." Anna closed the bedroom door. "There's something going on with Max. I've just spoken to him, and he says he went to the station in the middle of the night. The police came and picked him up. He says he went to be closer to developments. Kat left after him to go on Lyssa's trail alone. She didn't even tell Max

210

she was going and when I spoke to him, he said Inspector Keir hadn't let him know about Kat either. You did tell the Inspector?"

Gordon frowned, thinking. "Aye, and she hadn't known about Kat either. I thought it was odd."

"I'm telling you, Gordon, Max is involved in this."

"Now hold on, Anna. Max is the best dad I know. Look what he does for those children, and Katriina has never complained has she?"

"Well no, that's true."

"In fact, quite the opposite," he continued. "She's always singing his praises. You know how upfront Kat is. I don't think she could hide anything important even if she wanted to."

"That's what I can't understand."

"Though it is puzzling not telling Max what she was up to." He sat down on the end of the bed as he tried to frame his thoughts.

"I'm frightened, Gordon. What if this monster gets Katriina too?" said Anna, crying.

Gordon got up and took Anna's hands. "Perhaps they had a row and that's why they're not talking. The stress they're under is unimaginable. Though you'd have thought they'd pull together under the circumstances."

"I don't understand how Katriina thinks she can find Lyssa. If the police don't know, how can she?"

"I don't know." Gordon wrapped his arms around Anna and held her tight. Finally, he drew back. "Come on, we must get back to Louis. That lad needs all the support he can get."

CHAPTER FORTY-ONE

Serena

Gordon and Anna walked into the kitchen to find Louis leaning against the range and hunched over his phone. His thick mop of dark hair hung over his eyes, and masked his expression. Anna noticed his uneaten breakfast.

"Sweetheart, would you prefer something cooked? How about some of your Grandad's scrambled eggs?"

Louis didn't reply but flicked his fringe off his face and stared at his phone, distracted and troubled by what he was reading.

Anna put a hand on his shoulder. "Are you OK?"

"No I'm not." He hesitated, then drew a breath. "I've had a message from a girl who's seen my Facebook appeal. She knows this sicko." Louis spoke through his tears. "She swears it's him. I could hardly read it, but she says it's all true, and she's going to ring the police." He passed the phone to Anna.

Anna read aloud. "Louis, my name is Serena Chalmers. This man is called Corey. I met him last July, and he's a paedophile. Lyssa is in danger, but you'll know that. I haven't told anyone what happened to me because I'm ashamed. As I write I am shaking and crying. I'm fourteen but was thirteen when it happened."

Gordon moved and stood with Anna and Louis.

Anna continued reading. "He asked me if I knew the time when I was walking home from my friend's house. He started chatting about stuff - asked me my name, where did I go to school. He seemed nice, and I thought he was good looking. I think I was flattered. He told me he lived nearby, and would I like to come and have a cup of tea. I knew Mum wouldn't be back from work and decided I'd go but not stay long. I like sugar in my tea, and he put lots in, too sweet but OK. He put the TV on and sat close to me but didn't touch me or anything. He asked about my family and friends, what music I was into. Then he showed me some horrible porn on his phone, and I began to feel sleepy and I must have passed out.

When I woke up, it was dark outside, and I was on his bed. I felt sick and sleepy. He asked me if I'd enjoyed myself. I could hardly speak, and I didn't feel right. My clothes were all over the place, and I felt sore."

Anna stopped reading, clasped a hand over her mouth, and stifled a sob.

Gordon tore off a sheet of kitchen towel, placed it in her hand and put a loving arm around her.

"This is hideous." Anna blew her nose. "You shouldn't be hearing this."

"I've read it, Gran. He's sick and we'll have to tell the police. Do you think she's already told them? She sent it last night."

"We can't assume she has or will. I'll ring Inspector Keir," said Gordon.

Anna nodded and they continued reading in silence.

"He helped me up and gave me water. I didn't want to drink, but my mouth was so dry. I sorted out my clothes and told him mum would be wondering where I was. He said I could go, but I shouldn't tell anyone, that they wouldn't understand our relationship. He said we'd meet up soon. I was desperate to leave so I said it would be OK. I walked home feeling terrible. Mum screamed at me, said I'd been with a boy, what had I done with him? I ran to my room and Mum didn't say anything else."

"I knew he'd raped me. I should have told Mum, the police, but I blamed myself for being stupid and going to his flat in the first place. I've been warned so many times about strange men, what they might do, but I was stupid enough to think he liked me, that he wanted to be my friend. He's evil, and I pray you find your sister. Sometimes I feel grateful that he didn't kill me, so maybe he isn't that evil, I don't know. I was scared I'd get pregnant, but thank God I didn't. I won't tell you how I've been feeling inside ever since. Tell the police. I'm going to. They need to know, for Lyssa's sake."

"Have you seen her photo, what Serena looks like?" said Louis, through his tears. "She looks like Lyssa, and so young, just a kid."

"Oh Louis, my love," said Anna, and embraced him. "You need a hug. We all do."

213

Anna, Gordon, and Louis held onto one another and wept. They wept with fear for Lyssa and what she might be going through, wept with pity for Serena who had shared her terrible experience, but most of all they wept for themselves, because there seemed to be no end to the nightmare.

CHAPTER FORTY-TWO

Deep Water

Under the circumstances, I was about as prepared as I could be. My rucksack held a few basic supplies and the knife was hidden safely in my coat pocket. Although, if I needed to use it, I prayed I'd have the courage to.

I parked the car in an empty layby at the edge of a small loch and consulted my map. The well-trodden footpath followed the shoreline of the loch for a few hundred yards, and I passed behind a long line of wind-bent Scots Pine trees on the edge of a narrow stony beach, which leaned over the water like old men gazing down at their reflections. I clambered over a laddered stile, and even though the path petered out, the map showed the route veered left. I walked on and passed a herd of highland cattle that grazed a short distance away. A hefty bull raised its head and stared at me, and I quickened my pace. The long-horned creatures must have been used to hikers and he soon continued grazing, his curiosity satisfied.

As the altitude increased, the temperature dropped, and I drew up the zip of my coat. I recalled our hike up Benn Arum all those years ago, but the path didn't feel familiar. As I walked, I remembered that we'd passed a farmhouse and some aggressive dogs. Perhaps because the events of that day had been appalling and wonderful in equal measure, the memory that had sunk into my subconscious only now returned to the fore. Maybe the surroundings, the imposing sight of Benn Arum and the unspeakable fear that I might lose my daughter forever had reawakened such deeply buried memories.

I reached the top of a stretch of coarse grassland, climbed another stile, and found myself on an old farm trail. Deep wheel trenches revealed how generations of farmers had driven this way, journeying back and forth over many years and shifting seasons. I turned left, and the knife came to mind. Had I been rash to bring it? I'd heard that if anyone was foolish enough to carry a knife, then it could well be used by someone else to inflict damage on its owner. But I needed some form of self-protection, and if it could help to get Lyssa away from that sick bastard then I would keep it close. I put my hand over my pocket and traced the outline of the blade as I tried to recall any films where a knife had been used. The only scene I could dredge up was the all too obvious one with Norman Bates in *Psycho's* shower scene, as he gripped the knife and stabbed at the naked woman behind the shower curtain. We had it on DVD, and we'd watched it many times, though of course, I had never anticipated I should be garnering tips from it.

I had to be right about Lyssa being nearby. My dreams and visions, the sightings of my car, the death of Roy Simpson; everything pointed to this location. I remembered my nightmare, the forewarning, or whatever it had been. The carriage arch, the farmhouse, the darting shadows and then Lyssa's terrified face. My step faltered and I felt an excruciating ache deep in my core. I sucked my breath to steady my searing anxiety, then I set off again and doubled my pace and resolve.

The track ran level and headed towards thick woodland some way ahead. Two men came into view and strode towards me. They led two spirited dogs that pulled at their leads. As we neared one another, they talked and laughed over something. I was all set to say hello and walk on by, but they stopped.

"Afternoon. Have you been up the mountain?" asked the older man. He smiled with a glow to his cheeks.

The dogs, pretty beagles, sniffed and licked my ankles.

"Aye, I'm heading back now." I tried to sound upbeat. "I don't suppose you passed a farm?" I nodded at the woods.

"Aye, there was a farm, some way down a track," said the younger man.

"Do you live locally?" I asked, and thought he might know who lived there.

He looked wistful. "Sadly, no. I'm a city boy these days. Wish I did though."

One of the dogs whined and jumped up at me.

"Hey Leo, get down, yer brute," said the older man. He pulled the dog away and fed it a treat. "The farm is deep within the woods, but the track looked good enough. Are you going now?"

"Thought I'd take a look." I dug deep for a plausible excuse. "It belonged to my family a couple of generations back," I said. "I don't know who lives there these days. In fact, I don't know if it's inhabited. Did you spot a car or any signs of life?"

The dog jumped up again and looked at me with large brown insistent eyes.

"I didn't see any lights or vehicles. Did you Alistair?" He turned to his friend.

"No, but I wasn't really paying attention." He stroked his dog's ears.

"Leo likes you. Own a dog by any chance?"

I rubbed its back. "Just a rabbit."

"I reckon there's enough daylight. Though you wouldn't want to be down there when it gets dark, looked very remote."

"I'd better get going. Thank you. At least I know I'm heading the right way." I reached down and gave Leo a final pat as he tried to follow me.

The men didn't look like they were in a hurry to move on.

"Nice talking." I gave a reassuring smile and set off.

I heard the dog's barks and the men's goodbyes, but I didn't turn back again.

My throat tightened and my eyes stung. I pulled off my rucksack, grabbed my water and drank it straight back, then I tore open a cereal bar and ate as I walked. I felt my energy levels revive, my self-doubt evaporate, and I jogged along the middle of the track where it was most even.

As I reached the outer edge of the woods, the trail narrowed and drew me in. The long, spiny branches of the Norwegian spruces reached out to touch me, and it grew darker as daylight waned and struggled to permeate the tree canopies. The track felt familiar, though there was nothing that accounted for it. There were thousands of similar tracks all over Scotland, hundreds of which I had walked down before.

I stepped off the track and into the trees for a much needed wee. The bracken nipped as I squatted and the sound of pine needles cracked underfoot. I peered through the undergrowth and trees. Some way down I saw a faint but definite glow, and I knew it could only be coming from Deeren Farm. My map confirmed this and I continued my approach under the safe concealment of the trees, rather than take the easier but more exposed track.

Instinctively, I felt for the knife, despite there being no obvious threat of imminent danger. I remembered I hadn't turned off Dad's phone and my heart pounded. It hadn't rung or beeped in a couple of hours, and I guessed I was too far from any mobile masts. Even so, I couldn't risk it giving me away, assuming I was right about the farm. I turned it off and zipped it into my coat pocket.

Something disturbed the stillness, then a shrill cry from somewhere cleaved the silence and startled me. I spun around, senses frayed. It hadn't sounded human, and I imagined it was only an eagle or a fox out hunting. Nevertheless, I felt a heady spike of unease.

I threaded my way through the trees, onwards and ever nearer. The light appeared to ebb and flow as though it flickered. Perhaps it was candlelight and therefore no mains electricity. I heard a steady but soft rumble and I paused. It was the sound of water and within a few steps I stood at the top of a short but steep bank. I looked down at a fast-flowing burn.

There didn't appear to be a way past, so I looked for a narrow section to jump over. I walked upstream and down, but it was at least four-feet-wide at its narrowest point, too far to leap across cleanly. Maybe it wasn't too deep and I could step on a stone or branch to avoid a soaking. I scrambled down the bank and decided I had to risk it. I stood at the edge and realised it was full from recent rainfall, and impossible to judge with the water so heavily peat stained. I placed one foot behind the other and launched myself across. Straightaway, my foot slid beneath me. I fell forwards, and my hands raked through the mud on the opposite bank as I plunged into the ice-cold water. My feet skimmed the bottom briefly, but the force of the water flow dragged me downstream. I braced my legs to halt my progress, and looked for something, anything, to grab onto. I was frantic with every second and I grasped a clump of grass, which came away from the loose earth. My feet slithered through the muddy floor, and I sank beneath the water, as though clawed by invisible hands. Its strength carried me along. I thrust my head up and gasped for air, my mouth full of silt-laden water. I spluttered for breath as the current pulled me downstream, and I snatched desperately at the bank for a branch, a rock, anything to escape. My thigh scraped along something razor-sharp and I shrieked. I panicked at the sheer speed and ferocity of the current, which had looked more innocent from the bank. As I drifted with the flow I twisted onto my back. I spotted a sapling with wiry branches hunched over the water. As I drew alongside I made a determined grab for it, and felt the notches of the branch as my fingers scraped along its length. I doggedly kept hold. Inch by inch I hauled myself out until my shoulders and chest were against the bank, the flow still clutching me. I gained a lucky foothold and with one final motion, I dragged myself up the muddy embankment. I crawled away from the water's edge and lay on my back, shaken, as each breath came in sharp rasps.

"Stupid, stupid, stupid!"

Why didn't I just walk back to the track where there must have been a bridge over the stream? What an idiot. I'd almost drowned myself, nearly broken my leg and wasted god knows how much precious time doing it. The only positive was that I was on the right side of the water, though that was more through luck than judgement.

My legs regained some feeling and a searing pain radiated through me. I looked at my leg and drew back the material to reveal a three-inch gash with a thick flap of skin and a shiny ribbon of blood that oozed from it. I rifled in my rucksack for something to tie around my leg to stem the blood flow. I grabbed my spare fleece and used the knife to detach one of the sleeves. I fumbled with my soaked trousers, but managed to pull them down. I held my breath and tied the sleeve securely. Then I removed my sodden jumper, T-shirt and bra, and put on the dry fleece, minus a sleeve. If I didn't move I risked hypothermia, and I'd be no use to Lyssa then. I stood up slowly and took a hesitant step. The pain felt uncomfortable but tolerable, and now I was so close to Lyssa I wasn't going to let anything delay me further.

I scanned the trees for the light, but there was nothing, not a glimmer. I turned full circle but saw only scruffy undergrowth, fallen branches, and dense woodland. Now I sensed darkness descending. It trickled its way through the treetops and seeped with intent down the length of the trunks and dripped from branch to branch below. I had

219

lost my bearings, but at the same time I knew the farm was nearby and so I kept on. After a couple of uncertain minutes, I stepped through bracken and brambles and felt relieved to have found a well-defined path, lined with pine needles, bedded down into the soil by footfall. It had to be a public footpath or one used by the inhabitants of the farm. I kept low and continued over a hillock, until through the trees stood a large farm building just yards ahead. There it was - Deeren Farm. Wet, frozen and in pain, all discomforts faded as adrenaline coursed through me and prepared me for what was to come.

CHAPTER FORTY-THREE

Alone in the World

When Inspector Keir entered the interview room her demeanour held more purpose than it had all afternoon. Despite her outward vigour, her skin held none of its former healthy glow. Her appearance laid bare the few hours of sleep she'd snatched during the past three days, and she clung to her coffee cup for support and sipped intermittently.

She sat down and exhaled. "We have information about Corey and his family. I want to share it with you because we believe it is why your car was found in Arrochar."

Max sat up, alert.

"It's possible you might think of a location he has taken Lyssa, a place from his past that links with the death of his father," she said.

Max sensed the Inspector thought he knew more than he had admitted to. "But I only know about Benn Arum, where we found Roy."

"We've learned that Corey was briefly under the care of a psychiatrist last year. His GP referred him because he was concerned that Corey was becoming emotionally volatile and unstable, potentially dangerous. Initially, Corey was unwilling to undergo counselling, but he did attend two sessions, enough for the psychiatrist to make an assessment."

"How did you find out? I thought that kind of stuff came under patient confidentiality."

"It doesn't matter how we know. The point is we believe it to be true." She set down her empty cup and leaned forward.

"And what did it reveal?" said Max, unsure he wanted to hear the reply.

"In brief, that he was in danger of inflicting harm upon himself or someone else. The psychiatrist concluded it would most likely be someone else. Corey didn't attend his third session, and the

221

psychiatrist hasn't seen him since. We know that in cases like this, a person's emotional state can deteriorate in a matter of weeks or even days and so we can only hazard a guess as to his present state of mind."

A deep flush rose up Max's neck and face as he digested her words.

"I'm sorry, Max, but it's important you know," she said. "Given that he's abducted Lyssa, we can assume he's in an unstable emotional state. Shall I go on?"

"Please," Max replied, and walked across to the window. He parted the blinds.

As the Inspector continued, Max turned and listened.

"He's moved a lot during the past few years, most likely through being evicted by disgruntled landlords. His current neighbours report they rarely see him come and go, and that he keeps himself to himself. One or two told officers they didn't trust him, or like the way that he's spoken to their children. No one we've spoken to has seen him for about two weeks."

Max returned to his seat and picked up a pencil. "What do you mean how he's spoken to their children?" Max pressed his forefinger onto the sharpened lead causing it to snap.

She pursed her lips. "He wanted to engage them in conversation and find out as much as he could about them. In short, he wanted to befriend them."

"You mean he's a paedophile?"

"As you know, he's already been arrested and cautioned for hanging around a school and giving alcohol to minors, so I think we can safely assume he's attracted to children." She paused. "A female volunteer he befriended at a community centre has come forward. She recognised him on the news and told us he'd confided in her about the death of his father and how his grandfather used to own a farm in the Loch Lomond area. Corey told her how he used to visit with his parents, and then after his father's death with his mother and her boyfriend. Seems he wanted to talk about it, as if things were dwelling on his mind."

"Have you spoken to Corey's mother?" said Max.

"No, she's dead. Died twelve years ago of alcoholic poisoning, only thirty-six. Corey was sixteen at the time, still a kid."

"Perhaps he's at the family farm. Do you know where it is?" asked Max.

"We're working on it. We think it may be near to where you came across Roy. It's possible Roy walked from his father's farm that day. The problem is there are a number of farms in the area, but we're hoping the name Simpson will mean something to someone locally. We haven't seen any mention of a farm in his messages. Have we missed something, did he refer to any locations?"

"Not a farm no, but twice he asked me to meet up with him at Corrieshalloch Gorge, south of Ullapool. Both times I turned up when he said to, but he never showed."

She pondered. "Strange that he arranged to meet you that far north when he's living in Cumbernauld, Glasgow. He doesn't own a car, so perhaps he never intended to meet up and it was merely a ruse to get you running around."

"Maybe. Look, if you give me my phone I'll go through the messages, see if I missed anything. And, I need to get hold of Kat."

"No," she said. "That won't be necessary at the moment."

CHAPTER FORTY-FOUR

Childhood Matters

Natural light in the room faded, and Lyssa sensed nightfall approached. She watched him slumped in the chair, and the way his head nodded every now and then. How was this going to end, she wondered? Last night, the grey emptiness and the unfamiliar shadows had made everything unbearable. Her tummy grumbled again, and she wondered if she might starve to death. Every time she moved, her head pounded. The dryness in her mouth was unbearable, and she ached for home; for normality. She recalled how sometimes at night, if she woke up thirsty, she would creep upstairs to the fridge, take out the orange juice, and drink it straight from the carton - so wonderfully sweet and cold.

Why wouldn't he leave? She needed a wee and wasn't sure how much longer she could hold on. She knew he wasn't going to release her and felt a surge of determination rise up within her.

"Have you got anything to eat or drink?" She didn't disguise the suppliant tone in her voice.

He glanced at her and turned away.

"Excuse me, have you got any food or water?"

"Not much. I can go without food, so can you."

"I need the toilet. Please, can I go?"

Again, he didn't answer but instead began to tap his foot feverishly on the floorboards. "It was too much for Mum. First Jean, then Dad. Mum started drinking 'cus it took her mind off the bad things. Sometimes, she forgot I was there. She got dressed up and left me on my own. She stayed out all night, and I'd wake up not knowing where she was. I'd go down, make toast and watch telly but it didn't feel right." He got up and walked to the window.

"Mum met Ian. I thought he was sound at first. A good laugh. Got us takeaways, took me to the cinema, and fishing down the river. I caught a roach and Ian said I was a natural." He leaned against the wall and scratched his cheek. "Turned out he wasn't as great as we first thought. He liked a drink too, and when he got pissed, he'd shout, throw stuff and smack us. I hated him and I told Mum she should dump him. But Mum said he was a good man deep down." He snorted. "She finally threw him out after he beat her up so bad she had to stay in hospital." He paused, and remembered.

"This was Grandad's farm. It got too much for him, Mum said. She said he'd leave it to me after Dad died. My dad liked coming here, but I remember him and Granddad would argue about the farm. Granddad wanted him to take it on, but Dad said he'd never be a farmer. Said it was too lonely and miserable. I like it – the silence. And it was smart back then, nice kitchen, sofas, telly and mod cons. Dad made me a tyre swing in the woods that went right over the stream. I felt like I was flying."

He flicked his Zippo lighter, and adjusted it so that the flame flickered up and shrank back down again, then he reached for a cigarette tucked behind his ear, twirled it in his fingers and lit up. He dragged deeply and blew a spiral of smoke at Lyssa's face.

"One summer, Ian drove us up here. Mum was giddy, telling Ian all about it, the sheep and cows. Mum said he could have a go at driving the tractor and I might be big enough to have a go too." He drew on his cigarette and flicked the ash onto the floor. "Granddad knew me and Mum were coming, but he hadn't known about Ian. Granddad was mad as hell. Mum and Ian started on the booze and had a massive row with Granddad. Ian ended up punching Granddad and split his lip and broke his nose. Nan screamed at them to stop. Granddad must have been scared 'cus he stormed out and didn't come back in. I know, because I checked his bedroom in the night and only Nan was there. In the morning, he walked back in when we were having breakfast. Turns out he'd slept in the stinking cow shed. Anyway, we had to leave, and I never saw Granddad again."

As he continued talking about his past, she decided that if he kept talking, then at least he wasn't shouting at her, shoving her or making her touch his revolting feet.

"A few months later when the foot and mouth hit, Granddad had to have the cows and sheep burned in a huge pyre. He wrote to Mum and said he was going to sell up and move to the village. It was sad 'cus Granddad died just after they'd moved into their new cottage. He had a massive heart attack and died straight off. We came for the funeral, but there was hardly anyone there. Just me, Mum, Nan and a couple of old codgers. We all cried when they lowered him into the grave, but at the pub, I remember asking Nan if she was going to be OK. I'll never forget her reply. She smiled and said, 'Corey lovey, I'll be much better than OK. I 'spose I'll miss your Granddad sometimes, but life is going to be just fine from now on'. I thought that was a weird thing to say seeing as he'd just died. It made me wonder if she hadn't liked him much." He looked down at Lyssa and his eyes narrowed. "Does your mum like your dad?"

"Yes."

"Then she hasn't heard he's a murdering bastard." He stepped closer to the bed and watched for her reaction.

"My mum never got over losing my dad. Do you know why? He was a real dad and knew how to look after us. He sorted anyone who upset me or Mum. He'd be with me now if your dad hadn't murdered him."

Lyssa didn't attempt to defend her dad; it would only provoke him further. Unable to hold her bladder, a wet patch spread across the mattress.

He took a step closer. "What the…? Have you pissed yourself?" He kicked her.

Lyssa screamed and recoiled into the corner.

He stormed across to the window and stared into the shadowy darkness as he reigned in his rage. "Why didn't you tell me?"

"I still need the toilet." She stared into her lap.

"What for? You've been."

"I need the other."

"OK. But if you try anything, I will kill you."

Lyssa tried to control her breathing as the air caught in her lungs.

He grabbed her arm, and pulled her down the stairs, then through a darkened room and into a narrow passageway.

He pushed her roughly through a doorway. "And leave that door open."

She gasped as her arm scraped the doorframe. A waft of cool air brushed her skin and she wondered if the window was open. As she felt for the toilet seat a vile smell coiled around her and she pressed her sleeve against her nostrils as her insides cramped. Afterwards, she rearranged her clothes and touched her way back to the door.

"What shall I do with you?" he said, and dragged her away.

In the hallway he stopped and pulled open a drawer and rummaged inside. He clicked on a torch and lit their way up the staircase and into the bedroom.

He beamed the torchlight into her eyes. "I tell you what girl, I've had enough of you. I'm sick of you lying there pissing yourself, not talking. You're not right in the head." He directed the beam down to her feet and back up again to her face. "I thought you'd be a bit of company, a good listener… give me some comfort."

He clicked off the torch, which plunged them into darkness. Instinctively, Lyssa backed away.

He switched it on again, held it under his chin and jumped forwards, "Raaaahhh!" His repulsive features became distorted by the light.

He stepped out of the room and snapped the door behind him. Seconds later he threw the door open and pressed the torch against her cheek. "I'm gonna repay your dad for what he did to mine, like for like. Do you hear me?" He walked out, slammed the door, and the floorboards shuddered.

Lyssa heard the key turn in the lock. She collapsed onto the bed and sobbed. "Mummy, where are you?"

CHAPTER FORTY-FIVE

A Development

Max had remained locked in the interview room all day, and was furious at being treated as though he was the monster who had snatched Lyssa. Periodically, he paced up and down the room like a caged animal before slumping back into his chair. Inspector Keir and Detective Brooks broke his isolation every so often to ask him a question, none of which suggested they were any closer to finding Lyssa or to releasing him. The clock on the wall was a continual reminder that he could do nothing to help find Lyssa, and instead he was wasting time behind closed doors; locked doors.

It was a quarter to ten and still there was no word from Katriina. He knew how devastated she was by his deceit on top of Lyssa's disappearance and that she had every reason to be.

Detective Brooks opened the door and walked in, followed by Inspector Kier who held two cups.

She placed one in front of Max. "There's been a development," she said, watching him carefully.

He sensed it could be positive news and his heart pumped against his ribs.

"Two walkers were up on Benn Arum this afternoon, and they believe they've spoken with Katriina. She was heading to a farm she wanted to have a look at it. She said it belonged to her family. The walkers passed a farm a short while before and told her this. It wasn't until later that they linked her to Lyssa."

"Christ . . . how can she know?" said Max, and ran a shaking hand through his hair.

"A team are on their way to the farm. I'm going back to keep track of developments."

"Please, I have to know if they find Lyssa, Kat . . ."

Inspector Keir exchanged a look with Detective Brooks who nodded. "OK, but you cannot interfere with communications. Is that clear?" she said.

"Guaranteed," replied Max.

"Lyssa might not be there. You do know that?" she said, and touched Max's arm.

"But there's a chance," he said, and his tears fell.

CHAPTER FORTY-SIX

Nightfall

I looked up through the branches at the darkened sky. Nightfall couldn't come quickly enough. I made my way nervously around the farmhouse and prayed that I remained concealed by the undergrowth and trees. The farm wasn't precisely as I remembered it from my nightmare, but it was the same farm, with the same distinctive stonewall and carriage arch. If the situation weren't so fraught with danger, I would have been stunned by the amalgamation of dream with reality.

The yard at the front lay covered with timeworn gravel that had mingled with the cold earth. Nettles and thistles forced their way through, some newly grown, delicate barbs atop, others dead, dry, and decayed. I moved further round and saw a blue car tucked against the side of the house.

Fear and adrenaline had sustained me all day, and without it I would be an exhausted shell. I'd had little sleep since Lyssa's disappearance, but despite that I felt my blood surge through me to energise my limbs and mind and my senses were primed with dread and anticipation.

If Lyssa was in there, I had to get her away. I couldn't turn back, and I was more than ready to fight for my flesh and blood, all the way if it proved necessary. The doubt and anxiety that had threatened to take hold surrendered to an unyielding purpose, and God only help the monster who stood in my way.

A dark mist slunk its way towards me through the treetops, and I watched the farm as I awaited full darkness. I felt an all-pervading chill sink into my bones, which threatened to cloud my mind. Was I awaiting nightfall to avoid being seen or was I stalling, too afraid to risk going in? But if I delayed, I was leaving Lyssa open to any number of atrocities.

I slid my hand into my pocket and withdrew the knife. My fingers curled around the handle with a decisive grip. I made my way between the trees, but remained within the boundary of the woods and continued around until I met the walled carriage arch. I'd reached a point of no return, and I strode to the back door and turned the handle. I wasn't surprised to find it locked.

I noticed a sash window and I peered around its edge. I pressed my nose against the glass. Through the darkened maw I could make out some chairs and a table, upon which lay strewn packets and bottles. I crouched down and crawled beneath the ledge and around the corner to what looked like an extension to the original building. I came upon a small window and looked through to a dark and unoccupied room. I pressed my fingers into the gap between the frame and felt it give. I wriggled my fingers and the window suddenly flew open with a dull thud. I froze and pleaded that the sound hadn't travelled. The window ledge was shoulder level, and I looked around. I spotted an old metal washtub and tipped out the foetid water, turned it upside down and placed it beneath the sill. I dumped my rucksack, pocketed the knife and stepped onto the tub. With hands on the windowsill, I jumped up and eased myself headfirst over the other side. As my thigh scraped over the window frame, I gasped and pressed my palm across my mouth. The pain subsided and as my fingers touched an open toilet seat a foul smell hit me. I held my breath and lowered myself to the floor.

Automatically, I grabbed my knife and listened for voices or movement. But everything remained still, except for my heartbeat which raced in my ears. I wondered if I'd made a mistake and the house was empty, or worse, that Lyssa lay unconscious or dead somewhere nearby. I pleaded; please be here, please be alive.

Blinded by darkness, I touched the walls on either side. But then something stopped me. A sound. Undistinguishable at first. The soft scuffle of feet nearby. No, there was more than one person. I knew I must move quickly or be found. I slipped from the room, stepped down a short passageway and through an open doorway. I pressed myself up behind the door. Dryness filled my mouth, and my palms felt slick with sweat. I tightened my grip on the knife, and listened to movement in the passageway.

A man's voice, but I couldn't catch the words. Then it became worryingly quiet. A minute or so passed, and I heard movements close by, nothing precise.

Then a sudden whimper and a familiar voice filled my senses.

I heard footsteps retreating, then a man's vindictive tone, "What am I going to…"

Relief surged through me – Lyssa was alive. I wanted to jump out, grab him by the neck and stab his eyes out, but I held back such dark impulses. I knew it was unwise and that I had to be clever. A certainty of purpose restrained my fear and dulled its ferocity.

I wanted to shout out to Lyssa; to reassure her and warn her, but I didn't. As soon as I felt sure they were at a safe enough distance, I traced their receding footsteps, and felt my way into the deeper recesses of the house. I noticed the second-hand beam of a torch as it glanced from the walls and ceilings, and it illuminated my way. Sounds thudded up the stairs. Then his muffled voice, cruel and punishing. A door slammed and startled me, but I stood my ground. Seconds later, another door closed and I knew he was coming back down. I drew back into the corner of the room and fell against something, an armchair. I squeezed behind it and hunched down just as torchlight beamed in and scanned the room. The light threw chilling, unfamiliar shadows onto the ceiling. I held my breath and every muscle fibre in my body tensed. I was all set to react, certain he had seen me. He moved and I heard his every breath. Gradually, the light ebbed into silence.

I tried to slow my breathing, convinced the sound of my hammering heartbeat resonated through the room.

CHAPTER FORTY-SEVEN

Running

Corey lit the old oil lamp and placed it on the table. In the timeworn, long-abandoned kitchen, the light shone at just the right luminosity to give it a deceptive, homely glow. He picked up a can of lager, pulled the ring and slurped it and then wiped his mouth with the back of his hand. He paused, belched and drank the rest. After throwing the can into the sink, he pulled his phone from his trouser pocket and went to his favourite website. The screen kept buffering.

"You piece of fuckin shite." He threw the phone across the table; stared at it. No matter. He peered up at the ceiling and his eyes shuttered. He tugged at his flies and shoved his hand down his trousers. The skin across his face twitched as he fondled himself.

She would be ready for him.

He grabbed the lamp, walked up the stairs and reached for the key in the door.

Overcome by tiredness, Lyssa had found relief in sleep and so didn't hear the key in the lock. Didn't hear him set the lamp on the chair.

He watched her for a moment or two, then shook her. "Wakey, wakey!"

Lyssa screamed, her face alarmed and she sat bolt upright.

He snarled, and his face appeared flame red in the lamplight.

Whimpering, she shuffled back.

"Take off your clothes."

"What? No!"

"Do it! Or I will." He grabbed her ankle.

A dark shadow flickered across the floorboards. She glanced behind; saw something that made her think she was still asleep and dreaming.

Lyssa watched her mum hold a finger to her lips before leaping onto his back. She wrapped her arms around his neck and pulled him backwards.

"Run Lyssa! Get out. Find help."

"Mummy!"

Lyssa watched them crash to the floor. She paused for only a second before running past them and feeling her way down the stairs. With her arms outstretched she found the front door. She heard loud thuds and shouting from upstairs, but knew she must get away.

She scrabbled around and turned the door handle, but it was locked. Sobbing, she ran her shaking hands up and down, found a bolt, twisted and dragged it sideways. The door swung open and she ran into the darkness, gulping the air.

A wind bit at her skin, but despite the chill, her body prickled with fear and sweat. She wanted only to run away in any direction, but she had to be smart. She made out the dense profile of the treetops against the night sky, but to her left it appeared less dense. As she stepped forward the ground beneath her feet felt solid, flatter, and she guessed she was on a road or path. She walked on, and when she felt certain, she ran. As her eyes adjusted to the night she sensed the direction of the track, but there were no lights visible in all directions. A sudden gust of wind slammed at her back, and whipped up the leaves and branches in the trees around her. Certain she had heard a voice, she stopped and turned around, but now there was nothing above the wind as it swept past her, and urged her to keep on going.

CHAPTER FORTY-EIGHT

Violent Fury

We slammed against the wall and collapsed into a heap of flailing limbs and frantic minds. I'd caught a glimpse of Lyssa as she rushed past us and out of the doorway, free from immediate danger. Thank God. He rolled, and his back fell like a lead weight against my chest. His bulk crushed the air from me, and I pushed with all the force I could muster to get him off. My right hand was empty, and I knew I'd already dropped the knife. I scratched around on the floorboards and tried to locate it. He spun around and scrambled to his knees. I sat up; his black eyes narrowed and his top lip curled in anger. He straddled me, grabbed my wrists and slammed me back against the floor. I tried to wrench my hands from his grasp. His face hovered inches from mine and I watched the spittle as it ran down his chin and flash on his parted lips. "You cunt. How the fuck did you find me? Who's with you?"

"The police," I said, without hesitation. A shudder of doubt appeared in his eyes, and for a split second I sensed his fear.

He slapped my face, but I barely felt it.

"Don't believe you. I'm surprised Max isn't with you. Neglecting his husbandly duties is he?"

I kicked beneath his full weight and spat in his face. Then I felt his wrath as he slapped me again, but this time with full-force. My head cracked against the wall and my vision swam. Everything flashed white.

I hadn't planned for this. In my fury I'd thought I could overpower him. But I'd dropped the knife instead of ramming it in his back when I'd had the chance. Again, I twisted sideways, but it was hopeless. Then I lay still and hoped he'd relax his hold.

235

"That's better, missy. If you stop struggling, we'll get down to it. I was going to have Lyssa. She's been giving me the eye since I picked her up."

The only words I heard were, 'was going to,' and in that instant, I thanked God that he hadn't.

He would rape me instead. But to do that he'd have to move, and that would be my opportunity. He wasn't heavily built, nor tall. Yet my strength was severely diminished by fatigue from the past few days, and now a paralysing fear had taken hold and I couldn't overpower him. He grasped my hands and pinned them to the floor, and with his other hand he ripped down the zip of my coat and then yanked my fleece up to my chin. In the shadowy lamplight, I watched as he stared and leered, then he rubbed my naked breasts, and grunted like a rutting beast. I gritted my teeth as the terror welled up within me. He grappled at my trousers and wrenched them over my hips. He undid his trousers, and as he did I felt his weight lift. Without hesitation I seized the opportunity and swung my knee up. He didn't flinch. Instantly I swung it hard again, and this time I knew I had struck my target.

He howled and released his grip on my hands. I wriggled back and kicked him full-force in the balls. His face contorted in agony, and he toppled sideways with a thud and curled into a ball.

I jumped up and secured my clothes, frantic to get away. But then a glint of metal caught my eye. The knife, just inches from his head. Its reflection flickered in the lamplight, calling out to me like a gemstone. I reached for it, but as I bent and clasped it, his hand shot out and clutched my calf.

"No fucking chance." He spat the words like a venomous snake biting its prey.

I pulled my leg away, but his grip remained strong. I booted his face with my other foot but he barely registered any pain. He leaped to his feet and gripped my shoulders. Then he shook me with a force that propelled me backwards into the wall. He rammed his body against mine with one hand grasped around my neck. With the other hand he wrestled with his trousers, then pulled at mine.

"Get off me you bastard," I screamed.

Then he grinned at me; evil and repugnant. His breath smelled foul and his teeth were discoloured and rotten. I raised my knee, but he'd already anticipated the move and pressed his knees against my legs.

"Get off me... please." Petrified and powerless, I knew I wouldn't stop him. I pleaded with him, anything to prevent the inevitable.

He forced himself up against me and tightened his hold around my neck. I felt the air burn and stick in my throat, and I tugged and scratched at his wrists in a futile attempt to pull his hands away.

I met his eyes and saw into the deepest darkness of them and glimpsed Lyssa's terrified face. Then as her image paled, I saw laid bare the depth of violent fury and rotten hatred that had grown and festered within him for twenty years. Something within me snapped. An immense rage fired up from deep inside of me. I wasn't about to fail my daughter now, not after everything she had been through. If he thought I would lie back and let him kill me, he was mistaken. I gripped the knife, thrust it upwards and plunged the blade deep into the yielding flesh of his belly. I withdrew and thrust again. I didn't want to kill him; I wanted to live. As I withdrew the knife the second time the fury in his eyes faded and died, and was instantly replaced by stunned shock. He gawped at me, his mouth slack. I felt his hand slip from my neck, and he looked down.

The colour in his face drained and he clutched his stomach. "What have you done?" He staggered back and fell.

"Nothing you don't deserve you sick bastard."

Terrified, I staggered from the room. In the dark, I missed my step at the top of the stairs and fell. I turned a full somersault and slid down the last few steps. I stood up, disoriented, but a sudden breeze whipped my hair. I saw my escape route and ran.

"Lyssa!" I called.

My thoughts were confused and my actions out of control. What had I done? What if I'd killed him? What if I hadn't hurt him enough and right now he was coming after us? I no longer had the knife in my hand. Did I drop it in the room after I stabbed him, or had I released it as I'd fallen down the stairs?

Frantic and crying, I called as I ran, "Lyssa. Please baby."

How long had we fought? It hadn't seemed like long, so why hadn't I caught up with her? The wind gusted and I sensed a storm neared. I looked ahead to headlights that approached fast and I stopped in the middle of the track and waved my arms. The vehicle skidded to a halt, the doors flew open and two officers got out. I sank to my knees and sobbed.

"Mrs O'Donnell?" A female officer crouched beside me.

"Have you seen Lyssa?" I cried. "She should be in front of me."

"How long ago?" she said.

"About five, ten minutes. Oh, I don't know."

"Perhaps she's hiding somewhere," she said.

"She might have reached the village, it's only a couple of miles," the male officer said.

"No. She can't have gone that far. Please Lyssa. Where are you?" I screamed into the blackness.

"If she's not with him then she's out of immediate danger. We'll drive up. Reinforcements are coming."

"I'm Constable Newton," she said. "This is Constable Briggs."

In the car, Constable Briggs turned on the radio. "Tango Charlie 431 control. We've found Katriina O'Donnell on the lane approaching Deeren Farm. Lyssa has escaped her abductor, over. He paused. "Copy that. Another pause. "Negative, no sign of Lyssa. When backup arrives, flash the beacon to reassure her. She may be scared and hiding, over. Affirmative, heading up there."

We moved off and rounded the bend. Some way ahead I saw a hazy orange glow and what looked like clouds or mist. We drew near and I saw smoke. It sparked and swirled in small spirals above the trees.

"Oh Christ," I said, and craned forward. "The house is on fire. What if Lyssa's stuck inside?"

She slammed her foot down. Flames blazed from an upstairs window, and curled up onto the roof.

I flung open the door and shouted over the raging wind. "That's the room Lyssa was in."

"Is he locked in?" Constable Briggs said.

"No. But he's injured."

They glanced at me briefly, and after exchanging words, Constable Briggs raced to the front door.

The female officer turned on her radio. "Request fire service – Deeren Farm, fire taking hold."

"Katriina, we'll scout around and shout for Lyssa. She could be hiding and too scared to come out. It's possible Corey isn't in the house so stick close. Constable Briggs is checking indoors."

I nodded. "There are some outbuildings, we should check those."

She beamed her torch at the house and into the woodland.

"Lyssa," I shouted. "The police are here. You're safe."

The wind growled and intensified and thrashed through the trees to feed the flames. I glanced upwards. The fire was spreading fast, and I prayed that Lyssa wasn't trapped inside.

A figure appeared at an upstairs window, his face twisted and terrified. He smashed the panes of glass with his fists and leaned over the ledge as thick smoke billowed around him.

I grabbed the officer's arm. "Look there - -"

But he had hurled himself out and we watched as he landed with a bone-cracking thud just feet away. The officer ran up and shone her torch over him. One of his legs had rotated at an unnatural angle and blood swam across his abdomen. His eyelids wavered, neither fully open nor closed.

The officer knelt down and pressed her fingers to his neck. "We need to move him."

I felt sickened to be this near to him, but far more than that I felt relieved.

The heat intensified, and the flames burned through the roof. The fire had become an inferno. A window blew out – the ear-splitting crash shook me – and shards of glass sprayed down to the gravel like falling scalpels. More cracks and bangs followed as the blaze grew more frenzied. Its tremendous power raged through the corridors and rooms, and tore apart the walls and ceilings. The flames swirled and twisted, luminous-red, brutal and bloodshot.

Black ash and burning debris fell around us. We took Corey's arms and hauled his limp, trailing body under the cover of the trees. As we lay him back down, his eyes rolled, and he slipped into unconsciousness.

The officer called for an ambulance. "Deeren Farm, Tippelin. Adult male, jumped from a burning building - -"

"He has knife wounds," I added.

She looked at me and nodded. "Medics needed urgently," she paused. "Copy that." She returned the radio to her breast pocket and looked at him, then to me. "An ambulance is en-route, it's procedure." She put her hand on my shoulder. "Katriina, we will find Lyssa, and whatever you needed to do in there... all will be taken into consideration. Let's focus on Lyssa. And you need attention. You're limping."

"I'm OK. I just want to find her." I sobbed.

Officer Briggs reappeared through the smoke, hunched over and coughing. He collapsed onto the ground and wiped at his streaming eyes. He glanced at Corey, then up at the officer, in search of an explanation.

"He jumped," she said. "An ambulance is en route."

"I checked the... downstairs and Lyssa... wasn't there. I only got half way up the stairs. Too risky to go further." He struggled to speak and coughed hard.

"Are you all right?" she asked, and held his arm as he bent over and tried to regain his breath.

"I'm gonna need a few minutes, and I'll stop him from running off, eh?" He gave a crooked grin and coughed again.

"We'll keep searching," she said.

We moved off in opposite directions.

Where was Lyssa? It didn't make sense. Maybe she had got as far as the village. But, what if she was still inside the house? What if she'd had an asthma attack and had collapsed somewhere amongst the trees and undergrowth, unable to breathe, move or shout for help? I panicked that we might not find her in time. She couldn't have gone through all of this only to escape and for that to happen to her. My mind erupted beneath a wave of new fears.

The flames illuminated the surrounding area and into the woods.

As I ran I called, "Lyssa, it's Mummy."

At the carriage arch I met up with Constable Newton.

"Maybe she ran into the woods," I said.

"Let's get around to the front," she said.

The fierce heat, falling tiles and other bits of masonry gave us no option but to move back from the conflagration.

We hurried beneath the trees. Suddenly, I felt dizzy; my mind and body exhausted. I had reached my physical and emotional limit. I became aware of the reflection of blue flashing lights on the trees and knew that backup had finally arrived. I tripped and fell to my knees and the officer hooked my arm and pulled me upright. We passed the Nissan, which was now alight and with thick, acrid smoke pouring from it, then we turned onto the gravel. Wild flames and smoke billowed from the downstairs windows and doorway, but I saw through the curling smoke that there was an ambulance and several police cars. Officers and paramedics moved about, and then I spotted two people emerge from behind an ambulance. They walked towards me, one of whom was a girl with long brown curly hair - must be about eleven years old.

We both cried and ran the last few steps to one another.

"Lyssa! Oh my baby," I sobbed.

"Mummy, you came," she cried and held out her arms.

I grasped her like my lifeline, folded my arms around her, and as I clasped her tightly to my chest, I felt I would never let her go again.

CHAPTER FORTY-NINE

Retreat

I am floating, naked and unfolded in the semi-darkness.

My limbs are outstretched and my hair drifts in gentle waves. I raise my head and watch my toes break the water's surface. I feel whole, my mind is calm as it meanders gently through soft swathes of carefree thoughts. Such a blissful state of tranquillity finally allowed.

I am not alone. Lyssa is here with me. I am, we are, without husband, friend, lover, father... lawbreaker, villain and thief, hider of truths and keeper of dark secrets.

It has been three weeks and three days since I found Lyssa, and finally, I allow myself this time; a chance for renewal, a search for a new state of being. It is a time to meditate, to reflect and ruminate, to pass judgement upon them and on myself.

Corey Simpson is dead. He breathed his final breath before he reached the ambulance. Of that I am glad. Yes, I know that if it weren't for me he would still be very much alive... to continue controlling, drugging, abusing and raping. I have to live with that knowledge and a guilt-ridden conscience, and handle the remorse. I will learn to live with it, and yes I think I can come to terms with it. Some people will want to judge me. Let them. Others may understand.

I am eternally thankful to have Lyssa safely back with me. She is alive, my own flesh and blood. Throughout my forty years I have never needed anything more than this one thing. My precious, amazing daughter Lyssa is alive, and more than that, she is going to be all right. Of that I feel sure. Her counselling has begun, and her psychiatrist tells me Lyssa talks and opens up, that she is vulnerable, but also that she is strong. Lyssa talks to me too, about how Corey treated her, what he said, her fears and thoughts during her terrible ordeal, though some of the details are sketchy. We will continue to talk for as long as she needs to. I want to share her burdens, hold them and carry them far away.

My counsellor mostly sits and listens and allows me to talk about anything and everything. My fears for Lyssa and the after effects of what she has been through, Louis, Corey, my childhood, my family... guilt and murder. More than anything now I find I need to talk about Max, my profound anger at him and yet still my love for him. A deep love that refuses to fade, however much I want it to.

And finally, I think about how even despite my best physical efforts of recent weeks, there is a new inexplicable life which grows inside of me and wants to live. For all of these things I feel thankful.

THE END

"Take the life-lie away from the average man, and straight away you take away his happiness."
Henrik Ibsen

About the Author

Olivia Rytwinski grew up in Worcestershire, England. She studied English at Worcester University and later Marketing at Postgraduate level in Leeds. Today, she lives in rural Yorkshire, England, with her family and dog.

Visit her website at www.oliviarytwinski.com